WEDDING WORRIES

D0754263

STIG DAGERMAN

WEDDING WORRIES

Translated from the Swedish
by Paul Norlén
with Lo Dagerman

A Verba Mundi Book
David R. Godine · Publisher · Boston

This is a Verba Mundi Book
published in 2018 by
DAVID R. GODINE, *Publisher*, Inc.
Post Office Box 450
Jaffrey, New Hampshire 03452
www.godine.com

Originally published in Swedish in 1949 by Norstedts, Sweden.
Published in English translation by agreement with Norstedts Agency.
Translation sponsored by The Swedish Arts Council.

Preface © JMG Le Clézio, 1982

LIBRARY OF CONGRESS CATALOGING-IN-PUBLICATION DATA
Names: Dagerman, Stig, 1923-1954, author. |
Norlén, Paul R., translator. | Dagerman, Lo, 1951– translator. |
Le Clézio, J.M.G. (Jean-Marie Gustave), 1940– writer of introduction.
Title: Wedding worries / by Stig Dagerman; translated from
the Swedish by Paul Norlén with Lo Dagerman.
Other titles: Brollopsbesvar. English
Description: Jaffrey, New Hampshire: David R. Godine, Publisher, 2018. |
"Originally published in Swedish in 1949 by Norstedts, Sweden."—ECIP galley.
Identifiers: LCCN 2018012334| ISBN 9781567926156 | ISBN 1567926150
Subjects: LCSH: Man-woman relationships—Fiction.
Classification: LCC PT9875.D12 B813 2018 | DDC 839.73/74—dc23
LC record available at https://lccn.loc.gov/2018012334

FIRST PRINTING, 2018
Printed in the United States of America

Contents

Introduction BY J.M.G. LE CLÉZIO   7

List of Characters   11

Who's Tapping on the Bride's Window?   13

Who Can Know My Anguish?   47

Make Do With What You Have   137

Where Is the Friend I Seek?   243

Acknowledgements   256

The Last Novel by Stig Dagerman

Death Sleeps within Life,
Life Sleeps within Death

The novel is that thing you can't define, that stone that weighs on memory, that creature that bites its own tail, in which, unlike in poetry, dreams or music, so many have lost their way. And yet we turn to the novel, despite all the dissatisfactions and near misses, in search of its chimeric truth. Reading Stig Dagerman's *Wedding Worries*, I'm struck by the internal needs of the novel, by its inevitable absurdity, and at the same time by its exaltation of reality, its warmth, its life, its blood. The novel is a living being made of time, the very substance of our world.

What is revealed in this book's design, built brick by brick, like the secret map of memory? It is time—not measured in the duration of actions, but time as a whole, in what comes and goes, time marked by the tracks and words of men, the moment of birth joined to the moment of death. As I slowly read *Wedding Worries,* I rediscover what fascinated me in Dagerman's *The Snake, A Burnt Child,* or the strange *A Thousand Years with God.* The same fascination I felt when I first read *Ulysses, Light in August,* or *Journey to the End of the Night*: when I felt a towering wave wash over me, carrying all the force that had unleashed it on the other side of the horizon.

Wedding Worries describes the passage of time in the Swedish village of Fuxe, over a summer's day and night, after the war. Time pervades this place, magnifies it, turning its men and women into the heroes of an epic cycle. Time grows heavy and multiplies here, because of the impending marriage of Hildur Palm, "the Snail's daughter," to Hilmer Westlund, a butcher. The wedding is exactly this, a moment in time, a knot in the history of people who lack histories: it's a chance to find the sources of converging streams, to find life in the wake of actions, and perhaps even an answer to the riddle. Marriage is the moment when, according to tradition, we pause to look and listen. So the old tramp writes "eight stanzas for his wedding poem, six lines each." A love poem, or celebratory poem? Yet this human rite at life's zenith also reveals its nadir, and the poet must dip his pen into an "inkwell filled with blood": "We ought to write about death, not marriage. Like this: You little human creature, you bride! Your bed is made for your final night, your wedding night. Your dark groom sets his watch, and moistens his lips with only wine, and your lips, you know, will kiss them dry. Death is your only groom, soon you will bear his name. Soon your only faithful lover will make love to you, so undress, strip naked, his sheets are burning."

Everyone gathers around the mythical figure of the bride—goddess of life, and sorceress of death—Hildur, closeted in nervous waiting, under the halo of her coming metamorphosis. And then they all celebrate the rite that unites them with the world's rhythms, the grand nuptial parade, the world's oldest act played out amidst joking and fear, while the Swedish summer burns in all its fire. At this supreme moment of life, ordinary feelings and civilities are replaced by impatience, violence and sometimes hate, along with impulsive and brutal happiness, laughter and inebriation.

The wedding is more than a party. It is a trial, a revelation, where everyone has a role to play, from the three tramps who get drunk and fall asleep in the barn, to Hagström and Karlsson, the butchers' lackeys, and even to Nisse and Mary, the bourgeois know-it-alls from the city, and finally to the singer who knows only one question: 'How did I sing?' but who wants to ask: 'Who am I?' They seek and provoke each other, for the wedding celebration is also a game and an arena for combat. They search for each other as if, during that day and night when Westlund and Hildur are ritually united, no one has a name or identity, and each, taking part in a dance, wears a mask that frees the soul from its depths.

The dream of freedom: the wedding is the folk celebration that unleashes the wild creature inside every man and woman, through a plunge into collective violence. It is there that Dagerman takes us, just as the festival of Carnival once did. Drunkenness takes people beyond themselves, drives them toward their destinies. Can time be measured any other way, than by this haste? There is Svea's desire for bliss, carrying a child as if out of vengeance; there is the grotesque clash between Simon and Hilmer, the two butchers; there are the tramps who find shelter for a few hours, one of them finding, more than shelter, his grave. The songs and jokes are fired off, to banish death and doubt, while Rudolf and Sören, not knowing how to talk to girls, discover happiness in the river water, in the sun, in the thick of the birch forest. The wedding party is a celebration of life, making us forget for a time our fear, despair and loneliness.

J.M.G. LE CLÉZIO
Review of *Wedding Worries*
in *Le Monde*, May 14, 1982

List of Characters

The Palm Family and Relations

VICTOR PALM ("THE SNAIL"), old man and owner of a small
farmstead
HILMA, wife
RUDOLF, grown son
IRMA, unwed older daughter
GUNNAR, Irma's child
HILDUR, youngest daughter about to be married
SÖREN, farmhand
RULLAN, Rudolf's girlfriend
MARTIN ENG, Hildur's former lover
"THE SINGER," aka Johan Borgh, close friend of Hilma Palm
GÖRAN, his grown son

The Westlund Family and Relations

HILMER WESTLUND, village butcher, about to marry Hildur
Palm
FRIDA, dead wife
SIRI, teenage daughter
SVEA, maid
HAGSTRÖM ("ONE-EAR"), butcher's helper
SIMON, Westlund's butcher rival
KARLSSON, Simon's butcher's helper

Creek-Lasse's Family and Relations

CREEK-LASSE LARSSON, old man
ERIKA, wife
VILLE, son
THE PEDDLER

Three Tramps

FILIP, old man and poet
IVAR LUND, young tramp
"SIXTEN," a younger man joining them

Wedding Guests

NISSE JOHANSSON, a Palm cousin from Gävle town
MARY, his wife
WALLINDER, their friend from town
BJUHR, local farmer and important man
OLD LADY BJUHR, his wife

Who's Tapping on the Bride's Window?

Slow and steady—that's how God made snails, or whoever it was who made them. But whoever made them, he did it well. For what does a snail need speed for? Whatever he treads on is his. Wherever he turns in this world his building rests on its own ground. So there's no need for him to run his legs off to make it home for a court auction or forfeiture or forced slaughter. A snail, he carries his house on his back. That's the kind of back you should have.

But if you do—then you're not well accepted. Then those Saturday sodbusters, stone-pickers and barkbread-eaters in Långmo will stand on their stoops, gawking and sucking their dipping tobacco. Some people have nothing else to do. Some have one heck of a stoop in front of their rotten hovels. So big that from there they supposedly can see the slightest thing that's going on in Fuxe. So if you're sitting in the outhouse with the newspaper they can read it if it's just light enough. And if you add on another floor then they stand on their stoops and gape until their mouths are full of flies. Spit 'em out then!

Now Victor probably is completely off his rocker. Oh yes. That's been said on the stoops. As if the shack wasn't good enough for that braggart Palm, just like it was for his father-in-law Asp Johannes. But no! Add a shack on top of the shack! Maybe he had a manor in mind. A twenty-four-acre manor. Suppose you've got to call that old farmhand squire now. Heard the squire's one horse got strangles and heard squire's daughter got a position with an accountant in town. The one with the bastard, that is.

You see, the first time you're christened, it doesn't count. It's the other times that matter. The only name you've got is the one you wear with shame. The one you get from the whisperers and the acid-tongued. And if you've built a house that carries a house on its back, then you'll be called Snail till you die. Wherever you go you carry Snail on your back. In the end you get bent and broken. In the end you can't stand being seen. Then you lock your room tight and die in there. Then you sit alone in the house-on-top-of-a-house looking at your own back, for a life-time. Blinds down, so you can't be seen from the stoops. And the clocks are up there, all three of them, hanging on the wall, ticking and striking. Then you know how time wanders toward peace and deliverance. Slowly like a snail wanders. The old lady brings up the food. Walk softly on the stairs, woman, so the stoop folks don't hear you. And take the slop pail down, it stinks.

Fixed idea or craziness, this thing with the house? No matter, around here it's always been the same thing: fixed ideas and craziness. But late at night when dawn is breaking, the blind is raised. Slowly. You're a snail after all, and in no hurry. Why should you be when all you can see belongs to you?

They've just been cutting hay. Did he go down? No, the others had to come upstairs. *We thought we should cut, Pa.* I see—and is the knife sharp? *The farmhand sharpened it, Pa.* I see—and do you have help with the mowing? *We'll get Smelars from the poorhouse and Rullan, my girl, will do the raking. She's got herself some time off.* I see—well then, go ahead. But keep a tight rein on the mare. And get salt and whetstones. *Huh? Yes, Pa.*

And Rudolf, does he have a snail on his back when he walks? Yes, a small one. Someday it will get bigger. Then he'll probably move upstairs. Then he'll probably lock himself in and won't come down until he's carried.

At daybreak the rye glistens. Rye has its own sun. Although soon it will be cut. Again he hears steps on the stairs. *Should we cut, Pa?* Bring a spike here so I can taste. Guess I'll have to test the grain this year too, since no one else knows anything around here. Remember to grease the wheels. And the knife edge is sharp, right? *Yes, Pa.* Head out the gate then, son.

But now. Should he go down? Leave his house, venture down to the others? Down within sight of the eyes on the stoops? Just because the old woman, while putting the herring on the table, had said: *Yes, Hildur's going to get married now.* Is that so? And to who? To Martin, that pauper from Långmo, the one she carried on with on the stoop at night right under my window? *No,* she said, *Martin went to cut timber in Västmanland since his mother died, so that's over. And the ring was sent back. She'll marry the butcher, Westlund from Mon, the one who's been in America. We thought about having the wedding here at home. The banns will be read for the third time on Sunday.*

"For the third time." That's how slowly the news reaches a snail. But then again: what does a snail care about weddings? Would he leave his house for the sake of a wedding? No! A wedding counts for less than a hollow in the ground. The only thing that counts is death.

Now it's daybreak on Saturday, the very day the wedding will take place. He saw that Westlund was at the house yesterday. With a cigar and in his Sunday best. The old lady was on the stairs. *Won't you come down?* No, never. Better stay where he is, be who he is. Best to be the one they've turned him into. Those who do the turning.

But a door has creaked and all of a sudden the barn door is wide open. A fellow passes by the well, a long thin figure wading through the dew straight for the house. Cap pulled down over his forehead. Forward-leaning. What does he want? Probably someone from Långmo, one of the peepers. Best to slowly lower the blind. Best to let him come thinking he's unseen.

See, the snail lets everything come to him. And things keep on coming. That's why he walks so little. For as far as he can see everything is his. Although it's true he doesn't see that far. Last year he could see farther than this year. Last year he could make out Creek-Lasse's field of bush vetch from the window. He can't see that far now. So he's richer: richest of all is he who sees just as much as he owns. To thank God for bad eyes—that's the way of the world.

Of course he hears the tapping on a window down below. Sounds like Hildur's and the old lady's. But what's that to a snail? Little by little the light on the blind fades, and he walks and walks in the house that he built on top of the house. Makes his solitary run round the chimney stack that stands in the middle of the room, its whitewash glowing. Probably walks on and on until there is a groove in the floor. If he makes it that far. Round and round never getting to his destination. Like a snail? No, like a clock.

It's time to be rechristened. Time to die.

Hilma: Married to him up there. Never sleeps. Hears better and better with every passing year. The others, they hear how he walks. But she, she hears him best when he's still. Sits at night in the rocking chair with the black runners, with her hands ready on her lap. Ready for what? Oh, she knows.

You should take off your skirt, Ma, when you sleep. At the poorhouse in Lillnäs where I worked last there was an old lady like you. She never took her skirt off either. Said that in just the poorhouse rags, there was a draft between her legs. Although I know where the draft was. But she smelled so bad you had to tell the director. Then the skirt came off, Ma. This is what Irma says. Irma who pinches. Are you a pauper? Feels like it. But Hildur is nice. And today she will leave home.

Her shoulder is bare. Shines white as a sheet in the light from the crack. Cold? Now Hilma quiets the chair, gets up and puts the blanket on. Sees how her girl is sleeping with white arms under her head. Sees how the black hair lies like a mourning veil across her forehead. No lines yet, no wrinkles. Oh God. Caresses her a little with a fingertip. The forehead, the nose which is cold, and the down on the chin. Then Hildur sighs. But Hilma drops her shawl. She can't wake up yet. Children should sleep, they're only yours when they're sleeping.

Carefully she moves her chair over and sits by Hildur's bed. Kicked off the covers below now. Oh, her feet are so clean. She's always careful about that. If she steps out barefoot at bedtime, then out comes the washbowl. Is Westlund as clean? Is Westlund worthy? She places her right hand on Hildur's blanket where her breasts are. And there, it is warm and good. Does Westlund grab hard? Does Westlund scratch and tear? She leans far over and looks at her daughter's face as close as she dares.

My dearest dear, you mustn't waken. Dear God, let my children always sleep and let the night last forever. One day they'll all be gone and life will be desolate and empty. Then I'll only have my dipping tobacco in a twist, and a lonely chair rocking in the bedroom. Then I'll only be a poor old woman with dip under her nose, somebody no one cares about and no one writes to on Sundays. The world is full of robbers who want to take what I own. The earth is full of wolves that howl around the doorsteps. Dear God, let my children sleep eternally. For when they waken they don't love me. Why do we get old, tell me? Why do we get ugly? And why do we start to smell from mouth and body? Why must we live when those we live for want to live without us, push us away when we want to get close, leave when we want to approach?

Tears are raining onto Hildur's forehead. It can't be helped. They come when they come as the sorrow flows out of you. But Hildur is a light sleeper. Suddenly she sits up in bed and lifts her breasts into her slip.

"God, Ma, you scared me. Can't you sleep?"

Sleep! Hard when no one understands. Someone has to be awake when all the others are sleeping. True, the pastor had told her that the sleepless are those who do not trust in God. She trusts well enough, but it's him up there who has no one. In the darkness she hears him weaving his thoughts, thump-thump, a sound that only she can hear. But one night, she knows, this loom will stop. And God help the one who isn't awake then.

But Hildur herself can't sleep, she licks her lip and looks up at the ceiling. Probably sees through the ceiling up to him.

"Ma, do you think he'll come down?"

Hilma doesn't answer but looks at the mouth that is speaking. Soon it will be Westlund's mouth. Does Westlund bite? Is Westlund like that? Half a tooth is missing to the left in Hildur's mouth since she bit on a piece of buckshot. Westlund will probably have that fixed. Then she raises her gaze. Then she sees that Hildur is crying. Not shaking and not wringing her hands. It flows just like it flows with Hilma, a thin measured stream. So we are related. Runs clear and evenly as if snow inside her eyes was gradually melting.

"You mustn't let Westlund see when you're crying, Hildur."

"No, Ma."

But you're crying anyway, girl of mine. I'll sit with you. Can that help? Westlund is probably kind. But you are little. And he is big. You are young, girl of mine. And he is old, Westlund. Almost twice as old. And has a daughter who is already chasing after men. Siri. But why'd you take him?

"Are you with child, Hildur?"

That question is hard to ask. Harder, though, to answer. Hildur has stiffened in bed and the snow it melts and melts. Poor little feet, girl of mine. Poor you and poor all of us. May I hold you, your head in my hand?

"Yes, Ma," Hildur then says quietly. "I am."

"With West—"

But don't ask such questions. Don't ask what only one person should know.

"Be kind to Westlund, Hildur."

"Yes, Ma."

"And don't cry when he's drunk, Hildur."

"No, Ma."

"And never say no when he wants to, Hildur."

"No, Ma."

"And be kind to Siri even though she's not yours. Being kind is good. Then you can bear more, Hildur."

"Yes, Ma."

And after a while:

"You dropped your shawl, Ma."

While she bends down for the shawl she hears him lowering his blind.

"Can you see what time it is, Hildur?"

Her daughter turns her head. The alarm clock from Gävle is ticking on the dresser. Quarter to four in a bit. But the old man's clocks are starting to strike. One by one as if they had something to confide in one another. First the grandfather clock strikes. It resonates of ore. And then the one that hung in the parlor, bought at the parish clerk's auction. A chime of glass. The last one has a wretched sound, rattles like someone who's dying. The old man won it as a young farmhand at a shooting contest. Now the old man starts to pace. Around and around the chimney-stack, his slippers shuffle, his suspenders drag. That's the kind of father I have. A snail, an unsociable fool. Who doesn't go with to see the minister. Who won't come down for his daughter's wedding. She pulls the blanket up around her bosom and forgets the old woman who is holding her head through the silence. I must get him down, Hildur thinks, growing hard. For Westlund's sake he must come down, not for mine. Oh no. Nothing is done for my sake any more. But you must be kind to Westlund. Anxiety makes her throat dry and her hands damp. She clasps them firmly over the child in her belly and doesn't cry any more. The snow again becomes snow.

But the old woman has tiptoed to the clock and sure enough it's quarter to. Four, that is. But something is not as usual. Because when everything is as usual the old man stays in his hole until five. Best to go and listen at the stairs. But at the same time she hears what's new. A fellow is coming around the corner of the house. No one from the house because Rudolf walks like a soldier in his boots, stomping and kicking. And the young farmhand trots along, even if otherwise he's in no hurry. But this one is sneaking up, although he sneaks loudly.

"Hildur," she whispers, walking over to the bed. "Someone is coming."

She badly wants to pull up the blind right then but is suddenly stopped. Feels a hand on her wrist, so hard she can scream. When she looks over, Hildur is afraid. And she is strong, that girl—the blind has to wait. But the one who sneaked around the corner of the house is standing quietly by the window. Makes a shadow on the curtain, dark like terror itself. Then what they are expecting comes, the tapping, five light knocks, and the grip hardens. But Hilma no longer feels it, she is terrified. Not of him out there but of her in here. Terrified of Hildur. Fearful of Hildur's fear. The one who is fearful is a stranger to everyone else. And what does one know about one's own child? And at that moment her energy surges, she reaches out. The blind opens, and Hildur screams. Screams so that even he up there hears it. And stops walking.

But there's nothing to scream about. Only daylight, damp and bright, stands outside the window. And the sun quickly rises over the forest behind the lake. So Hildur dares to open the window. But where she doesn't want to look, she looks.

"What is it," her mother whimpers, like a frightened dog.

"Nothing," Hildur replies harshly, but closes the window.

Although she has seen the paths in the dew, the one coming toward them and the one going back. And the crow that flew up from the hedge, and in fright cawed down over the lake. And the faces in the washhouse on the marshy meadow where otherwise only the farmhand lives. And the sun that rises over one new heck of a day. She lies down with her hands over her hot face like a well cover over her worry. Skittish, the old woman retreats to the chair. That alone is hers, that and nothing more. Then sits down quietly with her head turned to the stovepipe. The stove is gone and they've stuffed a newspaper as a plug. But sometimes she hears God through the pipe anyway. And him above them, he whose blind went up again. Poor you. Poor all of us.

"Sleep now, Hildur," the old woman whispers from over in the chair. "You have a lot to do today."

"Go to sleep, Ma," Hildur answers.

But no one can sleep. Each and every one has their worries to think about.

And Hildur has ice behind her eyes.

Of course, Irma also hears the scream. But let her scream! Let Hildur scream at the top of her lungs! What does she know about screaming silently? A silent scream hurts more. A silent scream is the most painful of all. And the tapping, she probably hears that too. But let it tap. Let it tap on other people's windows. No one ever taps on mine. Why is that so? Why are some so lonely?

She feels an arm next to her in the bed. Thin, hard, hot. Takes it in her hands, harshly, like holding a stubborn handle. And suddenly she pinches. Not because she wants to, oh no. But she can't stop herself and afterward she screams silently, very silently. The boy doesn't wake up anyway, he just whimpers. Then she lets go and is free. Free for the briefest moment. It feels so good to hurt. The aches let go. You feel less lonely. And when you're less lonely you think that everything will be fine in the end. That someone will tap on your window.

Sleep now, boy. You can't help that you exist. No one can help that he exists. That's what's so aggravating. Nine years. Who knows how long nine years can be if they haven't put up with a bastard child that long. Like a shackle on your foot. Like seaweed when you're swimming. Like—but sleep now, boy, I won't do anything to you now. But once it was a close call.

She is lying in a bed up high. High so the ends of the bed almost touch the beams below the ceiling. She has a view of the whole dusky kitchen. The door to the bedroom, and the outside door, and the green leaky water butt between the doors. And the big meat and herring cabinet next to the separator, the Alfa Laval they call it. And the white newspaper holder by the window where a tramp painted three hearts last winter in return for food. And the daybed by the window, where Rudolf snores through the night. And the drop-leaf table by the other window with the alarm clock on it, the one they got to keep since Pa got his latest mania, the clock mania. And the plants in the windows that Ma waters with a cup ten times a day. Or fifteen. And then the blue stool that Pa once was about to hit Ma in the head with when he was drunk, but Rudolf, just newly confirmed, stepped between them. Instead, Rudolf took it hard across the back of the neck, and fell. The next day Pa took the ax and chopped the stool into big pieces in the woodshed. So big that it could be glued together again by someone who was handy. For three days Rudolf went at it. Then he carried it in one evening, setting it in the middle of the floor. "Take that stool out," Pa shouted. "It stays where it is," Rudolf said and became a grown-up. And now it stays where it is, but Pa is somewhere else.

However, she sees more than that from her bed. She sees through the years and they hang like dark clouds under the sooty beams. Her whole life is packed like darkness between those beams and the floor. The ceiling is low and anyone who has lived with a low ceiling wants a high ceiling. And so you flee, right? But you should know, Hildur, that some of us are tethered. Some always end up back here. Some always have to come back and be smothered, Hildur, you who'll get a ride to the butcher's villa today.

At the assessor's they had a high ceiling and no beams, and there was an even higher ceiling in town at the accountant's. But all of a sudden, Hildur, your belly grows big and under all those high ceilings you're alone with that belly. Then you take the train home and give birth. *I see—now it suits you to come home,* they say. Defenseless, at a loss for words, you lie pale in bed. The pains come and go and those beams run right over your head.

Then off again. In the factory there's a high ceiling. High like in church, Hildur. But the woman who takes care of the kid, where is she during the day? Out on the stairways, gossiping, she is. And the kid is about to die from hunger. So you lie alone at night under your high ceiling, Hildur, and think like this: Maybe that wouldn't be so bad after all. It'd set you free.

The daylight is sharp, pushing through the sides of the blind. A crow shrieks and someone runs past toward the stable. Probably the farmhand who's up to no good with girls. But between the beams the darkness gets denser. And who knows what freedom is? Ma once told us, Hildur, how one evening back when Ma was little, Kerstin, their maid—they could afford a maid then—comes running into the kitchen. That was of course before Pa came into the picture and decided to get rid of the land to be able to build. She comes running through the door there, in under these beams. She's been gone for two days, been in the forest with the cows. When she left she was fat. She's thin now. *Now it's done*, she screams, beside herself with joy. They wonder what's been done. She answers: *I'm free*. And her eyes flash. But how free they get to see the next day. Then they find the child in a ditch, crushed with a stone. And then, Hildur, they find the maid in the stream, outside grandfather's reeds.

Sometimes at night when Irma is awake she thinks the door opens. Someone is standing on the threshold with tangled hair, holding her stomach. Under the beams the dead girl enters with seaweed around her body and stained with the child's blood. Then Irma gets so scared that she screams silently. And has to waken the boy.

Here the ceiling is low. At the poorhouse it was high, Hildur. Higher than at the butcher's. So I probably should have stayed there, right? Would've suited me well, I suppose. But then my kid would never have come outside. My kid that crawled in the corridors, played with full spittoons, got pale as a pauper. Could I take it? No way. So back to: *I see, it suits you to come home now. Bitch!* And maybe that's what I am. Tugging on my leash, went off but had to come back. Back here to rot. Not like you, Hildur, who can take your bicycle and leave whenever you want. And now you're leaving for good. Leaving me behind. So go ahead and scream! And thank God that you can scream out loud!

Her brother is jabbering in his sleep. Probably dreaming about Rullan, the waitress at Bengtsson's café. Smokes long cigarettes, and blows smoke in his face so he won't see what kind of person she is. Laughs behind his back, but he's deaf. Pity him too. And pity the fly that buzzes on the flycatcher. And pity the horses in the stable. It hurts so much inside, she has to get up. Get up and walk around a little, that usually helps. Sit at the table awhile, press a cold knife against her forehead. One night she raised the blind, about halfway, unfolded the oilcloth and wrote a letter. It hurt but it helped. And no one saw it. She took the newspaper from the bottom of the shelf, tore out the announcement of the banns and stuck it in the envelope:

> The Butcher
> Hilmer Westlund
> and
> Freeholder's Daughter
> Hildur Palm
> Fuxe the 18th of July

That was the announcement and it was large. She drew another the same size on top of the paper. There was plenty of time and she wanted to be hurtful:

> Former Public Relief Worker
> Martin Eng
> and
> Snail Daughter
> Hildur Palm
> Homewreck, the 18th of July

She goes over to the cupboard and takes out a dish. Eating also helps a little. Sits down at the table and spreads lingonberry jam on a piece of rye bread. Rudolf wakes up. He doesn't hear when his sister screams like she's been stabbed, but when you take a bite he hears it loud and clear, the glutton. He yawns, scratches his chest and says, "Do ya think you can give a fellow a taste too?"

"Do you think you get served in bed? Oh no, Rullan can do that. If she can be bothered, since she's so special."

Sighing, he drags himself out of bed, his nightshirt clinging to his body. Whatever he does, he sweats a lot, Rudolf. No wonder Rullan makes faces. But otherwise he's good-looking.

"Hildur screamed," Irma says, raising the blind a little. Enough light for all her wrinkles to show. In the bedroom next door all is quiet. Are they listening? Do they know?

"So," Rudolf mutters with his mouth full of jam, "and why is that?"

"Someone tapped on the window."

The siblings eat in silence awhile. The light gets sharper and they look at each other furtively. So unaccustomed to talking to each other. But Rudolf is thinking. It shows. Because the vein on his forehead swells and he has a hard time chewing.

"Who do you think it was?"

"As if I should know that," she snaps in a hushed voice. "Should I keep track of everyone Hildur's been running with? However. It may have been the farmhand. Or one of his girls. Or Kalle Bjuhr. Or—"

Suddenly she falls silent. Rudolf sees her face turning red. And she puts her hands on her cheeks.

He sees that something is up. But he doesn't want to let on. She's so touchy, and mean at times.

"I'm gonna take a walk around the house," he says instead and steps into his work pants.

But his sister doesn't say a word.

The grass is wet but the sun is coming up. Sits up in the pines of Uvberg and spews light onto the lake. In the flowerbed the old lady's sunflower is standing with its head bowed. Have ya lost something, girl? A squirrel runs on the wooden fence. You should flay a few of those suckers for Rullan, he thinks. She's always complaining about the fur coat she doesn't have. He stands by the corner of the house and pisses onto a small uneven stone. The grass around it is singed. Once a month he turns the stone with his foot. If he lives and keeps his health, little by little the stone will become completely round. Then I'll take it inside, he thinks, and put it on the mantelpiece. Although first I'll clean it. This is one of his goals in life. And not the least one at that.

He makes a few turns past the lilacs up by the stables and woodsheds. A gnarled birch root lies on the sawhorse, wet from rain. He gets a splinter in his left foot and curses. Walks around the farmyard and the outbuildings, then comes to the row of birches he'd planted the day he came of age. Took saplings straight from the forest, so there wasn't any extra expense. Now they've grown up, like him. And some of them have scars from cow horns, just like he carries scars. He takes a leaf and chews on it, then remembers that it's today they'll be decorating with birch branches. It's today his sister will be married to the butcher. The youngest of them and first to get married. Only twenty-three. He himself is thirty-three (two in between died as infants) and if Rullan doesn't want to marry soon, God knows how it'll work out. It's not so easy for someone who doesn't own a motorbike. But Irma is thirty-five and will probably never get married. He can pity her. Maybe he should go back inside.

But just then he sees that the barn door is open. And he's enough of a farmer to get angry. One of the tramps has probably been out doing his business. They have to do that sort of thing too of course, even though they're next to nothing, but they should at least shut the door behind them. There are three of them and one is sick, couldn't even make it to evening porridge. Have to see now if he makes it in for the morning gruel. He's not lying there puking is he? *No, the old man had said, it's not that he's sick. Not in that way*, he said. So God knows how he's sick.

As he's closing the door he remembers the rake. It's right inside the shed and he brings it out to the yard in the sun. Such a magnificent rake has probably never before been seen on this farm. But then again, he's worked the shaft with sandpaper every free moment for a week. Then he painted it blue with yellow teeth and set a nickel-plated fitting on the handle. If Rullan gets splinters on her fingers from that handle, she can just as well rake with the dung-fork. Or a silver fork from Bengtsson's kitchen. Tonight, he'll give her the rake. Tonight, she'll hold it in her hand and think: What a man he is after all, Rudolf, even if he doesn't own a motorcycle. Does anyone care as much about a girl as Rudolf does? No way!

When he comes out of the shed again he sees the old man's white hair glow in the window. He must have seen the rake, and been wondering. But go ahead and glare all you want! Because now I'm the one in charge. Even if the old man thinks he is. Long ago you could hit somebody on the head with a stool. Now that stool is mine. So go on in and pull down the blind. Suddenly Rudolf gets so angry that he takes the birch root from the sawhorse and throws it to the hedgehogs in the lilac bushes. Now he'll have that to brood about too. The old fart.

But in the washhouse a door slams sharply like a shotgun firing. Rudolf moves quickly to the corner of the house. He sees a white skirt slink behind the bushes by the lake. And he hears a woman's heels tapping against the stones on the shore. I see. No wonder the farmhand almost falls asleep at the dinner table these days. In July he was asleep in a hay-load and ran it into the barn with himself on top. Loaded low as luck would have it, otherwise there would've been one less farmhand in the village.

But you wonder who it can be. For the fun of it Rudolf takes a stone and whizzes it down into the reeds. The girl stops a moment behind the farthest alder tree. You get a glimpse of white but nothing more. Then she laughs and disappears, the white devil. A loud, ugly laugh, like that of the river spirit, the one who together with her husband drags children into the lake when it gets dark. He's cold now. Yawns, wipes a piece of chicken shit from his toe and steps into the house.

Inside, the jam is still on the table and he takes a ladle. Just then Pa's clocks strike. One at a time but close to each other as if it was a competition. Last comes the farmer's clock in worn-out boots.

"Pa's clocks just struck," he tosses out toward the bed, as he's done a hundred times before, and crawls out of his work pants.

But Irma doesn't breathe a sound. So she's probably asleep then. Best to sleep awhile yourself. Because soon you'll be up cutting branches for the sister you like. And soon you'll be drunk. He swallows some jam and climbs into bed at four-thirty.

But Irma isn't asleep. She closes her eyes but still feels fear seeping from the beams. What have I done? Help me God so that it works out. Darkness falls around the beams and it becomes hard to breathe. But as she sinks, drowning in the black water of fear, she gets an arm across her breasts, and it holds her up. She clings fast to the boy's arm with both her sweaty hands as if it were her final rescue.

"Martin," she whispers. "My Martin."

At three-thirty Svea wakes up. Usually when she wakes she wants to leave right away. Because when daylight comes she is ashamed. Ashamed of the room she's lying in. Yet not mostly for the room itself, but for what the room is called. Because there are things she can do without being ashamed, things that aren't good but which have a good name. Drive-the-tramp-out-of-the-yard, for example, in the name of a love for order, not out of mercilessness. But the farmhand's quarters in which she wakes up have no name other than "the farmhand's quarters." That's what makes it so hard. And there's a dirty word on the wall. Or, to be exact, there was, because Sören has chiseled it out since the last time she was here. That he hadn't once carved it himself was an excuse but only a small one, as she'd told him.

Besides, it's cramped lying with a farmhand. The mattress Palm supplies him with is thin and she feels the springs as much as Sören's ribs. At the butcher's, there's a softer place to lie down. The butcher's maid should have a soft place to lie down. That's what Westlund had told her.

"Let me go now," she says half-awake to the sleeping Sören.

But Sören hasn't heard anything. She wriggles like a fish on land for him to notice. But no. He just takes a firmer hold of her shoulders and pulls her closer.

"You're out of your mind," she mumbles, content in any case, and pinches him between the ribs.

Then he blinks, Sören, like a sleepy horse. And he places his strong hard legs over hers. That's all. It's dark in the wash-house and the rats rustle in the attic. It sounds like they're reading newspapers. Outside it's probably full daylight already and she must be home before the village wakens. Because you know what people think about those who come home late on a Saturday morning. And how does she herself think about others? Badly. But she strokes Sören across his back and a thrill of sin and shame runs through her body like the sweetest shiver. Sören goes back to sleep and she lets him. Just a while longer. A little while like this.

She doesn't love him but you can't ask for it all if you don't have money. Once she saw a film at the Community Center. The man in it lit two cigarettes, and one he gave to Bette Davis. The next day she told the boy she was going with, an errand boy at Ohlsson's Hardware and Paint, about it. He smoked a pipe. *Hell, yes*, he said. *Take a puff then. But don't go gettin' any ideas.*

There's probably no one around here who can love like that. And who knows what it's like in town? People go there and come back unloved. Irma, up at the farm, went there. Then she came home after eight months. Alone, not counting the one she tried to hide under her coat that is. Coats were loose-fitting that year. Now she's alone all the time. No harm done. And it serves that snail-monkey right. But you have to watch out. It's not that easy to live. That you learn with time, that and nothing else. Like for Rullan at the café, whom they say you can believe just about anything about.

You ought to have a car, like the doctor's wife, a small one to drive around to better places. A car, said the butcher, that can easily be arranged; just do as I say. But what is that supposed to mean? You all say the same thing, she told him flat out. Promises, promises, and more promises! Then a girl is left there standing. Not even engaged. Or lying there, to be more precise. *I see*, said the butcher. *If it's the ring that's missing I've got nothing against it. But come now, let's hit the sack.*

So much for you, butcher-liar! For who's sitting in the car when you return from the village the next day if not Hildur

32

Palm. That wasn't the cow you were supposed to pick up from the farmer at Söräng. And then there's a steady stream of flowers, sausage, ham and what have you. So that in the evening it gets said flat out: "I'm not wearing out any more sheets in this bed. How will it turn out if something goes wrong?" And what does that goat of a butcher reply? *First, it'll have to be proven.* I see, it has to be proven. Westlund could have said that right away. Then it would have been easy to know what kind of bed warmer he is.

Sleep now Sören and don't dream anything bad about me. And nothing bad when you wake up either. Because you live as well as you can, and a bird in the hand is worth two in the bush. One girl gets a butcher, another a farmhand. And you're warm and good anyway. There are people who don't even think that about their own. Nisse the painter, who hits Aina with firewood when he's drunk, and Pump Johan with his artificial hand. Those in the know say Maja shudders every time he touches her with it.

But hush my mouth! And hush you who say: *And today they'll be married.* Today, Westlund, you shall stand before the pastor, the fillings in your teeth sparkling. Surely you'll be hanging by the mirror, Westlund, for half the day, combing the curls on your balding head. Gaping, so your fillings gleam. But one day, they too must hit a short circuit. *Has Svea seen so many fillings at any one time before? Made in America.* But make me here and make me there, Westlund. You won't see me on my back again.

But now Sören is awake.

"What are you lying there mumbling about," he says softly and quietly, pulling hard on the hairs under her armpit. Goat beard!

"Got to go home now," she answers, "before Westlund

wakes up. And today he'll probably be up early. So he has time to get married, the jerk."

And Sören is not one to hold you back. It's hot and cramped in the bed and he's exhausted, exhausted and content. Surely he could have had someone else. But you make do with what you have. Although if he owned a motorbike then, hot damn. Then he'd go farther away than the dance floor at Forsen. Then he'd drive to Lärkström and walk on his hands. Although those who have motorbikes in Lärkström come here. So somewhere along the line something is amiss.

At the foot of the bed Svea is on her thick knees, separating her clothes from his as if they were a lower sort. Sören stretches out, making the bed his again. Because this is how it is: first you have a crazy wet longing to have someone. But once you've had, then you thank God every time you get to have the bed to yourself. Every evening you can be on your own picking up stations on the radio. Just think of the ones he used to hear. One night he was lying there listening to the Chinese who have little bells in their mouths. And then to the amateurs: *Hellohello. Yes, thank you, I'm doing fine. Yesterday I was out picking mushrooms and got two liters of fine morels. Hellohello. Do you hear me 2 wc? Right now my wife is making coffee. Yesterday I spoke with DUM 3 ASS. I could hear fine except one time when a crow came onto the signal. On Monday I'll have coffee in the garden along with H_2O. The weather is nice here but soon it will start to hail so I'd better sign off. Goodbyegoodbye 2 wc and hello to the wife. Over from PI PPI.*

So go now Svea. And stick to the butcher's helper with only one ear. Who got punched on the other at Forsen last Wednesday. Yours truly will get a certificate instead, lie here in bed and be his own radio. *Hellohello India and Nowhere. Last night I washed my feet. And tomorrow I'll probably do my neck if all goes well. Tonight Hildur from the farm will marry Westlund the butcher, and this morning I saw a big stone lying in the middle of the road. I'm thinking about treating the stone to coffee if the weather is nice. But now I have to blow my nose so it's probably safest to stop. So goodbyegoodbye* ABCDEFGHI-JKLMNOPQ *3.*

He looks at Svea but his mouth doesn't water at three-thirty in the morning. He is satiated and the inner Sören, deep down inside, is close to throwing up. Because with Svea it's like with whipped cream, first you shovel in a load. Then all at once you're full. They say she ran after the butcher. Although there's so much talk in this village. It was different at home in Sågfors. There they only talked about one person. Sören reaches out his arm and raises the blind a little. Light outside, but light doesn't suit Svea this time of day. Ink under her eyes, and her breasts hang like lead bags over the fold in her waistline. He touches her, lightly. She is cold as an ax handle.

"Pull the blind down," she pleads.

And she has fright in her eyes like a cow brought to slaughter. But he raises it even more because he's tired now. Tired of her begging. And tired of always obeying. He turns her head hard out toward the day. Hang your beauty out for airing then we'll see if it holds! But she doesn't blubber like he wants. She startles and stares.

"Someone's knocking on Hildur's window."

A man is outside the bride's window and Sören's clock from confirmation does not yet show four. Cap, black trousers, a turtleneck sweater. Short and with a rather slender back. Running now, in a flash he's around the corner. Couldn't see who it was. But Hildur's blind goes up and there she stands. White in her window. They draw back from theirs, and close their blind.

Sören stretches out in the bed. Svea steps out on the farm-hand's rug. It is rough under smooth feet. The butcher's is soft as moss. Hildur is said to have walked barefoot on it only once. Perhaps she'd like to walk barefoot on other rugs than Westlund's? Maybe the one who's knocking has rugs on his floors?

"Yes, I've seen her on her back," she hears the farmhand testify from the bed.

Although that's probably plain boasting. Who among the boys doesn't hide in the alders when the girls swim? So she says quite calmly, and without her back turning red:

"If you'd stayed a little longer maybe you would've seen her belly too."

"Yes, Hildur's belly and Rudolf's rake," the farmhand says with a sneer.

Then he says something else. But it has no significance, because she's not thinking about the farmhand now. She's thinking about the one who ran. And about big fat Westlund. Someone knocks on the bride's window—someone rings the wedding bell. So, Westlund, who makes the most noise? He who has ears let him hear, even if he only has one. She's so happy that her mouth waters. Happy about the unbelievable thing that's now happening. And will rot in the butcher's well. Now, Westlund, we're in the same boat. And this levelling gives her the strength that getting on an equal footing can do. The back she's turned to the farmhand is firm. And the voice with which she kills his freedom is confident.

"I'm gonna have a baby, Sören."

She finishes dressing in silence, and listens to the silence of the farmhand. She will have time to finish, and then some. She will have time to leave if she wants to. And it is almost morn-ing so she must leave. But when she turns around, she hardly dares look at him. Because if she looks she may be lost. More lost than she already is. Because she already feels how her lie is taking hold, how it's glued on by terror. She sinks down on the bed beside Sören, and pain draws its drapery before her eyes. She presses her hands around his rough cheeks, tight like never before. Poor Sören. But I guess this is what living is like. Lucky that it's not like this at the movies because then it would be unbearable.

But Sören removes her hands. So gently that it hurts. And then it's time to leave.

"Guess I'll see you tonight at the Palms."

She says it quietly as she is already out the door. There's no answer. But no vexations linger in the morning air. It feels better outside. Really good almost. It's as if once it's been said, it's over. There is a breeze from the lake. She gets drunk on fresh air and feels a surge of happiness. The Palms' boat creaks against the dock. Fish snap at the surface. On the other side of the lake a stack of bricks glows red below the spruce trees. Kungsgårn is rebuilding its wall. But mostly she is happy about that which she doesn't see, but knows anyway. The blind is up in the bedroom window. So Hildur is waiting. Waiting for whom?

Up on the farm a noise is heard in the lilac bushes. Someone's coming probably. She sneaks behind the alders just in time to see that it's Rudolf, known as Little Snail. She runs on the pebbles along the shore, glad for the green cover. It's good to see, but best to be unseen. She hears a stone fall into the lake. The one Rudolf throws. But stones can't really see, can they? At the old clothes-washing jetty, she stops and laughs out loud at his stupidity. And at his rake. Then patters on in the cool morning.

Sören gets up. Stands up naked and opens both windows.

The one facing the lake and the one facing the farm. But it's still just as cramped and stuffy. How can you get a bigger place? How will you get away? In the east, the cliffs of Uvberget loom like an unpapered wall. In the west lies the snailhouse. A damned trap, that's what it is. Maybe he can run. The hell he will. Because the child welfare officer has long arms and hands. With glue on them. And suddenly his hands will be around your neck like Svea's just were. Then you become a customer at the post office, mailing checks for the rest of your life. Like Little Sven and Ture Olsson. Collection, they call it. Because of that.

No, no more radio! He takes the damned box and coaxes it ungently into the chamber pot shelf in the commode. Now the Chinese will have one less person to jingle to. And the amateurs, they can shut up. He finds some pipe tobacco, but his hand shakes, and the can spills. Furious, he bangs the pipe against the wall and the stem comes off. This must be what it's like to smoke in hell. And for a farmhand, this is what it's like to eat in hell: the pitcher of small beer falls into the bacon. Butter melts on the bread and runs down your fingers. The milk is sour and the porridge burns on the stove. The sauce runs from the spoon down over your shirt. And you drop the fork right into the mouth of the farmer's dog. You take salt with the strawberries, and thank the devil for his food. But worst of all is to make love in hell: It's too cramped in bed and you've forgotten to wash your feet. And she has never brushed her teeth. So you have to open the window to let in some air. The bed feels full of pebbles, and creaks like a lecturer. And you're afraid that someone will walk in. You're afraid before and you're afraid after. And probably you're afraid in the midst of it too. Because there's a rustling under the pillow. It's the child support order. And who's standing outside the wall sneering? Who is knocking on the window before the night is over? Oh yes, it's the child welfare officer. Who leaves big tracks in the dew.

The prisoner walks aimlessly around the room, from one corner to the other. This morning everything has edges, everything feels sharp. And bars seem to envelop his forehead. Stopping, he stands in front of the wall and stares at the mark from the defaced word. Then a thought takes hold with a curious force. The greatest force he's known so far. He runs into the washing-room, finds a rusty marlinespike in an old kettle and a large hammer on top of the stove. Finally back at the wall, he starts pounding it. Striking like a lunatic who knows what he's doing and yet doesn't know. Letter by letter, he hammers in the forbidden word until it is etched there forever. The nail gets hot. The hammer too. And warm sweat rains onto the rag-rug.

His pitiful youth pours off his body in hot streams.

Three tramps are sleeping in the hay. Or ought to be sleeping, it still being that time of night. But Filip, the old man, lies awake. And so does Ivar Lund. And the sick Sixten hasn't been able to fall asleep since he came in from doing his business.

So three tramps keep watch in the hay while God spreads light like honey on the shingled roof. They are each lying in a corner of the big barn loft floor. Usually, there is no hay here, but this year the farm got seventy loads and the old man didn't want to stack. So they put a layer in the loft until the rye is cut. Filip rests the deepest in the hay because he's the heaviest. And Ivar rests lightest because he hates himself. But Sixten is hardly lying down at all. Up walking again now. If the others cared, they could see him prowl around in the darkness of the barn. Stand awhile by the threshing machine with a hand resting on the feeding table. Turn the wheel fifty times although it creaks. Smell the thresher under the belly, over by the husk outlet. And at the end caress the tongue of the straw spitter.

There once was someone who loved threshers. But it wasn't this one. No, it was someone who walked long and far. So far that at last he no longer spoke of the many pairs of shoes he'd worn out, but of how many roads. He walked and walked but of course: he never arrived. Because an arrival probably doesn't even exist. If you walk, then you walk to arrive at the same place from whence you started. Him too. But he loved threshing machines. Slept at farms like all the others. Sometimes he was full of lice. But don't think that made him sleep in stables. Only barns would do, because in barns there are threshing machines. So what did he see in threshers? Well, some of it was probably the color, the red and yellow. The yellow of the body and the red of the joints. And he was particularly fond of feeding tables that were blue. But didn't like the ones with wooden extensions in the front. He loved threshers more than animals, and naturally much more than people. Mostly he liked them at rest when heavy with sleep and calm power, they stood motionless on the barn floors with their six or eight feet screwed into the floorboards. Captives, yes, but captives who wore their captivity the way others wear freedom. There was a calm about a sleeping thresher that was greater than the calm of all other sleepers, because a thresher had no dreams. In the twilight, he sneaked around the sleeping threshing machines and in that way felt a peace that grew with the years. His soul became like a barn after harvest, a calm place where no one enters. When he died he'd die like a thresher: silent hands unscrewing feet from their captivity to the floor. For the first time free.

But naturally he was not unmoved by the beauty of a threshing machine at work. The brute force in the jaws as they grind. The yellow sides quivering with fury as the life of the grain is torn apart in its hot body. The frenzy with which a chewed-up sheaf is ejected into its meager components: grain, straw and husks. The rumble from its dark bowels: a volcano in controlled eruption. And the smoke from its hot breath, hovering like a cloud in the barn. *Such is life when life is at its very best* he used to say to anyone who listened, and there weren't many. Life is a threshing machine that whips the grain out of us, bangs the straw out and frees us from husks. When life is at its best, it takes life from us.

How he ended his days? Well, one evening at a paddock, Filip was told there'd be no more tramps on that farm. So why's that? he'd asked. *It went very badly last time, see. Is that so? What happened? Well, a tramp came along in the middle of threshing time. May I sleep in the barn, he said, I love thresh-ing machines, you see. And that was fine. And the next day he asks if he can help out with the threshing. We reckon that if he loved threshing machines he'd probably be able to feed them too, although he looked old and frail. But it goes badly. The maid has to rescue his fingers. And he can't stand in the load or carry hay. So finally, the old man has to be content with the husks. And the threshing is in full swing and all of a sudden the old man's gone. Probably just as well because he was mostly in the way. But at noon the farmhand is removing the husks from under the machine. After the first fork load, a foot is visible. And completely covered, under the husks, the old man is lying dead. So he sure didn't get much for loving threshing machines.*

And now we won't take any more tramps at this farm. As I said.
No way. G'night.

This third one here tonight, is he like that? Although he
seems incapable of loving. Thin, silent, flat-chested. *Hit there*
by a stone, was the only thing he'd told about himself that first
evening. And the following night: *It could've been the end of*
me. I see. Thanks for sharing. If you'd had a tweezer perhaps
you could have pulled out a little more. But why does a person
need to know? It's enough to know that the earth is round.
And that all tramping routes lead back to the same hayloft.
About this a poem should be written.

A poem has actually been written, but it's not yet finished.
Filip carries it in his pocket from hayloft to hayloft. It has
twenty-four verses but that's far from all. Someday when it's
really finished, when it has a title and an ending, it will be
printed at a print shop in Tierp. There must be one there.
Then Filip will sell it to all the homesteads along the road.
Does he go around peddling? No, ma'am, I'm selling a poem.
But I bought one last year, so I'm not sure. That was probably
a different one, ma'am. This one has a hundred verses. And
costs one riksdaler. One öre per verse, ma'am, you won't get
cheaper poems these days. Not even in Stockholm.

Perhaps it will never be finished. Once he'd thought to
himself: Mine eye hath seen all this. And now others will
find out what I know. But time passes and poems never get
finished. Time passes and statements become questions. If in
the first stanza he'd say: See here a soul I deeply know, then in
the final, he'll lament: Who can know my anguish?

Now someone comes and shuts the door after the one
who's sick. And Filip sees how terribly scared he gets, the one
by the name of Sixten. Or at least that's what he calls himself.
Ivar Lund sees it too. How Sixten crawls away behind the

thresher, lies low like a hare until the one who shut the door is gone. So who can know his anguish?

Where do you come from, they'd asked him that first evening. *Skåne*, was the quiet one's quiet answer. Ivar and the old man had seen him from afar, standing under the signpost by the road to Mellanhede station. Himself a signpost, but with lowered wings, pointing inward toward himself. To My Pain 2 km. Carrying pebbles in his shoes and his sorrow on his back. Not used to walking at all, at most used to standing still. That was the impression they got as they approached.

I see. So you're familiar with Lackalänga then? Filip asked. *No. How so?* Well, it's literature-related, Filip replied. It was the first parish of the poet Esaias Tegnér. Then Ivar Lund burst out: *What business is that of mine?* and he spat in the Mellanhede gravel. That was a day he was even touchier than usual, Ivar. But the new fellow breathed hard: *Did I say Skåne? No, I meant Östergötland.* I see. So how do things look in Sörping nowadays? *Well it's probably as usual. You see I mostly stayed in Frövi.*

A man who lies, Filip and Ivar Lund had added, silently. Best to keep eyes open and mouths closed. And if he hadn't had a pencil it probably would've been "so long" at the next fork in the road. They would've said: Now we'll go our way and you go yours. But he had a pencil. And Filip had lost his in a Willbo hayloft. And at any moment, a verse of a poem might come to him. Then he'd head down into a ditch or to the nearest pasture to give his pencil free rein. But a person with no pencil writes no poems. No. His poems are lost. And what could be a worse thing to lose? Earlier that day Filip had told Ivar the same thing four times. In Willbo in the morning, in Skärpe at noon, in Treng at four and in Mellanhede in the evening. He'd told Ivar that at the next store he's going to ask for a pencil. And every time, his face increasingly ashen, Ivar had replied: *We're not beggars. We're just out walking. Remember that!*

So he's just out walking, Ivar. Nothing wrong with that. Each and every one has their own way of suffering. But if you want to get a free pencil, you can't be proud. And now this fellow had one, so he got to join them. Pencil-less now. Although he doesn't exactly look like he writes. He also has a knife hidden in his pocket. To sharpen the pencil? A Mora knife with a sheath! There are some who like to cut horses at night. Is he one of those? If you walk across the barn loft from where they are lying, you come to the stable, and from there a whitewashed door leads to the stalls. And he walks that way, the one with the knife. Takes small steps in the hay and sighs four times. And his whole face looks like the white of his eye. But he stops in the shed, rattling the horseshoe nails and discarded horseshoes, and picks up halters. Searching for something. And finally Ivar gets mad:

"Yes, take a horse, dammit, and run off with the threshing machine so we don't have to look at you."

It works. Silent as a barn rat, and just as quick and frightened, he scurries into his corner, into his hole, the insomniac. Stays silent, and disappears into the hay so he can't be seen. Spreads the hay over himself as if he never wanted to get up again. But what is he doing here? He who got so sick when Fuxe Lake was glimpsed from the Tyr ridges that he turned pale as a sheet and lost his appetite. *We're not going to that farm, are we?* Of course, we are. The old man is crazy but he's in the attic. The old lady is nice, but the son is stingy. And the farmhand is lazy. The oldest daughter is ugly, but the youngest one, she's fine. *You go on,* Sixten had said, *I'll sit here in the ditch awhile, I'm worn out.*

44

It's mostly quiet now. Only the horse stamps. Up on the roof a bird is scratching. Somewhere in the thresher body there's a popping sound. Then a hen is making a damned racket. Best to sleep while there's time. But it's at that time, when it's dark, when you should sleep, when you're tired as a worn-out beast of burden, that a verse arrives, carried to you through the air. Where's that pencil now, and the paper? The paper is here, but the pencil is gone. Up on your knees, digging for it in the hay. But it's dark all around, and the tiny holes in the shingled roof shine like small cold stars.

"What are you doing?" Ivar snarls from his corner.

"I've lost my pencil," Filip whines and tumbles over.

"What do I care! Be quiet."

And little by little, it does get quiet. Although the cock crows, and the horse noisily eats in the manger. Ivar falls asleep first, his hand covering his face like a lock. Filip lies there awhile in pain. Feeling an ache that comes when he's lonely. A burning on his left side. A fire that corrodes like lye. He puts his fist over it, to keep it from spreading. But sometimes it spreads anyway like all our pains. At last, he falls asleep, a moan hanging from his mouth.

But the third one perhaps won't sleep at all.

Who Can Know My Anguish?

Westlund is lying in his oak bed. A sizeable man, in a sizeable bed. Whatever's bigger, that's to Westlund's taste. But can he really help it? A bigger farm, a bigger slaughterhouse, a bigger mare, a bigger dwarf. Not simply big, because there's no consolation in big. Consolation is found in bigger, in what isn't the smallest. In being superior.

He was in America once, you know. Arrived there with a sizeable sum. Left there with one not as big. But that was long ago, so long ago actually that he's forgotten most of it like a dream. And so long ago that often he finds himself there when he is somewhere else. Mostly it's right after he wakes up, as he lies waiting for Svea to bring coffee. Around eight, that is.

So there he lies in his oak bed. A bed of oak in America. Under a ceiling of oak. In America. Between walls of oak. In America. And above his head on the oak bed's oak headboard are three oak buttons. The first is for Mary. If Westlund pushes it, well yes, soon he's no longer alone in bed. For in through the oak door comes Mary in silk underwear. Then there's the second button and that one is for thirst. The whiskey button called—a toast to oak, between oak walls. He presses. *Yes Massuh.* Here comes Joe, the colored servant, honking in the oak mezzanine. Westlund moves the oak lever, the door opens and in rolls the truck, bringing the beer and whiskey cart. Joe honks again and drives out. And the third? The coffee button! More worn than the others, gets used a little more. You can get tired of all the extravaganza, as Westlund says. Probably have to let the oak carpenter take a look at it sometime.

Westlund tells Joe: Send 'em in! Na! Send 'em up! Na! No, call the beef manager to take an order! While the beef manager is on his way Westlund goes through today's mail. Look here. Another signature! It wears on you being the butcher of the hour. And all the paupers begging for sausage and bratwurst. But see now! Yet another medal, this one you'll simply have to wear on your fly. Hmm, ugh. What about that factory in Arizona that wants to get bought, the meat cleaver factory. Okay, just hold your horses and the price will probably come down some ten thousand dollars.

Beef manager here. I see, good. Well, how's it going with the beef? Eighty-three thousand! Not bad, huh? Should probably get the ham manager in here to hear how things are going with the hams. But you'd better put on the white coat today, manager, and wash the hogs and scrub the cleavers with Sunlight soap, because the president is coming at four o'clock.

At eight o'clock Svea arrives. Knocks on the door like a sheriff. Come in, Joe! Westlund is lying in his oak bed, Svea stands at the threshold. He must have pushed the third button by mistake. She is short and round. Rounder soon, from what's been said. So Westlund is back home again, and doesn't grieve over that at all. Because Westlund has imagination. But no illusions. Some have illusions but no imagination, and things go badly for them. For Westlund things are going pretty well. Or better. Svea trots in over the rug, holding the tray at a slant. There's the usual on it, the petty usual.

"Haven't I told you that the mail should be on the tray,"

Westlund scolds. This is like his morning prayer, because the mail doesn't come before eleven.

"How many times do I have to say that the mail doesn't come until eleven," Svea hisses. Today she's like a stove fired with oak logs.

"So," Westlund grunts, "that's going to change."

But darned if Svea believes that. Sly, she looks. And tired as a nightshirt at nine o'clock in the morning. The chipped cup on the tray again! As if he couldn't afford whole ones. She sneers a little as she pours, sneers but keeps silent. And Westlund saves on words too. Westlund ponders as he looks at the first button. To push it or not to push it, that is the question. Westlund's answer is yes, so when Svea turns her back to move the chair up to the bed for the tray, he touches her hips slightly. It's a long way to her legs, and Westlund feels like grabbing her really hard. Feels like taking her. But this time Svea isn't going along.

"Today when Westlund is gonna get married," she says, wrestling herself away. "And all."

"Goodness," says Westlund, round-eyed with surprise. "Is that today?"

"Yes, he doesn't remember that?"

How happy the poor thing is. Until she understands: he's just joking, the jerk. Although then, she's happy anyway. And that's not good. Because if she's happy she's dangerous. Then her eyes glow and her serpent tongue wags. *I'm probably gonna have a baby, Westlund. With Westlund.* That was back then. But he pushed back until she'd shut up and her fire went out. He should put it out now too, he reckons. But not before pushing the second button.

"How about a little drink this morning?"

"Today when he's getting married and all," Svea blathers on.

But she walks over to the secretary desk and unlocks it. Gets the cognac, but only one glass. And that's probably just as well, so it'll last until tomorrow morning. They'll need plenty of drink then to quench the hangover. Because the cellar is still full of aquavit and the village of Fuxe full of thirst. An amusing memory tickles the corner of his mouth. Oh yes, before Lillsvängen was carried out drunk last night, he'd said: *One has a slight but solid education, said the man who could sign three liquor ration books in one go.*

"Do you know anyone who has a slight but solid education," he asks Svea, watching as she pours, already feeling the drink warming his chest. But she's holding the bottle at a stingy angle.

"That must be Westlund himself," she hacks at him. "But does he happen to be so educated that he knows who threw up on the stairs last night? Because when I came home . . . "

Then she bites off her tongue, swallowing it whole. Because even though he throws up on a stairway, his very own no less, after his own bachelor party, he's not so drunk that he doesn't know what time it is. Three o'clock, Svea! So last night you got to bed late, Svea. Into your own bed, that is. And that's probably just as well, but don't come here shouting about child support and support for fallen virgins thinking Westlund will stand for it.

"Hand me the cigar!"

So Westlund lights his morning cigar with a sure eye and sure hand, and blows the first smoke down between his shirt and his chest hair. A custom from America. Then you smell of Havana through and through, a smell worth some eight thousand dollars.

"Have a seat, Svea."

She sits down and glares, her elbow on her thigh, her chin in her hand. But deep in her eyes she has something that must go away. She has all the weapons of the puny coward: *I, I know something about you. Something you don't know.* So Westlund sits up against the headboard. Oak at his back. Svea only has elm. He clears his throat and then goes at it with all his might:

"Well, circumstances will change here as of today and this date. If you understand what I mean by what I mean, Svea."

"Sure, a person probably understands what Westlund means," she says. "And as far as circumstances are concerned I'm not the one who will have any circumstances with you, Westlund. More than the circumstance that already is, that is."

Westlund drinks up. Then drinks up some more, truly touched by the simple words. He pulls out the drawer of the oak bed stand. There is a brooch there, and he takes it out.

"You can have this as a memento, Svea," he says, all parts of him moved. Someday he'll pin the Medal of Patriotism onto Svea's old woman's breast. This here is only a practice run but with tears on the ready. Svea takes the medal for brief and unfaithful service, immediately shoving it into her apron pocket. Then she sits down again. Time passes. Both in the room and outside. Westlund is lying in his bed of oak. Svea sits straight-backed on a chair of elm. In the know. Knows what Westlund won't know yet for a while.

"Send for my assistant," Westlund says. He's a little scared, maybe it's his nerves. He sometimes feels them in the mornings, treating them like friends.

Svea is gone and the butcher's helper arrives. Enters with his cap on. It's a habit he has, a good one at that. Because then his half an ear isn't as noticeable. Some call him One-Ear, others Half-Ear, Westlund hasn't been able to decide yet on which. He puffs on his cigar, letting the helper stand and stew on the rug, at last all of Westlund is smoke.

"You must rake the walkway up to the slaughterhouse." Smoke rises from his command, and inside the smoke there's lightning and thunder. "Because today it must be tidy as hell."

"In honor of the day," the butcher boy chimes in. Another habit of his, chiming in instead of talking. Then he avoids thinking of anything to say himself. Sometimes he simply chimes in too much, but he sure knows how to butcher.

"And don't leave any goat skins hanging outside," Westlund barks.

"Oh, no. Young brides, they've got good noses," the helper says. "But the fact is that we haven't butchered a goat in three months. Because of Simon. There's no stopping him."

"That's going to change," Westlund says. "And if I ever see that bastard in the middle of the road again, I'll run him over."

"Probably better wait until you get the marriage license, sir," the helper suggests. "But Simon brought home his new car yesterday. And went around the village bragging that now Westlund will soon be driven out of Långmo as well."

"That's going to change," Westlund says.

But that's a prayer, and barely that. War is just around the corner or a storm is raging. That's going to change, Westlund says. And so there will be a change. "Where was I?" Westlund asks, "Right: That's going to change!" But the butcher's helper stands there grinning. Before long he'll probably be a butcher boy for Simon. And Svea, Simon's maid. Then the Medal of Patriotism will be no good. Then it might be handy to have a farm up your sleeve. It's generally good to have things up your sleeve. But that butcher boy won't be grinning for much longer.

"Take off your cap inside," Westlund says.

Cap comes off and the half an ear is bared. That sure put a stop to the laughing.

"And don't forget to go to Bylund's at noon for the calf, because I'm still the one who picks up calves in Långmo. And at two o'clock I'm the one getting a ride. You know where. But if you spot Simon's car before then, hit it. It's probably nothing but a junky old Ford anyway."

"Yeah, but this year's model," the little shit adds. Mean now for the doffed cap's sake.

As if a '29 year's model wasn't good enough for animal transport. But he can brag, that Simon. That's all that chiseler is good for. But not good for getting a lady, he's not. Much less six or seven of them.

"You can go now, Hagström," Westlund says. "And send Siri in if you see her, Hagström. And lock up the dog because today no one must get bitten. There's a party today, Hagström. Hagström!"

"You" for the small moments. And "Hagström" for the bigger ones. Fancy having someone whose name is Hagström. My assistant, his name is Hagström. Yours, Simon, what's his? Karlsson, right. Jeez. Though Hagström will never get a woman with that ear. Westlund listens with his. Hagström shutting the door to the porch. It will probably be a while before Siri comes.

There's a hand mirror on the bed stand with a loop handle, and sometimes, when he is on his own, Westlund sets his thumb in it to take stock of himself. Looking this way, and that, his cigar in the middle of his mouth, his cigar on the side. He wipes the shine off his nose with the corner of the sheet, he lets his forehead be at rest. And the fillings, there are plenty of those. Seven at least, although only three are visible. Even so he has a yard-size smile. He tinkers with the light, glowers and twists, Westlund has many different looks but only one that is good. If he's patient, it finally shows up in the mirror. Then he can put the mirror away, and look like that for the rest of the day. Oh yes. You still have the charm, as Hildur was saying, even if you're past draft age. You still have that special thing, Hildur said, even though you're a little wide around your belly, rising like a ridge out of the bedding. But what's that to him? Not chicken shit. Go ahead and glare, he thinks, although no one is glaring. Not yet, though no doubt there'll be glaring when he arrives with Hildur in the car. The '35, as he'd told her. True: a six-year lie but what does that matter, the buggy looks the same as it did six years ago and in six years' time he'll have a new one.

Go ahead and glare, he thinks. And this time he says it to someone specific. To Frida who's sitting in a chair within glass and frame on the wall. Sitting in a rocking chair, to be exact, staring. It was taken the year before she died, before the blood clot reached its final destination, a year when she just sat and stared out into the empty blue. And the empty black, because for a long time she was sleepless. And the empty white, because she died in the winter. A year in which she even left the statute book untouched on the shelf. Before then, there'd been plenty of speed in her page-turning. She inherited a bed of books, see, from the parish clerk in Kilfors, her stepfather. The bed you could lie in. But it was worse with the books. The fact was that most of them you couldn't read at all, however much she kept on bragging about them. There were theosophists and philosophers and homeopaths, the whole oak bed full, and she was going to read them all. No wonder she went crazy. At the very bottom was the book of statutes. It was from the 1700s so there must have been laws then too. It was written in a slant, and the cover was golden, parish-clerk golden. She sat in the rocking chair and pored over it from cover to cover.

So one night, he comes home from Sara Kristoffersson— that was while Kristoffer was in the national guard in Värmland, so she was lonely, the poor thing. Frida has the light on and the statute book open. As soon as he sneaks inside, she says: *In the past, they had the death penalty for people like you.* And then she reads him a section about double fornication. Westlund gets chills down his back. Earlier that day he had threatened the helper with five lashes because he'd borrowed an ax over the weekend. Finally his chills give way, he gets mad and turns off the light. If you want to read the law to me, he screams, then pick up the constitution of 1809 dammit. So there! *Or the stud farm regulation,* she snaps back at him.

After that, it got quiet. That night. But not on others. Although yes: at last it was completely silent. The books gradually went into the furnace. And Frida went up onto the wall. Silent and without a book. Frida went, and Kristoffer came home.

But it's time for her to come down. She's glared enough, with her cussed eyes. The years of mourning have passed: four, five, six. And tonight Hildur will be a bride in the parish-clerk bed. Siri arrives, just in time to see him acting on his decision. But her eyes are red. Has she been crying? Or been peeling onions so early in the day?

"Come on in and have a seat," Westlund says, "and close the door behind you."

There she sits right where Svea sat, and now things are not so easy. Because sticking together, that's what they did, Frida and Siri. So who dares guess what Siri's thinking today? Her hands on her lap, small, thin, delicate. She's hardly had to wash dishes yet. Only page through books. Paging her way to secondary school in town. She's cost him some money too, if you'd like to take that tack. Although, it's clear she's been crying. So best not to forget the piano.

"I've been thinking about the piano," Westlund says.

That had been a good approach with Frida: "I've been thinking about the piano." Sometimes it helps with Siri too. Although not today, Siri's not talking. Although it's an expensive piano he's thinking about. But it was the same with Frida when there was something that had to be said; a piano didn't help. Then they'd both stay silent, silent and waiting each other out. So it's just as well to strike first.

"Well, it looks like there will be changed circumstances around here," Westlund says and looks at Frida. And Frida, she looks back.

Then he looks at Siri but Siri is looking at her lap. A skinny little lap. A bony little girl with a large red mouth, and big eyes that are dripping. Dripping more and more. Westlund swallows.

"It looks like there will be changed circumstances," he says, louder. "In the sense that there will be one more in the house."

But she knows that. It's known, known even in town like they said at the brewery. Soon it will probably be known nationwide and be in *Expressen*. So why say it?

"You're getting a new mother, Siri."

Westlund ties together the threads, the whole thing turning into a granny knot. A new mother? Is that true? Sixteen years old—and twenty-three. Perhaps better to have said sister? But what's said is said, best not to say anything at all, he reckons. And sister? Sister Hildur! No, best to keep quiet altogether. He gets his hairy legs out of bed, and he lets Siri sit where she's sitting. Just strokes her golden hair awhile. But what does that help a poor little thing? Quietly he unhooks the picture and sets it on the floor. She can think whatever she wants. He patters out to the kitchen, clears his head in the cold water under the tap. Sees through the window how his assistant is raking the broad brown walkway up to the slaughterhouse. The wall shines white and sharp through the greenery. And no skins are hanging outside. And no buckets are making a mess. No beasts are howling in the stalls from the fear of death. The tables are weighed down with apples, everything seems good. But Svea comes strolling out of the bower, with a letter in her hand. So Svea is writing letters to the farmhand instead of being useful. That's going to change! Everything's going to change. Westlund fastens his suspenders and slams the kitchen door. Then slams one more before coming back to the bedroom. At last gets really fired up.

But when he comes back to the bridal bed, there has been no change. Siri is sitting like before, crying. And a fly is hovering in the corner. Then he notices that something has indeed changed: Frida is back hanging on her place on the wall. Holding herself firmly in the chair. Holding her place on the wall. Heat rises to Westlund's head, a little fire-devil. He grabs hold of his daughter by her slender shoulders, one in each large hand, and lifts her up toward his anger. But he encounters a fire no smaller than his. A bigger fire, actually. He looks into a pair of eyes, a pair of eyes that he knows. That he usually closes his own eyes to. The eyes have a voice, and the voice is saying: *Thus says the law, Westlund. If you had been living then they would have beheaded you.* And that's how it is with the dead, you can't look into their eyes. Just close your own.

So Westlund releases the shoulders he is holding, and sits down on his bed of oak. Siri stays sitting where she is. And Frida rules. Sometime that must change.

"I'll have to see about changing the sheets," Westlund says in a tired voice.

But not even an echo answers.

There is a road to the poorhouse and it is long. The one leading there is the longest of all roads. Hilma will walk it, but she keeps quiet about why.

"You can at least take your hat, Ma," Hildur says.

But Hilma takes the shawl anyway.

"Give me the basket," is the only thing she says, "whoever knows where it is."

Irma knows, but stays sitting at the table, looking at the coffee grounds. And Hildur knows too but she has other things to tend to. Because now it's like she's built around a stone. A stone that grows and grows. So heavy that soon she won't be able to get up. But around the stone the steps of fear ache. Like his upstairs.

The clocks strike eight. One by one the clocks jangle. Glass, copper, bell. He stops in his tracks and listens. They all stop and listen.

"So no one's getting the basket?" Hilma asks from the doorway.

She has to search for it herself. The others have their own searching to do. Irma shows Hildur her cup. There are lots of grounds at the bottom. Grounds for the dark stranger, the long visit, the short journey.

"Are you waiting for someone?"

It's Irma who's asking. Asking, and moving ever closer. Hildur has always been scared of her sister. Always avoided her eyes, the ones that burn like a bunch of nettles.

"Should I be waiting for someone?"

"How do I know! But it says so in the cup."

Leave me alone! The stone is growing. My last time here in the kitchen, and what happens? Only uncertainty follows and a long, long day of fog. She places her hands firmly on the table, as if holding on to it. Holding on to what is. Holding yourself in place. Protect what is against what is to come. Irma leaves, the cup stays put. Hildur pours some milk in it, it only takes a moment.

"Wonder why Ma is going?" Irma asks from over by the window, pinching the geranium. "What business does she have at the poorhouse?"

The old woman in black moves in the light under the apple trees, black and alone. The dew hasn't yet dried, her boots glisten black under the black skirt. They watch her move between the branches, picking ripe apples and placing them in the basket. One hand picks, the other supports her with the help of the branches, like crutches. She is like all the other old people Irma has seen: she shrivels up outdoors. But Hildur, who is not as familiar with old people, becomes afraid. Afraid of everything she won't get done before death arrives.

"I'll go out and help her."

But Irma puts her arm over her shoulders like a yoke. And Hildur is kept standing at the window for some time, carrying Irma's pain through the silence and loneliness. Suddenly she's afraid of losing what still belongs to her, and crazed she clings tight to her sister. But Irma has enough problems of her own, she wishes for no more. Retracting her pain, she says harshly:

"There's still coffee in the pan. But who's been pouring milk in the cup?"

The one who is afraid of dark strangers. The one who wishes that they will come, the dark strangers. Irma empties the milk into the slop bucket.

"You're leaving," she says quietly, bitterly too. "And someone else stays behind."

They stay sitting, in silence, stirring the cups, the clocks upstairs ticking, moving toward the time of the wedding. But no one is dressed yet for a wedding. Irma is in her black skirt and her tattered cardigan, proudly wearing it like a silk shawl. There's a hole on each shoulder, the bare skin glistening like two medals for suffering withstood. Suddenly she grabs Hildur's cup from her. Not to taste, but to look.

"Just think, how much money you'll get, Hildur!"

There are bubbles blistering all over Hildur's coffee. Though no fault of hers, she starts bawling over her coffee anyway. Escapes into the bedroom on noisy feet. Irma noisily after. Stands right inside the door waiting Hildur out from under the pillow. At last, she appears with swollen eyes and a hiccup in her throat.

"You mustn't think that Hilmer is rich. You've seen that truck of his. The thirty-five. And the other evening . . ."

"He didn't borrow money from you, did he?"

"No. No, of course not. But he did show me his bankbook."

"He did?"

Irma moves closer and sits down on the daybed. Velvet-gloved. Soft and tender. Don't tremble, sister of mine! But, Hildur, she's trembling anyway. Ready to flee like everyone else. How do you get someone to stay the person they once were? Why do people pass by on the road, laughing? Why have they made us into what we are? That's another question to ask.

"Yes, six hundred and ten. And that was to brag."

Hildur turns her back. Looks out the window that someone tapped on. Down by the lake the men walk carrying their axes on their backs. They're going to cut birch branches. For my wedding, they'll cut the branches. For my sake, young birches will be felled. And before the birches turn yellow, it will have taken place. So soon. So distant. But it's all the same.

"That's enough for a subscription to *Good Housekeeping* though."

Easy for Irma to say as she'll be able to read *Good Housekeeping* in peace on Sundays from now on. Hildur could easily retort: Maybe it's enough for a new cardigan too. Or for yarn to mend the holes. Or for child support. But she leaves it alone because it makes no difference. Because there's a stone growing big and strong. The stone of indifference.

"And then maybe you'll get your tooth fixed."

She could reply: That's exactly what I'll do. But who is going to fix your stinky sweat or the wart under your chin? But she leaves it alone.

"Or a new windowpane."

"A new windowpane?"

"Yes, if someone were to come knocking, and knock hard. Harder, I mean," says Irma.

There's no escape for the living. Where it still can hurt, it hurts.

"Did you see him?" Hildur whispers.

Her voice cold and pale, her eyes seeking a friend. But there's no friend to be had. Just Irma. And Irma says, "Just heard him."

"Like me, then."

Yes, like you. But not like you. Because those who are used to lying awake, they hear more. Know better. But now they hear the outer door creak. The sound of steps scraping. Tramp steps. Short, one at a time. Then a tramp knock on the kitchen door. Quiet, as if it didn't expect an answer, sorry to disturb.

"Here are the tramps," Irma says, getting up.

She stands tall and pale, with a light in her eyes. But Hildur lies there, makes herself little. Begging her not to go. The stone aches. No questions, Irma! But Hildur must have asked her too quietly, as quietly as a tramp begs. As quietly as one who knows that nothing will be offered. Irma is gone, already outside the closed white kitchen door. Hildur listens to her hushed inquiry. Her questions about that which should not be asked about. There's an equally hushed reply, then feet shuffling toward the kitchen table, toward the coffee. Irma returns, her hope vanished, she stands at the bedroom door, the light of her eyes gone, her cheeks yellow. You're like a bon-bon, sister of mine, one that life has sucked on for too long.

"His name is Sixten," Irma whispers, defeated.

And silently she turns back to satisfy two tramps' quiet hunger.

But who satisfies mine? And who will keep my stone from growing? She lies in the bedroom, on her left side, the one that hurts least. She hears all the clocks strike. Like alarm clocks. Waking one up to action. You upstairs, just wait! Because today you're coming down! With a sigh, she mounts the steps to him as if for the last time. Sighing but not afraid, for what does the stone of indifference know about fear? Heavy, weighed down by the death of hope, she opens the window she once knew. It faces east toward Grandpa's reeds. She hears the coughing-like sound of axes chopping from under the sunlit trees across the lake. Soon the stoop will be decorated, and all the gates too.

Decorated for me. For me! But myself, I feel nothing.

She must get through this spruce hedge, one meter deep and fifty meters long. Growing along the road, a shadow in the

morning, a patch of darkness in the evening. It smells faintly
of buried forest. It protects the living dead from being seen
by those who supposedly are alive. Or is it the other way
around? But is it strange if she draws back, and looks over her
shoulder? Strange if she shrinks as she nears the poorhouse
hedge? When she puts her basket down, it's as if it is pulling
her toward the gravel of the road like a false friend. A small
figure by the hedge, gazing about. She looks at the valley,
and the lake. Her chest wheezing after the hill. Take out the
damned bird, like Victor says, when she climbs the stairs.
Hilma, sit yourself down awhile, now when you're up here. So
Hilma sits down on a stone by the road.

    The hedge at her back now. And at her back is the poor-
house, that makes so many people feel faint. The old folks
home, the young people call it, and so do those who never
go there. But is old age a consolation for the poor? The tallest
building in the municipality. It frightens with its power of
height, frightens like all towers terrify those of us who are
below. Once, it was smaller, not even the roof was visible,
other than from the lake. But as luck would have it: the poor
had no boats and no water, so it didn't matter. But the building
grew, and the poor became both poor and old. They added
a story. The ones who decide, and at the very top they had
two chimneys of black metal. They should have put a cross
there too. Now the building rises tall on the Tyr ridge saying:
Here rest the lives of the poor. Visible from every window, but
most visible, strangely enough, from the small openings, the
tiny windowpanes of those who count for least. From Victor's
too. One evening, he comes home from town drunk. Brought
home on the floor of a building contractor's car. Staggering,
slurring: *Pissed my pants, is that what you're thinking? No way!
'Cause now it's a done deal. It's happening! Now I'll get to say:*

Us too, I say. You hear? Us too! Huh? Adding on, is what I'm talking about.

She sees a snail crawling out of the lake. Motionless, it crawls. It's good to have him there. She caresses him from afar. Right across the valley, right across Bjuhr's fields and Creek-Lasse's desert, she extends her boundless love. Come unto me, all whom I love! But no one comes. No one appears on the road, only an urchin on his shiny bicycle. No one is on the lake, the horses run loose in the pasture, the cows all huddle in a heap, thinking of something, surely. If only Hildur would come, and stay put at the farm. But all who come to the farm now look like nothing to her. A tramp or an agent. Some of them parking their cars behind the barn. Like Westlund does. Is he ashamed?

No, no one comes. She's sitting on her cold pauper's stool, and no one comes. Perhaps it'd help if she could cry. But nothing helps, she knows. So she'd better get going. Walk through the hedge in to where she is headed. But it hurts. What was lost stings like iodine. The times she could have but didn't. Could have loved, but held back. Like you do when you think: There's plenty of time. Like you do when you're young. The first times are just crap anyway. The last time you love, however, you love mightily. When it's all the same to others, then it's not all the same to me. But listen, one thing is the most frightening of all: To encounter death without once, not a single time, having taken someone, someone willing, into your heart. The stone is cold, the stitch stings, the chest wheezes. Kalle Bjuhr's three boys are in the field, smoking, their scythes likely in the ditch. Those who smoke in fields are no farmers. Playing cards for who will muck and who will groom. They go through a pack of cards every month, Kalle Bjuhr says. As if that was something to brag about.

"So, you're sitting here crying, Hilma."

At her back there's someone sniffing. Babble-Lisa makes her rounds through the village seven times a week year in, year out, the same apron on the same stomach. She snaps up news and spreads it. Her pocket full of sugar, that she sneaks from the sugar bowls when she thinks no one is looking. Bent as a bow. But no arrow. Calls everyone by their first name, even though she owns nothing, except her apron and a little sugar. And her running mouth. You can't love her. Tonight the whole village of Fuxe will find out that on the morning of the day Hildur marries butcher Westlund, Snail-Hilma was sitting on a stone, outside the poorhouse, crying.

"Oh dear," Hilma says stingily, as she crosses the road, the basket lighter. "Must've got something in my eye."

"Yeah, a tear," Babble-Lisa says, "apples you've got in the basket. I'll get myself one. You wanna know when Creek-Lasse last changed sheets? A month ago it was. And how did they change? Well, Creek-Lasse took Ville's, and Ville took Erika's and Erika got Creek-Lasse's. They were the filthiest of them all. Lice crawling on the table. Saw them myself. One was in the sugar bowl. Look for yourself!"

And now Babble-Lisa takes all the gray sugar cubes out of her pocket, and lays them out in the grass under an apple tree inside the hedge. Hilma sees a pair of black-rimmed glasses on an empty chair. Takes them unnoticed. His!

"Look here," Babble-Lisa calls out, crawling on the ground, twisting and turning every single cube.

On her wet knees, drooling, she pokes the sugar with her crooked fingers. At last she finds an aphid. Picks it up in her newly scrubbed hands, Sigrid at the poorhouse has a hard brush. Babble-Lisa cups them around it like around something valuable. Then up after Hilma, who's slowly fleeing toward the steps up to the porch. Three old women in black skirts are standing there, blocking Hilma's way. Forming a prison. There is Nodder, nodding worse than ever now after her second cerebral hemorrhage. And Mrs. Sandbom, a new arrival. Old man Sandbom died in the bailiff's barn one night in June. There was calving, and he had a stroke. And Klara, who's a Baptist. She stands there with her hands folded, her eyes heavenward. As if she was peering for an airplane. But the way things are now, there are no airplanes to be seen over Uvberg.

"God sees everything," she says, as if that was news.

Then she lowers her head and stares, looking at Hilma like God himself must look. And Nodder nods and Mrs. Sandbom waves a magazine, the parish publication, the pastor must have been there. But there is something they know that she doesn't know. As Babble-Lisa catches up with her, she sets the aphid out on her palm. Then says to Hilma, "Look, here he is! The louse. You're in a hurry, I know, but surely you can give me another apple. And the Singer, he will soon die."

She almost drops the pair of glasses she's hidden in her shawl. The old women dig in her basket with their worn fingers, crooked after their finger-pulling with life. Are they digging for the apples or for her heart? That little apple, that little blood-filled apple, soon full of worms.

"Is the Singer not well?"

Yes, Nodder nods. Klara clasps her hands around her apple, God mustn't see that she has taken one.

"All of us will take that road," she says.

Says it as if she was the one who made the decision. As if she wrote letters to God saying: Now I think it's time you bring the Singer home. Or to the other place. Hilma slowly breaks from the old ladies' prison, takes one step, then two, then the whole stairs. The basket in her left hand feels heavier, though it's emptier. She has the eyeglasses in her right hand. The door stands open like a toothless mouth. The opening is dark and the breath bad. The poorhouse breathes on you its odor of impoverished old age, of years that lie rotting, of the cancer of life. She finds him almost at once. He is standing in the corridor between two white doors, leaning against the gray wall, heavily burdened with himself. Dead he's not. Not even dying. So saved from a great pain she moves toward him. He notices her as she stands in the light, her shadow caressing him. She stands beneath the fly-stained lampshade, extending the glasses.

"They were on your chair, Johan."

But a new trembling has come into his hands, and he can't put them on. And his skin has yellowed some more, soon there won't be enough of it either. Under his green skullcap hangs a white curl of his hair. His singer's hair, gypsy black when she first saw it. She puts the basket on the floor, and places the glasses firmly over the old mark on his nose. Then they start walking down the corridor, not saying a word, just walking. Not looking at each other. Not daring to. His room is at the far end, in the last corridor where the last lamp shines. Mad Anders is sitting in the day room, on the floor under a palm, singing to his sock, the one he's taken off. Otherwise no one is there. The Singer stops and gets him up on his feet. Anders grins and stops his song. His hands hanging, head hanging, his tongue hanging out of his mouth. The Singer whispers something in his ear, he turns pale, tongue runs in and out, and he's off with frightened leaps toward the red lamp. There is a puddle where he was sitting. The Singer is embarrassed, he places a chair over it.

"Let's stay in here," he whispers, looking around but no

one is listening, "because Malm doesn't have long to go. The pastor is sitting with him."

Malm and the Singer share a room. Malm has cancer. They sit down in the day room on the yellow wooden sofa, in the shadow of a palm. Senior accountant Lindman had left the palms in his will. The dust is like snowfall in the yellow ray of sunshine.

"I brought some apples," Hilma says.

The Singer looks in the basket, sweat forms like dew on his forehead, his eyes are tired and red, as if they had seen too much lately. He takes an apple, and bites into it as best he can. Holds it with both hands, although it's not large, his hands shake a little more than last time. Fearful, she asks, "Has Göran written?"

She can see that he hasn't. And he hasn't sent any more cigars. Probably smokes them himself now, the factory owner. A furious hatred boils up inside her. Hatred toward the young and cold. Those who don't even bother to take their pipes out of their mouths when they're talking to those who love them. And who start all their letters with: *I have so much to do that I never get around to writing.* And end with: *I have so damned much to do that I have to stop now. And everything is so expensive that I can't afford to come home this year either. I've just bought a car, it wasn't that cheap.* But the Singer takes the apple from his mouth.

"Göran has so much to do," he says. "Fourteen men in the factory, three in the office. And you can't very well expect his wife to write, her mother was an aristocrat."

Pride struggles with pain, and pain wins. He places his hand on hers so heavily, it almost falls there.

"Dear," Hilma says, holding his hand tightly.

Holds it hard. Hears how he is crying inside. Crying for someone to hold him.

"And your Rudolf," he asks at last, "how's he?"

"He's fine. Works hard. Gets mad. And sulks. But I guess he's alright."

"Does he sometimes say: Come over here, Ma! I'm so happy you're here with me. So happy you're healthy and just the way you are. Come here so I can give you a hug."

"Goodness, when would he have time to do that!"

But it isn't true. It's not time that's the problem. But if it's not time, then what is it? Leave me be! Let me believe! But the Singer inches closer, and asks, "And your Irma? Does she ever take you by the arm? Does she take your hand sometime saying: Today we'll go to the cemetery together to tend to the graves! Just put your coat on and of course wear your shawl, although we're going to the village."

Take my arm? Yes, to pinch! And: *Put your hat on when you go out! And wipe your nose! Oh, by the way, stop using snuff. At the poorhouse in Lillnäs where—*

"I guess I knew that," the Singer says, as if he'd heard everything inside her. "I guess I knew that. And Hildur?"

But not a single bad word about Hildur! There Hilma is quick, see. Common sense is there first, and whispers: Not her! Not the only thing you have!

"Yes, Hildur is getting married today."

Then the Singer gets up from the sofa, and looks down on her from high above. Standing on the heights of the Opera, looking down onto a meager audience. And she shudders before him now, almost as she once did. Because she remembers with fear what he once was like. How he once stood and looked down at her in a green arbor, while the birds sang.

His forehead was smooth, his eyes clear and black, and a curl of hair had fallen forward. He smelled of sweet liquor and hair tonic. And she remembers, no longer with fear, but with something far greater, how he slowly pulled her toward him without so much as moving the tip of his little finger. And how she leaned forward with soft fingers to right the curl, not white back then. And no skullcap. That's the way it was. But did it all happen? Have you really lived? She looks down into her basket, as if that's where she might find the dream. But it's nowhere, that's the truth; it's gone.

"I see," the Singer mumbles. "She's getting married today." Then adds: "And you're here."

He can't understand that of course. Coming here, to him, where Malm sighs in the shadow of the valley of death. And where Mad Anders sings and pisses under senior accountant Lindman's palms. But, on the other hand, it's really not that strange that she's here. From somewhere afar, from somewhere above, she gathers courage to ask what she wanted to ask: "You will come and sing at Hildur's wedding, won't you?"

She sits and looks at him as he walks over to the window. With short shuffling steps, barely a foot long. All the kids in Fuxe can imitate his walk. That's probably why he only goes out when it's dark. Say those who talk. But some kids have lanterns. Or search for one to borrow.

"It wasn't yesterday that I last sang," she hears from the window.

But it was yesterday, my friend. And it was the day before yesterday too. Because everyone knows what takes place in the forest every afternoon. They keep talking about it, if they're not talking about anything else. How he goes to the forest and sings. What for? Well, for his future, the bright one. And how now and then a letter gets dispatched to Stockholm,

70

a letter addressing an important question. He slowly turns around now, coming toward her. Not the one he just was, but a different one. And the closer he comes, the starker the difference between who he was and who he is now. He seems to have grown a few inches and takes longer steps, his skullcap is grand, lordly green.

"I'm not asking for mercy, as you know, Hilma," he says. "Not mercy, but justice. Sooner or later the management has to understand that they acted wrongly. That they conducted themselves outrageously toward an esteemed artist. Yes, I don't hesitate to use the word 'esteemed.' There are flowers that bloom beautifully but briefly. I wasn't one of those. This is what they are soon going to realize. And that is why I dare say to you today, Hilma: Johan Borgh is soon again going to stand on stage after a brief absence. And when that evening arrives, I will not forget my faithful friends from here."

"No," Hilma whispers, more like a breath, a sigh of pain.

Because it hurts to see him standing there. Hurts to see your man drunk, and then your friend, your only one, deranged. Hurts to hear your only friend call thirty years a short time. Your only one—yes, that's true. Because loneliness gives its own only one friend. One just as lonely.

But the Singer goes and gets his binders. He is always on his way to those binders, or going away from them. They are black, with metal fittings, heavy from everything he has collected in them over thirty years. Thirty years of abuse and pain. While he's gone, Sigrid, Klara's daughter, comes with a rag to clean up. She's young and always whistling. Will probably whistle the loudest the day a person leaves this vale of tears, Klara says herself, when she's not in heaven. But now Sigrid looks at her carefully. Maybe too carefully. And says, "So she's getting married today, Hildur."

"Yes, I guess she is."

"It happens quickly for some. And never for others. Hah."

And she's off with her rag and her whistling. So it's known then? What if it's already rattling in Babble-Lisa's pocket, what no one should know. No one except one. Just then the pastor enters with the Singer in tow. The Singer without his binders, and with skullcap askew. The pastor with hat in hand and a prayer on his lips. Slowly, she gets up.

"He's not going to die, is he?"

The pastor shakes his head, the Singer takes off his skull-cap, they walk toward the red lamp, all three of them. Rather quickly because the pastor is probably in a hurry. But suddenly the Singer falls behind, Hilma senses a prayer at her back. She slows down and turns. The Singer's face is white and twisted. His trembling hand seeks hers.

"But he will."

Barely a whisper. But she stops and understands. And it's like this: *Don't let Malm die and leave me. Don't let Malm die in my room. Because he's part of my room. Because he's part of my life. If he dies, I die. I'm so afraid, Hilma. I have so much left to do.* She takes him by the arm while the pastor leaves.

"Come and sing, Johan."

And then, no longer feeble, he makes the leap. Even before the pastor reaches the lamp, he has again raised himself up on this earth. His color returns. And the skullcap is back in place. He follows her to the door. "Thanks for saying that, Hilma."

"I'll bring the basket with me when I come," he mumbles, as happiness snares him in its steel wire.

The song swells in him, he stumbles out the back steps, blind as a mouse. Stumbles into the woods behind the bush of song. The pastor offers Hilma a ride. They walk down the path together, the young pastor and her. And she looks around but none of the old ladies are standing there watching her. None of the old men either, although they usually hang around. Only Mad Anders is leaning against a birch tree with his hands on his behind. But what does he understand of such things? But something is happening even in his world, as they near he sets off toward the outbuildings, his back bent and his laughter lingering beneath the birches. Annoyed, she walks past. What is Mad Anders laughing about that no one else knows? Babble-Lisa is crying where they pass. Laying down in the grass, and searching. Probably a sugar cube gone missing. But she has eyes only for her sugar, she doesn't see the pastor and Hilma. "Had thirteen when I went. Only have twelve now. Huh."

Hilma gets into the car first, the pastor following like a shadow. He drives off but hasn't gotten far before the pastor moves closer, she retreats in the corner of her seat. Looks out at Bjuhr's field, the boys cutting the rye, cigarettes in their mouths.

"Mother Palm," the pastor says gently. "He doesn't have much time left."

She doesn't respond. Stop thinking about Malm, tomorrow is already knocking at her door. But the Bjuhr boys ought to fix the fence instead of playing cards and smoking cigarettes. And feel ashamed for letting their cows out on the road, it's good only for Creek-Lasse's undernourished beast. Lind has to stop the car for the cow in the middle of the road doing her business. Hilma feels herself blushing on account of the pastor. But he looks upward to heaven, like Klara, and all the angels in Fuxe. If there are any.

"How long?" she asks; you have to answer the pastor, no matter how you feel.

"Before Malm," the pastor says quietly.

For a moment all becomes still. The cow moves off the road, Lind drives on.

"That voice of his will be missed in church on Sundays," he whispers.

It's the Singer who will die. When she understands this, the blood runs out of the apple she carries in her chest. It becomes empty, shrivels, soon the worms will get to it. She hangs on tightly, in the greatest of danger. Because if she loses the Singer, she loses everything, she loses her last remaining hope: to be able to finally do some good for someone else. Slowly, the dark river of sorrow surges in her.

"Does he know?" she whispers.

"No, no."

Then, as if through a gray veil, she sees that she has arrived home. Lind stops outside the gate. And the pastor probably wants to say something well-meaning but is too young to be able to help. You have to be old for that, yourself close to what is approaching. As she gets out of the car, she catches sight of the old tramp, cranking the well. The pastor also sees him, no doubt, and she knows that he's no friend of tramps. He puts his head out the car window and says, "You're a very kind person, mother Palm."

She glances at the sky, but even so can't forgive him for being so young. So she simply smooths out the back of her black coat, and waits for what else he has to say. Lind sits waiting idly at the steering wheel, wants the tramp to leave. She can't stand him. Once he hit Palm's cow with his car. Deliberately, it was said.

"Look out, mother Palm, that you don't get fooled," the pastor says in his silken voice.

Then Hilma's anger flares up, she hates everything that is

young and superficial. And although she ties the shawl firmly under her chin, she can't hold back:

"Jesus was fooled too. But he was kind anyway," she hisses.

Lind steps on the gas. He must have heard too, and that's good. She walks over to the well and gets hold of the tramp. The well pole creaks, it is old too.

"Will you be staying?" she asks.

"Yes, there's another one sick in there," he answers, pointing over toward the barn. "So your daughter said we could stay today and help."

But working the bucket has made him turn blue. And he almost drops the well cover on his toes. He could use a pair of shoes.

"You're old," she says.

"Well, yes, about sixty-five."

He pulls the cart with the barrel of water. Gunnar's cart and Victor's barrel. She walks beside him, he runs into a rock and is embarrassed.

"You should stop tramping if you're so old. Because you're just out walking, right?"

"Oh, well, some of us write poems too," he brags.

Sounds just like boasting, she thinks, he doesn't seem educated. But she must be kind, she must love everyone before all the apples fall.

"Then write one for Hildur, for she's getting married today."

Yes, sure, he can do that. So she follows him into the arbor, lets him sit on a green chair. She sits on a white one. She doesn't look into the old lilac bushes, she looks beyond and up, north, to where the sky rests on the tall chimneys of the poorhouse. Don't let him die, she prays silently, holding him in her folded hands. And she lets the song he's singing in the poorhouse woods enter her wide-open portals.

"One probably should say a word or two about the groom as well," the tramp says, biting on Sixten's pencil.

But that she does not hear.

Hildur can't keep from looking at the clocks. And he must notice that, but let him notice. He has hung them in a row, all at the same height, like three crucified thieves. One whimpers on its nail. And the pendulums are like three extracted hearts. Hanging mine there would make four. The clocks are almost all she looks at, she hardly looks at him at all. But while she sits there with him, the hour is struck. She hears him get up and walk across the floor. He stops in front of the clock that is striking, his back to her... And because she hasn't looked him in the eyes she looks him in the back. And there isn't much to see. He has always been thin, is thinner now. His hair worn like autumn grass, his vest hangs every which way. And she doesn't really want to now, but at last she can't help feeling a little sorry for him.

He stands there talking, as if to someone. She thinks: *To me I suppose*, and she walks up to him on the rag rug. But he doesn't hear her.

"That may be as it may be," she hears him say. "But one thing I will tell you—and that is that you can sooner tear the skin off my body. And the bowels out of me."

She moves closer. Now he becomes silent, lets the clock finish striking. Nods his ear toward the belly of the clock, the clock probably agreeing. Then she finally understands that her father stands there, talking to clocks. That too.

"Pa," she cries out, as if rescuing him from great danger. A bull, the kick of a horse.

He grabs her arm and pushes her aside. And she sees that he seems to have forgotten that she was there. The second clock starts to strike. He wants to let go but she holds onto him. She counts the strokes, her heart pounding. He is tense as a wire, straight as a pole. The tenth stroke, done. She holds him by the hands and feels him shrink. She helps him to the bed, no steadiness left in him. Just tiredness, old age, soft as soap.

"Kulla," he whimpers, "when will she get well?"

Kulla, the cow? Oh my God! What's wrong with me? Hildur thinks. So wrong, that she wouldn't ask herself: When was I last up here? When did I last talk to him? When did I last have a thought other than: The Snail, crazy old man; so shameful, she could die. It's all my fault, she thinks, starting to cry. But while she's crying the third clock strikes. Her head buried in her hands, she listens. She has let go of him, he can get up if he wants to. There's a long time between the strikes, like three eternities. But not a peep is heard except for the rattling of time that's ailing.

"Pa," she says when it's ten. "The clock struck."

She looks down at their feet, hers and his. He is barefoot, his feet shriveled and yellow. All of him is probably like that. And he smells sour, she can tell from close up.

But it has done him good that she cried. No one comes up here and cries. They only come up here and say: Now we're going to do this or that. And a slop bucket goes up and down. And a serving dish is slung on the table. But there's never anyone who cries. Although he has forgotten what to do with one who's crying. He probably never even knew. So in that way he hasn't changed much. When she asks him to come down he says just one word: "No!"

But he doesn't want to be contrary, so he adds: "I can't."

"Why not?" she asks, sitting closer.

Then he walks over to the window to think about it.

"I don't have any clothes," he says, slyly listening for her reaction.

"And the black suit you had at Grandpa's funeral?"

"And I'm not clean," he says.

"There's hot water in the tank, Pa."

"Who'd like to wash my back?" he asks scornfully.

"I'll do it, Pa."

Just then a car drives into the yard. She hears from the sputtering whose car it is. The '25, Rudolf says, teasing. The '35, Westlund says. But the old man probably thinks someone is coming to get him, and quickly moves away from the window.

"A car just drove into the yard," he whines anxiously.

Soothingly she takes him by the arm. His shirt is tattered at the elbow, the bone sticks out white and sharp.

"No worry, it's just Westlund's."

"I see. Just as long as he doesn't run over the mowing machine."

She brings him to the window and shows him how far the truck is parked from the shafts of the machine. That mower is the old man's darling. Rudolf came home one night from Rullan's lounge. Came quietly across the farmyard, it wasn't completely dark. He saw the old man sitting on the mower, pretending to hold the reins in his hand. *Giddy-up*, he shouted at the invisible mare. Seemed like it took off, and Rudolf had himself a laugh. He sneaked inside to wake Irma and Hildur. And Irma had a laugh too. But Hildur stayed silent.

Now she notices the old man looking at her sideways, with an unusually knowing look.

"You're lying," he says with a sneer. "Since when is that son-in-law so puny?"

She stands beside him and looks out. One-Ear is standing in the yard in a filthy apron, taking pork chops out of the truck. Probably sat on them like he usually does, the pig. But soon things will change. A calf bellows on the truck bed. The old man grabs her hard by the hand.

"It's just Westlund's helper who's bringing the meat, can't you see?"

She looks for Svea but Svea isn't there, she's probably still lounging in bed. But soon she'll be done lounging. That lazy loafer. The old man squeezes her hand tighter. A look of triumph, conceit even, shines in his face.

"But that calf, that's from my barn," he cries out, prancing. "Rosa's calf. My son-in-law comes and takes calves out of my barn. And a person is supposed to shake hands with someone like that? Go down for someone like that? Huh!"

She sighs and walks toward the door.

"Come with me then and let's check that the calf is still there."

She stops, enticing him. But it's as if he's rooted to the floor. She sees how he longs to come but doesn't dare. She sees how he reaches toward her with all his longing, but he's still not coming. She walks out on the stairs, stands there and listens. One, two, three—steps moving in her direction. Pleased, she goes down. The door to the parlor is open, she hears Irma's voice through the opening, less contrary than usual, so she peeks in. Yes, Irma is tying wreaths with one of the tramps. He's standing on a chair, and she stands below and watches

79

as he attaches one to the beam. Hildur only needs a glimpse for her to see that now it's that way again. Irma has changed her blouse. And her manner. Changed manner and blouse for a tramp, even if he is handsome. And a second tramp is standing in the entryway, hat in hand.

"My friend was wondering if he could get some milk."

While Hildur takes a pitcher and cup from the cupboard in the entryway she has a thought. But she doesn't want to show him what she's thinking, so turned toward the herring and pudding, she says: "Go get some water, I'll bring the milk myself."

The tramp coughs and pants, spits out the doorway.

"He's not much to look at," he says. "Weak, ornery and skinny."

Then she turns, filled with courage, and looks him in the eye.

"What does he look like?" she asks in a whisper.

The tramp puts his hat on his head, scratches his behind.

"Like ropy milk," he makes up.

She almost gets angry. Ropy milk—what type of an answer is that? He must have noticed, because he goes on.

"Yes, long and tough. Gets stuck and just hangs in one place."

Without being any wiser she goes into the kitchen with the milk. The tramp huffs and puffs, taking out the water barrel. One-Ear is sitting on the bench legs crossed. Already made himself at home. His cap on, the cutlets on the table wrapped in newspaper. Upstairs, a clock chimes, a fine one that strikes the quarter-hour. With a sneer, he points one finger to the ceiling. What is he after? What business does he have with Pa, who doesn't understand a thing? And when the clock is through striking, he's still sneering. But, now, at whom?

"So there's a law now to wrap pork chops in newsprint?" she fires off, happy to have thought of something to say.

"It's not from today," he says as an excuse, getting up to check. "It's last week's."

So that backfired. But she doesn't want to let him off because if he gets off, he's dangerous. Even Hilmer has said so. So she forges right ahead.

"And Svea? Shouldn't Svea be here to do the frying?"

"She's coming, she's coming. But she had a few other things to do this morning see."

Now he can barely hold back his smirk. Angrily she goes outside, the butcher's helper in tow. Sneering, and scratching behind his one ear. He's a sly fox with something up his sleeve. And the fox glares right at her apron and says, "Soon there'll be a crown and a veil, I hear."

He has the guts to tell her. She walks a few steps ahead in the grass, feels the pain. A crown? Well, a two-crown coin to rattle in the keg. And her veil is black. *You'll wear crepe de chine*, Westlund said. But when it came down to it there was neither crepe nor chine. But it's all the same. That butcher boy has no reason sneering.

"No, a person's not expecting a fancy crown. Just a paltry half-ear."

On top of it all, she gets mean. Remorse stings and tears at her. She slows her pace and waits for him. Wants to let the sun shine on him too. And on the tramp pushing the creaking cart. She stops and offers her hand in farewell. He looks at the cup and the pitcher.

"I'm taking milk to the cat," she says in her softest voice.

"Hell of a cat to swill milk," the butcher's helper says with a smirk, and looks at the pitcher. "And if he drinks aquavit too, I'll go get my ration book."

Then he laughs so hard he almost loses his cap. Slaps himself on the apron, his false teeth flopping, then he jumps into the truck. But Hildur hurries toward the barn. She has seen the old man in the window with his nose to the glass. The calf is mooing behind her. And the cows are mooing in the pasture. Westlund's helper starts the '25. Probably wants to show farm folk how it's done. Puts it in reverse and backs up. There's a crash at the barn door. She turns to look. He's got the wheel right onto the shaft of the mower. It has cracked like a reed. And the truck engine died. It is silent for a moment, then there's a clinking sound. A window breaks. And the old man's arm dangles out through the opening. But the butcher boy cranks the engine. Would he think of stepping out to say sorry? Of course not. Instead he honks at the tramp with the cart who's not getting out of the way fast enough. And drives through the gate with a broom of smoke behind him. Honk and drive, like Hilmer says. Just honk and drive, and put the tuxedo on for the wedding. But where that tuxedo is, he forgot to mention.

She is afraid to look toward the old man. She slinks into the barn with her heart in a knot. It is quiet, nobody goes there to cry anymore. Not that long ago she was lying in the straw in the feed passage. With tears in her heart and a letter that came in the mail. And Westlund's words ringing in her ear: *If you want to see some more, then come home with me on Friday.* So what was it she wanted to see? Well, there was a collar of silver, but was that really so special? Kulla was slated for slaughter, fifteen years old, and all dried up. But Pa bought her back, he didn't want to lose her. Once a month Rudolf went up to him. *Isn't it time to bring Kulla to slaughter?* No, that's not going to happen. So when Westlund came he had to park behind the barn. She sneaked back there and saw him arrive. He whistled and tossed the collar. She'd never seen such a grand collar before. Its silver gleaming. She kept her hands in her apron pockets on her stomach, in one hand the ring, in the other a letter. Martin's letter asking her to wait. Wait just a couple of years until the finances are in order. The kid will do just fine where he is. Thanks and goodbye, she thought, closing the latch on the door to her heart. Become like Irma? A poor shrew that no one looks at? And below her hands, the fetus was growing, month by month.

What drove her out there behind the barn? She knew from five steps away. Found out from the collar that swung in the butcher's big hand. I want him. I'll get him. She took the collar in her hand, the butcher stood still. In the barn, the butcher boy was lifting the boom from the back gates. "Nice collar you have, Westlund," she said, smiling. Westlund's dog barked by the haystack. He was a foot taller than her, had his sleeves rolled up, and blood on his fingertips. He came close, and she did not retreat. "If you want to see more, then come to my house on Friday. Come round at seven." He sounded hoarse, she lifted the collar and stuck her neck in it. He led her around a turn. The collar was good and the only thing Westlund's old man hadn't sold for drink. It was found in the attic at the estate inventory. "I'll take it," Westlund had said.

But now the butcher's helper was standing on the threshold of the barn, watching. And nothing could be undone. It was as if it had been both written and printed. She took off the silver collar and looked Westlund in the eyes; they were blue and slightly bloodshot. She smiled. "Come along," she said, walking into the barn. She swung the collar as if it belonged to her. She went ahead of the butcher and his helper and his dog. She stepped into Kulla's stall and said farewell to the cow. She undid Palm's own collar and put the butcher's on. Kulla turned her head, saw the men and the dog in the passage, let out a bellow of terror. "Leave," Hildur said, "I'll bring her myself." They went out to the truck. She cried a bit before leading Kulla out, thinking she was leading herself toward the ax. But she was thinking so without regret, only with a kind of fright.

"Hell of a collar," the butcher's helper said to Westlund when she arrived. They were each throwing back a beer. Westlund wiped his mouth, and tossed the bottle into the haystack. The helper tossed his into the ditch. Hildur climbed up the gangway, tears running, a few drops at a time. "Silver for farmers, brass for sharecroppers," said the butcher. The helper sneered as Kulla, one step at a time, tripped her way toward death. The butcher closed the tailgate, standing in the road with his legs apart. Suddenly he threw out his arms. "Jump," he said, and Hildur stepped onto the tailgate. She fell into the butcher's arms, the letter rustling against Westlund's stomach. Then she ran the back way to the house, into the bedroom. There she sat herself down to write in fear and fever.

One night later, the letter had been written and mailed together with the ring. It didn't carry a return address, but it came back to her anyway. Every night until the banns were all read and for a while thereafter. Came back to her in her dreams. In her dream she is sitting at the table with a thick stack of papers in front of her, papers she must fill out. But before she gets started a spider comes running across the table toward her. It's a big one and she gets scared. She takes some paper to squash it. The pile falls over, and the spider scurries under some sheets. She throws a couple over it but can hear him moving still. Then she squeezes the paper until the moving stops. The spider must be under there somewhere. One by one she lifts the papers, until she reaches the bottom sheet without having found it. That's when the awful thing happens. The bottommost paper rises up on its own, riding on the spider's back. And the spider grows bigger and bigger until he becomes as big as a fist and comes rushing toward her. She wakes up, her chest full of fear, and she searches the bed. But the only thing she finds is the child she is carrying.

She reads a dream book from beginning to end but without finding anything about it. So she prefers to stay awake. At some point it will all pass. Here she is now standing with the milk in Kulla's stall. Pa has been asking about her. Probably senses what has happened. In the mornings he counts the cows as they amble toward the pasture. That first morning, one was missing. He knocks on the windowpane calling Rudolf. Rudolf goes up the stairs. *So where is Kulla today?* Well, she's sick so she's in the stall. *Send for the veterinarian then.* And the next day the pretend veterinarian comes. *But I didn't see him.* No, he came by bicycle. The car's in the shop, see. *And how long does Kulla have to stay inside?* Well, all summer. Whatever will they come up with on the first of September?

She goes to the pen and gives the calf a drink from the dipper. She wants to stay here, keep herself hidden until it's all over. But it's probably close to eleven, only four hours left. She gets a fright. Feels like someone is behind her, like so often nowadays. But this time, there's someone there for real. But it's just Irma's boy. Gunnar. She puts the milk down and hugs him.

"My little boyfriend," she says, putting him on the milking stool. "Did your mother pinch you again?" His left arm is blue.

"She'll be better when she gets married," Gunnar says, spitting onto a piece of cow dung, "that's what Rudolf says."

She twists his light hair, which he got from his unknown father. The Palms are all dark. She looks at his eyes as he turns away. Irma has turned them old. And Rudolf has turned the rest of him old. Taught him to talk like a farmer, about mating. And to spit like him. And pee on the same stone. But what has she turned him into? A plain nothing. Hugged him when she felt sorry for him. That's about it. And now she wants to make amends before it's three o'clock. So she sits down beside him on the stool, gently pinching his ear, nose and mouth.

"You'll come to see me where I'm moving, won't you?"

"If I get to watch when he butchers," Gunnar says.

She kisses him on the cheek.

"Don't be mushy," Gunnar snarls and stands up.

She sees something black around his mouth. But not the usual black. She reaches up to sniff him. It's snuff. And she sees something bulging in the left pocket of his short pants. Quickly she puts her hand there. First she finds two earthworms. And then a piece of chicken shit, hard as stone. Last comes Pa's snuff box. Then Gunnar wants to get away, moves up against the wall, afraid of being hit, afraid of being beaten, his eyes gleaming with hate.

"I didn't steal it," he hisses. Like a mite, a small animal. "Found it under the mower."

She opens the box, there's a mirror in it. Sees a bit of herself in it. A bit of bride, gray and teary-eyed, ugly in the feeble light. She closes it. So last night the old man had been down again. But he doesn't want to let on. Doesn't want to say: *Go and look for the box, Hildur, lost it outside.* One of these nights, he will go farther than to the mower. He'll go to the barn. He'll go up to the empty stall. And that night, she won't be at home. That night she won't be able to do anything. She puts the box in her pocket.

86

"I won't hit you," she says to Gunnar, in a tired voice.

Then he edges closer, until he's right next to her.

"If you don't get mushy I'll show you something," he says.

"What's that?"

"A heart," Gunnar says, walking into the milk room.

She follows, carrying the milk.

"Where is it? In here?"

"No, in the stable. A brand new one on the wall."

A new heart on the wall! A heart carved last night! Her own becomes rigid but bigger, her fear of spiders takes hold in her chest. When they leave the barn for the yard, it's full of unfamiliar cows. She is so immersed in her dream that she at first doesn't notice. But then she sees that the butcher boy left the gate open, and Creek-Lasse's cows are sniffing paradise. Because at Creek-Lasse's, the grass grows down instead of up, say those who are unkind. The tramp hasn't started filling the water bucket yet, he's sitting in the grass by the well, probably wore himself out just getting there. The younger tramp stands in the door, smoking, as if he is the man of the house. Victor is nowhere to be seen. But the glass shards sparkle on the stoop.

"Drive out the cows and close the gate," she shouts at the old tramp.

She's stern today, but her spider grows and grows. Soon it will fill her to the brim. She takes the boy's hand, and together they enter the stable. The boy leads the way quietly, she spills milk in the hay as she follows. On the left wall between the halters there's a freshly carved heart. She puts the milk on the chaff-cutter, and pokes the heart with a fingernail. It hurts as if it were her own. With her hand covering the boy's mouth they steal into the loft, silent as a good conscience. The door to the stable is closed and so is the door to the chicken coop. The floor of the loft empty. She walks up into the hay and touches the hollows made by those who slept there. The third one is still warm. Afraid, she hurries back to the stable, stands in the middle of the doorway, bangs the cup against the pitcher four times. While the sound travels, she looks around herself so she can face the danger. When the banging has rung out a last time and everything is still quiet, she calls as gently as calling a frightened cat:

"Martin."

Just then the stable door opens behind her, in a flash she's turned around. She drops the pitcher, drops the cup; she goes to meet her enemy halfway. The boy screams. The well pole moans outside as if from an old pain. And a hen falls like a feather bomb from the stable brood almost right over both their heads.

After ten birches have been felled they take off to the lake for a while. The axes flash on their shoulders, the grease shines on their boots, it feels like a major holiday. It's dry this summer and the water is dwindling in the lake. The reeds bloom, and in some awkward places they cut it down, then sit and gaze at the surface of the water. Rudolf spits in the lake, feeling good. The farmhand spits too. A big dead fish is bobbing by the lakeside. The farmhand pokes at it with the shaft of his ax.

"Creek-Lasse was here this morning. He raised your trap too."

"Did he get anything?"

"He probably got a couple. I saw some splashing at the bottom."

Rudolf's face darkens, it doesn't take much to make him angry. Sören starts to regret having said anything.

"Get me a forked branch," Rudolf growls at him.

The farmhand cuts one off an aspen. But Rudolf, probably now a bit crazy, sticks it into the rotten fish, and starts walking with long strides toward the creek.

"Today Creek-Lasse gets to serve a person some fish. It's not a wedding every damned day."

Suddenly he is cheerful, hey ho, swinging the fish. The farmhand shuffles along, the ax is dangerous and sharp. Soon they're standing at the black creek, not big, a wide ditch really with rocks in it; they step across on dry stones. A high creek bank leads up to Creek-Lasse's property, Rudolf tosses his ax up ahead as a warning.

"Maybe he didn't get any after all," the farmhand mumbles.

But what is said is said and there isn't a wedding happening every day in the village. They struggle up the steep incline, the farmhand with the ax in his hand.

"And we should have a wedding drink too," Rudolf hollers, shouldering the fish, shouldering the ax.

But the farmhand strews salt in open wounds; he chops off a thistle with the ax, but doesn't get any braver.

"We're not the ones getting married," he frets, falling behind.

Rudolf turns and sees the farmhand blush. Something must have struck a nerve. They set off through the field, walking right through but there isn't much to trample. The field reeks of neglect, the thistle stands thick in the oats and the oats stand thin in the thistle, on its knees begging for its miserable life. Their steps stir up dust, their boots sometimes striking rusty cans. Rudolf swears, the farmhand glares down at the thistle. Ashamed, like a dog, at their errand.

"He should have oats in the field, not cans. Because I'll be damned if any anchovies grow here."

Now, Rudolf feels strong, tossing the ax and catching it,

they each had a shot before they left. Reymersholms Aquavit. "Are you about to start drinking this early in the morning?" Irma yelled, Ma shaking her head at them. "It's never too early for a drink," Rudolf said, "and it's not like anybody gets married too early in this house. Huh?" And Irma shut up, but the farmhand shut up too, though usually he sneers. So today he's not so eager for a wedding.

When Creek-Lasse's house is just an ax-throw away, they stop and stare at the potato field, no one has seen them. It's only a ten-minute walk from Rudolf's house but it's been twenty years since he was last here. Was here as a boy sometimes, then came home and got a whipping. *You don't go there. Why did you? Be quiet when I'm speaking, you little brat! To that swindler! Who feeds arsenic to the horse. You may get a spoonful and die too.* Now, Rudolf pauses for a moment in the field, some memories fly around the broken barn door with the swallows. The farmhand lights a cigarette. In the dirt below lies a hoe with a broken shaft, a box with a broken bottom, a watering can with a broken spout. The barn roof sags as if a giant sat there at night. The stable door hangs crooked, it's empty inside. The old man had gone around and borrowed horses for mowing, but he didn't come to us. At last he had to buy a nag from the butcher for a pittance. One you can blow out like a candle, Westlund bragged. And it collapsed on the road right in front of the horse-drawn mower. The veterinarian was called, then the bailiff came in his Ford, maybe he'll be charged with cruelty to animals.

The farmhand's legs shake, Creek-Lasse has a son, one who's strong as hell. But Rudolf with his ax stands rooted to the ground, remembering. It was all the same back then too. The old man had stood by the woodpile and made arrows for him and Ville. Or shot crows in the lilacs with buckshot. One time, old Bjuhr got an arrow in his straw hat. That was only fair, Creek-Lasse said, 'cause Bjuhr paid so little for the gusset that it's a shame. Back then they had started trading their land. Creek-Lasse to get liquor, Pa to build on.

They move a little closer; the potatoes are feeble, the last part of the flagpole is lying on the sawhorse by the woodpile. The ax reminds Rudolf of something. Here he beheaded his first rooster. At age eleven. Ville: *I dare you to cut the head off a chicken.* Rudolf: Go get the ax, I'll get the rooster. He had to get the rooster from a hen in the wagon shed, Ville steadied the chopping block. The rooster was pecking, Creek-Lasse was sitting in the arbor drinking with a swindler, his old lady was at the cemetery. Rudolf: Give me the ax and hold the rooster. The first chop took off a leg, with the second one it was dead. We'll bury it in the dunghill. But they ended up throwing it in the lake.

There are wooden shoes on the porch, just one pair. And Erika is standing there, the sister of a woman who just died. She's old and filthy, people say. On the bench three bream lie, she is about to scale a fourth one, the carving knife glows with rust.

"Good day. I see, they've been biting today. Is Larsson there?"

The old woman is frightened by the men and the axes, shining on their shoulders. And Rudolf is again terse, the farmhand stays behind him. The old woman nods, yes, Larsson is there.

"And is Ville here?" the farmhand asks, looking around, wanting to protect his back.

The old woman wipes her eyes with her apron, the bream scales stick to her nose; she's been crying.

"No, Ville went to Gävle this morning. And he's probably never coming back home again."

Rudolf knocks with the ax handle on the door, no answer. He opens the door, enters, almost turns around at the threshold. It smells like a pigsty in Creek-Lasse's kitchen. The fly-catcher under the roof beam is moldy, and in every corner there's a bucket. Creek-Lasse is sitting at the table and neither hears nor sees.

"Good day," Rudolf says, stepping forward, ax on his shoulder, the bream on the forked branch. The old man does not move an inch.

Rudolf looks at him a long time. All he intended to say about other people's traps and fish poaching rots away inside him and he tosses the bream into the nearest bucket. The farmhand tries to open the bedroom door, intending to remove a bucket with something green in it. But the door is locked from inside, he puts the ax down by the doorpost.

"Good day," Rudolf says again, louder; as he's slinging his ax off his shoulder, it chips a beam.

The farmhand tries to open a window, but these are storm windows, the wadding is still there. Creek-Lasse lets flies climb on him, his hands asleep in his lap. Rudolf walks up to the table.

"What's going on with you?" he says, pushing a moldy plate aside, holding the ax in his left hand. The farmhand slips over toward the bedroom door.

"Get out of here, you bastards," Creek-Lasse says.

"Now then!" Rudolf says loudly, then he sees that the old man has been crying, and says no more. The shotgun is hanging on the wall, the old man gets up from the table. Death-mold blooming on his face, he hasn't shaved for a month. Rudolf puts his ax on the table, the farmhand puts his eye to the keyhole. Creek-Lasse's pants are torn, he takes hold of the gun.

"Get out of here, you bastards," he roars. The old woman rushes in screaming, the barrels stare Rudolf in the eyes, he gets up quickly. The farmhand runs out on the porch, trailed by the old woman, carving knife in hand. Rudolf strikes the old man across the wrist with the ax handle. The gun rattles to the floor, the old man swoons, and Rudolf catches him in his arms.

"Where's Ville?" he asks into Creek-Lasse's swollen ear, sitting him down at the table, putting the ax on a chair. The farmhand returns, white as chalk. The old woman follows and takes his ax and throws it outside.

"Ville," Creek-Lasse mumbles, tears trickling like from a rock, there is something he is trying to remember.

The farmhand steps forward, axless. Bends down and whispers, "It smells like a corpse in there."

Rudolf grins.

"The bedroom door is locked," the farmhand whispers.

Rudolf stops grinning, and places the ax across his lap.

"Go outside and peek through the window."

"Can't you come along?"

"Take my ax if you're scared."

The farmhand leaves. Tears run out of the rock, clear as crystal, as if they come from someone other than this filthy old man, from someone clean.

"Where is Ville?" Rudolf repeats.

"Ville is dead and buried," the old man says solemnly. Rudolf hugs his ax.

"Yes, he's dead to me," the old man adds.

"Just to you, huh?"

"Rudolf," the old man says, "shake my hand."

Rudolf shakes the old man's right hand. Then there's a commotion behind the house, and the old woman runs out. The old man's tears keep streaming. And Rudolf's right hand gets wet, the ax handle gets wet too.

"A person has a son," Creek-Lasse continues, "you toil for him until your bowels crack. You toil for him for thirty years. And why do you toil for him for thirty-five long years? So that one morning he can call you a thief?"

"Rudolf," the old man cries, "is Creek-Lasse a thief? Is Creek-Lasse a poacher? Is Creek-Lasse a fish-poacher? Has Creek-Lasse ever been a moonshiner? Does Creek-Lasse deserve a wallop from his son when he comes home with bream for him at seven o'clock in the morning?"

Rudolf lets go of the ax, a crowd seems to be coming around the corner of the house, he takes the old man lightly by the elbows, rocks him to settle down.

"You're a good man, Creek-Lasse," he says, "the best in Fuxe." He is tender-hearted. Later in the day he has a party waiting, he wants to share a little of his joy with the old man.

"But where's Ville?" he whispers, carefully coaxing the ax onto his lap.

Now three people enter through the doorway. The peddler first, bag in hand, then the farmhand with his ax halfway raised; the old woman last, with a bright red face.

"This son-of-a-bitch was in the bedroom," the farmhand says, hitting the peddler on his back with the ax handle, "he was climbing out the window just as I arrived."

Rudolf gets up. Creek-Lasse couldn't care less, just sits dripping his tears onto the table.

"What kind of peddling were you up to in the bedroom?" Rudolf asks, his hand clenched around the ax.

The peddler's hat is crooked, he's not having his most sober day, his bag hangs on his body, his nose is shiny, eyes wandering like a swindler's eyes.

"When I came in, the old man yelled at me to get out of the kitchen. *Don't want anything today.* So then I headed for the bedroom. What's so strange about that?"

"If you've pinched any money, put it on the table," Rudolf says, raising his ax. Now the peddler's head is between two axes. Then the crazy old woman comes charging.

"You leave my second cousin alone," she shouts.

"That's right," the peddler says with a nod, stepping away from the axes. "We're second cousins, you see. Please keep that in mind."

The old woman takes hold of the farmhand's ax, Rudolf lowers his.

"Ville left me," Creek-Lasse says, crying.

"We'll sue the two of you for trespassing," the old woman whines, "in court."

Rudolf's temper rises.

"A person stops by to say hello," he says.

"Axes in hand," the old woman hollers. "And you chopped the beam to bits."

Rudolf gets so mad he drops his ax, the farmhand tries to hide his behind his back.

"A person stops by to say hello!" Rudolf shouts. "And this is what you get?!"

He takes the chip and puts it back onto the beam. The peddler pokes it down. The old woman juts her stomach out at Rudolf as if she wanted to spear him.

"Now I'm the one who's going to the bailiff," she hisses, her stomach making a chirping sound.

"And the moose," Rudolf screams, "what are you doing with the moose?"

"The moose?"

The old woman turns pale as a corpse, Rudolf moves in on her stomach, gently poking it with the ax handle. The peddler slips out the door.

"You think a person doesn't know you've got moose in your buckets, even though you've tossed green moss on top? I wasn't born yesterday. And not in the shed, either, for that matter. Take the goddamn moose outside and bury it. It's been rotting here for a month."

Rudolf puts his ax on his shoulder, the farmhand puts his ax on his shoulder and they're off.

"Rudolf," the old man shouts after him, "if you run into Ville, tell him to come home. Then he'll get some buckshot in his ass."

And Creek-Lasse cries like a child for his son, bellows like a calf for his son, strikes his forehead on a plate so that it cracks.

"Jesus," the old woman says, as she closes the door behind them. The last thing she sees are the axes.

The peddler is standing in the middle of the farmyard, grinning at them, the tomcat steals by, sticking its claw into a bream. Rudolf spits a few times, the farmhand's face is white, he wants to throw up, and puts his ax against the corner of the house.

"Right now a drink would be just the thing," the peddler says. Patting the top of his bag, he strides off toward the potato patch, near the creek. Rudolf follows, the farmhand throws up at the corner of the house, before catching up. The peddler and Rudolf slide down the steep slope alongside each other, Rudolf throws his ax across, the farmhand's hits the water. The peddler missteps and gets water in his shoes, the farmhand dries off his ax, and Rudolf puts his on his shoulder. In the clearing on the other side, an air surveillance tower can be made out.

"I know someone who spent nights there on screw-watch," Rudolf says to the farmhand to perk him up.

"Hell if I did," Sören shot back, he's in no mood to talk about girls, not at all. But the peddler is.

"Come along, boys, I'll show you something," he says with a grin, and walks ahead with the bag, his shoes squelching.

"At home I have a stone that I piss on," Rudolf says. "It counts for eighty times more than you."

The peddler grins, Rudolf and the farmhand follow. They sit on a pile of cut birches, the peddler in the middle. He unloads his bag, there is a bottle of aquavit among the trinkets. They put their axes under a big birch in the pile, the wind rustles in the reeds.

"You stole that from the old man," Rudolf says, screwing off the cap sniffing. It's pure moonshine. The peddler grins, Rudolf takes a little nip, the farmhand takes a big one.

"And what would you like today?" the peddler asks.

They look in his bag, the usual junk, Rudolf takes a comb and sticks it in the peddler's dirty hair. Sören looks for something that is good for "deterring children," as the peddler calls it. From the bottom of the bag the peddler takes out a locked case, he opens it. It is full of brooches, clasps and other ladies' things.

"Buy a brooch for your girlfriends."

Now he's grinning like a mad man, spits once on the farmhand's ax, and holds up a brooch in his hand.

"Westlund bought four."

Rudolf glares.

"What would Hildur do with four brooches? She doesn't want to walk around looking like a peddler's box, does she?"

The peddler swallows hard, and grins, looking as if he has said too much.

"I'm sure Hildur will get one. And Siri, she'll probably get one too. And so on. Et cetera."

"What do you mean by that?" Rudolf says, eyeing his ax. The farmhand takes another big swig. "They're getting married today. Don't you know that, you packrat? When did he buy them?"

"Yesterday," the peddler lets out, his eyes playing a brazen little tune. "I got them from the jeweler in Gävle."

The farmhand drinks up, Rudolf takes a couple of fingers worth, puts the bottle between his legs, grabs hold of the peddler's shoulder.

"Put away that knife, lad."

The peddler throws his knife over toward the axes, staring at them from under the brim of his hat.

"And now out with it before you end up in the reeds."

The peddler loosens his tie, looks at the axes, looks at the knife, picks a leaf from Hildur's birches. The farmhand gets up, looking drunk.

"Well, yes, it was yesterday," he says, unburdening himself. "I'm walking through the village, and slipped into Bengtsson's café."

Sören's eyes light up, Rudolf lets go of the peddler, drops the bottle, lets it lie. Damned if it isn't Rullan! The farmhand moves over to Rudolf's side, the peddler continues, beaming now.

"Westlund is sitting there, having coffee. Rullan is out to get some rolls. Won't you buy yourself a comb, Westlund, a person says. Nah, but if you have a lawnmower I might get it, Westlund says. Ha-ha, I say, because Westlund's head is as bald as a croquet ball. Ha-ha, anyway and anyhow."

"Don't talk so much crap," Rudolf says gloomily; the farm-hand wipes his ax off with leaves, the peddler scratches his head under the hat. His eyes darting.

"Since you're getting married tomorrow maybe you're in need of some trinkets, I say. Straight from the jeweler in Gävle, I say. Trinket me here and trinket me there, says Westlund, but bring the case on over here so we can take a look. I'll be a monkey's uncle, Westlund says looking. This here is fancy. He takes a brooch and places it on the plate. Oh my, now I know a bride who'll be happy. Give me four, and I'll be done, he says. One for Hildur and one for Siri. That will be six crowns even, I say. Best to take out my pouch then, Westlund says."

"Dammit, I'm getting my ax," Rudolf says. He stands up and grabs the ax. The farmhand sits down in fright holding his. Sweat trails down Rudolf's forehead, he twirls the ax a turn, cross-eyed with anger. Like a cat, the peddler arches his back.

"Are you going to spit it out any time soon," Rudolf shouts, testing the ax's edge with his thumb. The peddler leans over, Rudolf puts his foot on the knife.

"And then two others," the peddler continues trembling, "that's my business Westlund says. But this much I can tell you, that I know what color panties she's wearing today, the one who went out for the rolls."

The farmhand lets out a laugh. Rudolf swings the ax over his head, the peddler crouches down begging for mercy, the farmhand hunkers down on Hildur's birches, Rudolf's ax drives into the biggest nearby birch. The wood quivers, the ax hangs there like a leech in the birch's chest, Rudolf leans down over the trembling peddler, uttering something incomprehensible.

"Huh?" the peddler squawks.

"What color?" Rudolf howls, grabbing him.

"Light green," the peddler whispers, whimpering in his grip. The farmhand stands up, biting his ax handle trying not to burst out laughing.

"That bastard," Rudolf mumbles. "And my rake." His knees give way, and he collapses on top of the cut birch pile. The peddler is free, he leans over for his knife. The farmhand can no longer contain his laughter.

"The story isn't over yet," the peddler says in a louder voice, louder than he has been for a good while, again grinning. The farmhand is done laughing, both of them now all ears.

"And this much I can say, Westlund says, that I know on which thigh she has a birthmark, the one sitting in the car," the peddler continues. The farmhand gets up, his eyes glowing from moonshine and worry, heavily he puts his ax in the peddler's lap.

"Yes, I saw it through the window," the peddler says, placing his hand on the knife. "In one word: it was Svea who was sitting in the car."

The farmhand falls to his knees beside the peddler, Rudolf stands up with his back against the big birch tree, in the farmhand's wild eyes there is a question; the ax weighs on the peddler's knee.

"Left," the peddler whispers, and with that the farmhand gets up. Bam! Sören's ax cuts into the big birch, a handle's width from Rudolf's, both axes nursing from the same breast. Both men look at each other, for a second, no more is needed. The peddler wriggles himself to standing, puts the lid on the trinket case.

"So no brooches then," he whines, but they don't hear him. Rudolf tugs his ax loose, the farmhand his.

"Let's go get that bastard," Rudolf says. Their eyes meet an instant, both of them touched, then they move apart.

But the peddler thinks they're talking about him, puts his bag on his shoulder and scampers away. They hear him splashing in the creek, they hear how he flees up the steep slope. Probably taking off to his second cousin to steal more liquor. He left the bottle behind. From each side the axes bite into the birch, they chop as if possessed, their sweat runs hot and steady, the cut into the flesh of the birch is getting deeper and deeper. They don't give themselves time to breathe, the axes whir, the chops resound around the lake, the echo plugs their ears. The birch begins to sway. It leans toward Rudolf, it leans toward Sören, the edges meet like brothers inside the birch, there's a clanking sound and a spark. The big birch totters, then falls toward the lakeside.

"Let's trim that bastard too."

They start at the base, the branches fly, the last ones are under water.

"Let's throw that bastard in the lake."

They take hold of the trunk, lift it, then push it out. At last it's afloat, the trunk bobbing on the water, long, white and sleek. They look at each other, startled by how big it is. They throw the axes into the grass behind them.

"Now let's blow that bastard up," the farmhand says.

He's been carrying a blasting cap in his pocket, as a wedding salute. Rudolf walks away beneath the birches, he's afraid of anything that explodes. After the blast he returns. The birch remained whole, only drifts away toward the mouth of the creek. It's deep there, two black whirlpools like mouths, drinking loads of water. Then fish float up belly against belly, a whole flotilla spinning around the whirlpools, the birch resting on the current.

"Now let's fish," the farmhand says, feeling strangely happy.

They undress close by their axes. Naked and white, they stand under the birches and look at the stump, feeling an unreasonably great sense of freedom under the sun and the birches. Sweat running down their thighs, they march out into the water, swim out to the birch in a few strokes, straddle it, take the fish by the belly and throw them up onto land. The whirlpools tickle their legs, they feel a sense of boundless happiness in this water with the dead fish. Suddenly Sören starts laughing, he laughs so hard he falls off the birch log and sinks into the whirlpool, his mouth open. Rudolf pulls him up. As soon as his mouth is above water he laughs again, and sinks. At last he pulls himself up onto the log.

"What are you laughing at?" Rudolf asks, getting the last fish onto land.

The farmhand is so full of laughter that he can't answer. But he just remembered that it's Westlund who got Svea pregnant. The sky is blue over Uvberg and free from worries. So instead of answering he starts singing an old ditty.

> *I bought my poor mother a golden brooch.*
> *I bought a ring for my girl.*
> *I bought my father some raggedy shoes*
> *And my sister a necklace of pearls.*
>
> *I bought a comb for my louse-ridden brother.*
> *I bought a strong drink to swirl.*
> *Paid with the brooch I bought my poor mother*
> *And the ring I bought for my girl.*

I bought a flask for my drink, then another.
I bought a giant flask to swirl.
Paid with the comb for my louse-ridden brother
And my sister's necklace of pearls.

I bought a saloon for my drink, then another.
I bought a saloon to swirl.
Paid with the shoes for my barefooted father,
And the ring I got from my girl.

But Rudolf leans out over the water and then he sees himself and the farmhand in its black mirror, sitting naked riding on a birch. He starts laughing, he howls. Laughing at the sun and at the water, and at the fish on land, and at the air surveillance tower in the distance, and at Creek-Lasse and the peddler. At the moose in the buckets, and the moonshine, and Westlund, and Rullan, and at the rake and the axes that glisten in the grass. The last thing he laughs at is Gunnar, who comes running toward the lake. Gunnar throws a stone at them, he can't swim.

"What's wrong with you?" he screams. He's out of breath, has a lot to tell. The old man's gone mad and broke the window, and Mom was in the parlor kissing the tramp, and One-Ear ran over the mowing machine with the truck, and Hildur is running around with milk that no one wants, and Grandma has put the old tramp in the arbor, and the ones in the stable were completely crazy. All of them are crazy. And you too.

"Forget it," Rudolf says, "there's a wedding at most once a year. But hell! Do you know where Creek-Lasse lives?"

"He used to make arrows for me," the kid says.

"Take the fish there," Rudolf says, "more fish than he's ever seen before."

They paddle the birch log to shore.

"Damn, that's a lot of fish," Gunnar says, "how did you catch them?"

"With our hands, lad."

"But what should I carry them in?"

"Take them in my shirt," Sören says, and he gets it and ties up its sleeves. They scoop it full of fish.

"Just empty the fish on the stoop without anyone seeing you," Rudolf says, "and then run like hell."

The boy leaves.

"But bring the shirt home!" Sören shouts after him.

They get up and dress, and drink to their swim from the bottle. A car honks up the road, the boy splashes in the creek, a cow bellows in the pasture, a fish leaps in the lake. They hear all the sounds so clearly it's as if they'd been for ear cleaning with Nurse Marie. Their bodies feel cool and good, they smell delightfully of fish and water and birch and aquavit. It's a real holiday, a holiday like no other.

"Now dammit, let's get to decorating with branches," Rudolf says.

He picks up his ax from the ground and lobs it firmly into the biggest stump; the farmhand thunders his in alongside.

Westlund has an office. It's where he often sits and thinks, from where he sits and runs it all. It is on the back porch, Siri's balcony is above, she only gets to be on it in the evenings. Are you crazy, girl, are you going to clomp around on top of the office? But she obeys, she does, it was different with Frida. She put the gramophone there and for a while the spinning wheel turned all day playing "See Grandpa Dance his Old-Time Waltz," from morning to evening. But now it's all spun out. Grandpa no longer dances his old-time waltz, must have finally broken his leg; Westlund is not much for gramophones, he wants to both spin and dance himself. And Siri is respectful, not telling him that he could run that little shed of a slaughterhouse from a stool in the kitchen, he doesn't need an office for that.

But an office is just what he needs, and one day he will have both a safe and a phone extension, on the wall he'll hang a map of Fuxe and the surrounding area: Bölö, Karlhäll, Bruket, Sjösta, Långmo and Lärkström. He had a map once, Siri had painted one with roads and crossroads and forests and chapels and churches and secondary schools and elementary schools and general stores. The bell tower she had painted violet. Then Frida came in and saw it. *Jesus,* she said, *but you shouldn't have it on the wall, you should have it with you in the car so you can find the farms when you're out driving. And you missed adding Sundqvist's new henhouse, so you'll probably turn at the Tailor's instead of Sundqvist's to behead a rooster.* And back then he was proud, always proud, so the map came down from the wall, and went into the wastebasket in fifteen hundred pieces. Siri came in, wanting to see how it looked on the wall. Poor Siri, she cried, it hasn't always been so easy for her.

Today Westlund is not sitting at his desk and driving things. No, he's being driven, driven by strange thoughts that come and go, by memories that flash like axes in the glow of the carbide lamps, he sits there and settles up with someone or someone settles up with him. He is almost alone in the house, his assistant has left and Svea has taken the bicycle and gone to the Palm's. But Siri is in her room crying; if she were on the balcony it would be heard down below. The only thing that can be heard is the rustling of the birches outside the window and, from time to time, the aches of the old wooden house. Eventually, he had taken the picture down, and put it next to Siri's chair. He didn't say anything, just went for the comb and arranged the strands of hair on his skull at an angle, so he looked like he should in the mirror. But then something must have burst inside her, suddenly a gurgling sound was heard as if she was gargling with her tears, then she got up, suddenly she was out the door, then upstairs, then she was in her room, gurgling the whole time. It hurt Westlund's ears, he went into the office and poured a shot. A big one.

Now it feels better, soon it will feel fine. He sits and covers a piece of notepaper with scribbles while he feels better and better inside. See, he's not mean, Westlund, although sometimes he does mean things. But he always regrets them, he regrets them so bitterly that he gives up his night's sleep, and lies in bed wondering why things are arranged so that you have to do what you don't want to, that you're forced to do the kinds of things that you come to regret? Creek-Lasse's horse, the one ready for slaughter that he'd sold him, sometimes comes at night and bites on the ends of the bed, the oak bed, its hooves scraping against the rug. Then he felt a strange desire to make it good again, so he went to Öhman at the post office with a fifty-crown bill in his hand. I'll send this anonymously to Creek-Lasse, he thought. But when he filled out the money order the pen gave way, turning it into just twenty—but that's not that bad! Usually when he is nice, he's nice to ladies, for the sake of being nice. Sara wasn't much to look at but she was alone in that cabin deep in the forest, the moose were prowling around outside at night, she was afraid. And Svea was alone too, and she got a brooch, so he must be nice after all. Hildur will get a brooch too, and coffee in bed. But here comes what's strange: sometimes, he also regrets the nice things he's done, maybe they weren't so nice although meant that way, because he notices that if you're nice to one person, then at the same time you're mean to another. And then he has no idea what to do. Then he has a drink.

But now he won't drink anymore; he puts the bottle in the wastebasket, because that's the bottle's place. He takes firm hold of the pen, he has an idea. He takes a fresh sheet of paper and starts writing a series of names on it, the first ones quite large, then they get smaller and smaller. He has to get another sheet of paper. He sits and writes down the names of everyone he has been nice to, and there are more than he thought. He feels really moved, as he often does from being nice; finally he can't think of any more. He counts the names, there are forty-two. Then he notices that Siri is missing, that hurts him. I must add her, he thinks. And right away he knows what needs to be done: the picture will go up on the wall, Siri will come down. Look, he will say, you mustn't think that I'm too proud for that. He adds her name, printing it big and thick; he puts the pen down and reads the forty-three names, when a car approaches on the road. He looks out over the barberry hedge, blood barberry well suited for a butcher, as the hedge agent once had said. A shiny new truck has stopped on the road, green with a silver radiator, Simon gets out, slams the door; Karlsson drives on. Surprised, Westlund becomes rigid and heavy as an iron rod, because then his gate creaks, Simon is coming to see him. But the moment before the knocking on the front porch, something has time to happen in West-lund's strange body, the desire to be nice is still there but it is wavering. Simon needs to be on the list too, he thinks walking to the door, he has forgotten Siri.

Simon doesn't look angry either, he's dressed for a holiday, has his blue jacket on. Under his arm he has a package that looks like it comes from the state liquor store in Gävle.

"Come on in, Simon," Westlund says. This is the first time they've met indoors, Simon is from Bomhus so they've always wondered what he's doing in Fuxe.

"Let's go into my office," Westlund says.

They enter, Westlund rubs the office dust off his hands, Simon sets the package on the desk, then says something that Westlund won't soon forget.

"A person should have an office, he really should," he says, sounding really sad.

So he doesn't have an office. Westlund offers him a chair, he's almost moved by the fact that Simon has no office.

"Yes, it's a fine thing to have an office," Westlund says, sitting down. He leaves the papers with the names on the table, Simon can think that it's a list of customers.

"I'm just dropping by," Simon says, "just came from town, I was there to get some liquor."

"You were right to do that," Westlund says, offering a cigar, swelling up in his chair. Simon probably measures a hundred and sixty-five centimeters tall in his socks, he himself is a hundred and eighty-six.

"And then I did a little business," Simon adds.

Westlund pricks up his ears, and he sucks on the cigar, he still wants to be nice. Simon unwraps the paper from the bottle, and puts it in the wastebasket, Westlund's half-liter is in there of course, just as well to put it on the table too.

"The maid is gone preparing for my wedding," Westlund says, "but I can always arrange a bite of herring."

He goes out to the kitchen. When he comes back, Simon is sitting there reading his list; Westlund swears to himself, he's going to get mean soon.

"Are these your customers?" Simon says. He's not grinning, he carefully puts the list back.

"Yeah, those are the butcherings we have," Westlund says, he lets Simon pour, Simon's hand trembles a little.

"Sara Kristoffersson, does she have livestock?" Simon asks, but not slyly at all.

"Yeah, she has a hog nowadays," Westlund says, sweating a little and folding up the papers.

"And Svea Larsson, she has livestock too?"

Westlund laughs.

"Nah, that's not that Svea. This is one in Skutskär that I did butchering for as a child. So to speak. And now she won't have anyone else."

Simon is impressed, that's obvious, although he probably came to brag himself. Says:

"Yeah, I was in town and bought a gadget."

"A shaving gadget?"

"No," Simon answers without getting angry. "Even better. One that slices sausage and ham and the like. Electric, you see. You could use one like it too with all your customers."

Simon lowers his eyes a little, Westlund continues to be nice, they toast.

"I have another deal in my sights," Westlund says at last. He grins and rubs his newly shaven chin, remains silent a moment, Simon is on pins and needles.

"Yes, you know, in America," Westlund starts cautiously, "there they have special blades that they saw meat with."

"You don't say," Simon says, not distrustfully at all, but all hundred sixty-five centimeters are quivering.

"Well," Westlund continues, blowing Havana over the whole office, "I've been offered this kind of sawblade by an old acquaintance in the States. You know, you just take an ox or a cow, prop it against the wall and start the blade! In two minutes you can carve up an elephant, in half a minute a horse."

For some time, Simon is speechless, Westlund refills their glasses.

"Such a sawblade must be expensive," Simon blurts out at last.

"More or less the same as your truck," Westlund ventures.

Simon's eyes get their shine back.

"Did you see it?" he whispers eagerly.

"Yes, it's parked behind the hedge."

"Did you see the gadget too? It was on the bed of the truck."

"Nah," Westlund says, happy that he's not lying, "I just saw the radiator."

"Then the damned driver stopped too soon!"

Now Simon is good and angry.

"I'll just have to see it another time then," Westlund consoles him, "I'll ask my assistant to drive me up to your place some time, Hagström that is."

But Simon is no happier for that, he remains silent and chews herring, stays silent and chews his beer. Westlund makes his triumph complete, even as he is being nice, sitting and drinking with Simon on his wedding day.

"What's your assistant's name?" he asks.

"Karlsson," Simon answers dejectedly.

"I see, Karlsson."

For a while, Westlund holds the name in his mouth to taste how bad it sounds, so at last Simon has to apologize to him.

"Yes, he can be good even so," Simon says, turning a little red. "But yours goes around saying bad things about you."

"Really, what does he say?"

Westlund's ears prick up, he stuffs a piece of sausage from his own slaughterhouse into his mouth.

"Yeah, he goes around saying that you intend to run over someone once you've got your marriage license."

Westlund gets red, takes a piece of herring in his large hand and throws it into his mouth, his teeth giving off sparks.

"That was a big fat lie," he says, "You know what they're like, these butcher boys! If they're called Hagström or if they're simply called Karlsson, it's all the same. But do you see the customer lists on the table over there?"

Of course Simon sees them, he sees almost too much of them. Westlund takes them and tears them into a hundred pieces right over the wastebasket.

"If there's ever been a bone to pick between us, Simon," he says solemnly, "may it hereby be torn to pieces like these lists are now."

They toast to that, Simon's eyes are starting to get misty with good will, Westlund's too.

"I was in town," Simon says. "And when we came to the road to Fuxe I thought to myself: A butcher is always a butcher, you shouldn't just pass by a colleague even if he lives in the same village. So I told the assistant to stop."

"You did the right thing," Westlund says, drinking down his beer in one gulp.

"Especially today when there's a wedding and all," Simon adds.

Westlund looks at the office clock, an alarm clock from Älvkarleby, there's still many hours until the ceremony. Simon sitting here thinking about weddings—that's so funny that Westlund laughs until he has tears in his eyes.

111

"There was a painter in Skutskär," he says, "who had seven shots before the wedding. And he stood up straight anyway. But then he tried to put the ring on her thumb."

Westlund's forehead shines over their glasses like the sun over Fuxe Lake. He takes his big hand and places it over Simon's, he is kind, he is happy, he has the desire to do something big. Something bigger.

"Then Westlund will have eight," Westlund says, pouring. "And put the ring on the right finger."

Simon thinks this is so grand that his eyes fill with tears in admiration. There is no more herring, so they drink taking sugar cubes. Simon remembers a story, something to do with sugar, grins again.

"Well, there was this house painter," he starts up, "do you know how he got his old lady? Well, he was living at Lundkvist's boarding house in Gävle, you know, where he fell in love with one of the serving girls. But she was strictly brought up, her mother stood in the doorway and made sure she didn't go around cuddling with the male guests. After dinner there was coffee, the guests would line up at a table in the corner. The girl stood there pouring coffee and adding sugar. Sometimes during the day they met, because in the evenings she wasn't allowed to go out. But his hours varied, so they agreed that if he had time at three o'clock then he would say: Three sugar cubes, please. And that worked out fine for a while. But one time he got off at twelve o'clock. How many sugar cubes, the girl asks. Twelve, please, the house painter says. The girl turns pale and loads up, the cup gets full and the saucer gets full and the folks in the line think that he's gone crazy. And then he drank his coffee and got sick, the next day he gave notice at the boarding house, and proposed at the same time."

"That's a funny one," Westlund says, and gets the desire for something even better. Fifteen cubes, perhaps. "What happened to him?"

"Then he got the DTs," Simon says. "I went to visit him at the psychiatric hospital. He sat upright in bed, swinging his left arm; he was left-handed you see. What are you doing? I said. Can't you see I'm painting, he said. Painting the fence at the sulfite factory. The bastards want it blue-yellow this year. Blue-yellow, I said, I think that's green. You're color-blind, lad, he shouts. Like everyone from Bomhus. And like you've always been."

Westlund's eyes hang in fascination onto Simon's thin lips, an extraordinary idea starts to form in his mind, at first there are only a few feeble shoots.

"You mean that painters paint when they get the DTs," he says.

"Of course," Simon replies. "And chauffeurs drive. Sitting in their beds, honking and driving. Shift gears with their bed knobs. And step on the gas with the footboards."

Embers of inspiration are burning in Westlund's red eyes; he puts both hands on the table, he almost has heart palpitations from delight.

"There must be butchers who get the DTs too," he says.

"Of course," says Simon, "what about it?"

Simon holds his breath with excitement, he notices that something is brewing, he almost gets a big sugar cube stuck in his throat. Westlund says, "What I'm trying to say is that perhaps you could bring home a devil like that on loan."

Simon thinks about it, scratches his nose, Westlund looks at him with giant eyes, the vein on his temple pounding.

"I have a sister who's a nurse at the Psychiatric," Simon says thoughtfully, "so that could be arranged. What about it?"

"Listen, you bring home one of those lads on loan. Give him a drink and when the DTs start you stick a cleaver in his hand. Go out to the slaughterhouse, lad, and bring the cleaver and the ox and the cow. It'll be the perfect detoxification cure. And cheap for both the government and the municipality. And for the individual butcher."

This is almost too much for Simon, his tongue gets tied, minutes pass before he can speak, he leans heavily across the table, sticks his hand in Westlund's, there is room for three or four of his sort in it.

"You're a genius, my friend," he says hoarsely, and almost grows to a hundred and sixty-seven in delight.

The spark leaps from Westlund to Simon and back, halos of inspiration are lit over both their heads, a smaller one over Simon's, a larger one over Westlund's.

"I've always thought like this," says Simon, "that there is one butcher too many in this village."

Westlund squeezes Simon's hand, but not angrily, he understands.

"Well what I mean is," Simon explains, "that there is one slaughterhouse too many. More correctly stated. So one could merge, I mean. Think about it: Simonsson and Westlund!"

"Or vice versa," Westlund says.

"Yeah. Or—and company," Simon thinks. "First we could borrow masons and blasting foremen, then we could borrow carpenters and painters and metal workers from the Psychiatric and knock together a slaughterhouse as big as the sawmill in Skutskär or the Community Center, at least. Then we'll bring home a dozen butchers on loan and get some of those sawblades from America and some of those gadgets like I have from Gävle. And we have trucks, I have my brand-new one and, well you have your. . . "

"Thirty-five," Westlund adds.

They take their fifth shot, the office growing bigger around them, and at last they both have double halos. But then Westlund notices that he is sitting in this glory in just his nightshirt and pants.

"Come, my friend," he says to Simon, "for now Westlund is getting dressed for his wedding."

Together they enter the room with the oak bed, Simon helps Westlund with the collar, he waits on him like a servant. Westlund shines, Simon shines, their four halos reflecting in the bedroom mirror.

"Maybe I should have worn a tuxedo," Westlund says, "but a person is inclined toward the simple. But when we bring home that blade, then hot damn!"

They pat each other's shoulders, when over Westlund's shoulder Simon catches sight of Frida sitting in the frame on the floor. Simon picks her up, looks around, finds the nail.

"No, not there," Westlund says.

Now he needs help, now he needs support from a true friend. His eyes wander around, he finds Simon's faithful eyes and at once he is ready to do anything, whatsoever, simply to be loved.

"Siri should have it," he says, "she lives upstairs."

"Then let's take it," Simon says, he understands.

They take hold of the frame at opposite sides, Simon walks backward, their knees bang against each other, not because the frame has grown bigger, but it has never been as heavy as now. The stairs creak, suddenly Simon thinks it's so funny that he's almost sitting down. Westlund is sweaty, soon he's laughing too. At last they stand outside Siri's door, howling with laughter. Westlund knocks. No answer. Westlund takes hold of the door handle. The door is locked.

"Siri," Westlund says, "it's Simon and me. Open up!"

But she doesn't open up, not a sound is heard from her and she isn't on the balcony, but Westlund has been good to a friend so he can handle it. They hang Frida on Siri's door and wander off to the stairs, they pause, then at last they walk down next to each other, close together, squeezed by the railings, the big butcher and the little butcher.

"How many are left?" Westlund asks.

"Yes, there must be three or four," Simon answers.

"Let's say four then," Westlund decides. "For the sake of orderliness."

In the middle of the stairs he stops, gets the ring out of his vest pocket, takes Simon's hand and pushes the ring firmly on his little finger.

"I hereby invite you to my wedding, Simon," Westlund says, having another try with the ring. "I'm not yet as drunk as that painter in Skutskär! Keep your hand still!"

"No, his old lady got so fed up at last that she mixed Antabuse in the liquor," Simon says.

The halos shine with an ever-clearer sheen, they enter the big slaughterhouse office, they sit down in the leather armchairs, feeling grand, and run their future businesses with ever greater and greater genius. The big butcher and the little butcher. The bridegroom and the wedding guest.

The milk is spilled, you shouldn't cry over it, crying doesn't help. Silently they push against each other, the sisters, last year's straw rustles under their feet, Gunnar is scared and silent in a corner of the loft, even the hens stop their clucking. Not a peep is heard, it's like this: whoever speaks first has lost, having opened the door to her innermost secret cellar. So what counts is to keep silent, for as long as you can, say things another way. Irma says them with her nose, her nostrils quivering as if her nose could fly away. Hildur says them with her ears, they glow under her black hair like a fire at night. Both say them with their hands, Irma presses down on Hildur's young shoulders, Hildur gets hers in the fat under Irma's heavy breasts. For a while, they stand in place and wrestle. But soon everything that it is possible to say silently has been said, big fish move in their water, start to bite, their tongues bob like floats. Gunnar stands next to the fire hose his body hot all over, a great, crazy joy filling him. Just go at each other! That is what he wants. Tear each other apart you two, you two that I hate! He takes the hose and bites on it, the water in the pump feels quite hot. Then Irma loses.

"You know about it," she shouts, loosening her grip, her eye sockets become too small for their bulging eyes, Hildur's ears shine red.

"No more than you," she screams back.

Welded together by hate and desire they stagger out onto the floor, tumble over each other and fall into Ivar's cold hollow.

"You witch!"

Gunnar can't hear who is screaming, it's all the same to him. But let them kill each other! Wings are burning on his shoulders, soon he'll be free. Sometime everything will burn, the flames will fling off the roofs, the horses will fry in the stable and crazed cows will tear around the farmyard, their burning tails raised like torches. Then Gunnar will laugh, he will lie under the lilac bushes, and listen to the fire follow the burning bridge of the lilacs to the snail house. But Irma and Hildur are up again now, they are quiet again, and stand linked together on the barn floor. Don't let their fire go out! Gunnar raises the hose, lifts the handle, the green water stiffens the hose. He pumps like a madman, pumping fire; he wants to destroy. The jet strikes the sisters' heads hard.

The rusty water runs like rivers of tears down Irma's cheeks, Hildur's newly waved hair starts to lose its curl. They look at each other, watching while the hate runs off with the water, suddenly break out laughing at each other's silliness. They writhe with laughter, freed from pain they fall into each other's arms, laughing at it all into each other's ears. Gunnar stops pumping, becomes like he was before. No, things will never burn. But Irma remembers something.

"What does he look like?" she asks, the laughter almost smothering her.

"Like ropy milk. And yours?"

"Like a clean broom handle."

That does it. They can no longer stand being stuck in these cramped quarters feeling so much happiness; happy as seventeen-year-olds at five o'clock on a Saturday they go out into the yard. Gunnar stands and spits in the pump, forgotten. He throws the pitcher of milk on the floor, he takes an egg and throws it at the beam. It will never burn!

"Good Lord," Irma says as they come out.

The old tramp is pumping water, bringing up a ladle or so each time at the most. But that's not what's catching her eye. It's the old man. He has come down, not just down but outside. He's sitting on the rusty seat of the mowing machine, making himself miserable, crying over the invisible horse, crying over the worn-out reins, crying over the shaft that is broken. Hildur runs over, but Irma isn't in such a hurry.

"Pa," Hildur whispers, lifting the shaft. "Rudolf will fix this in no time tomorrow. Thank you for coming down to my wedding."

The old man shakes his head, she carefully puts down the shaft in the grass, the snuff box chafing on her hip.

"You have arrived now, Pa. So you can get off."

And he does, and he walks from the machine toward the house, not to the barn thank God, she takes him under the arm, and guides him in through the gate. Irma is sweeping up glass from the broken windowpane.

"Don't worry about it, Pa. Larsson will fix it on Monday."

He seems comforted by that, but seems so endlessly tired, she gets him up the stairs, helps him onto his bed.

"Undress, Pa. Now you're going to get a wash."

When she returns with a wash basin and soap he is standing in front of one of his clocks holding up his underwear with one hand.

"Have you ever seen such a filthy old man?" he asks.

She caresses his back with the warm wash rag.

"You have such a fine back, Pa," she whispers, "as straight as a lieutenant's."

"My old man was a soldier," the old man says proudly, his pitiful skinny back shaking. The clock strikes, carefully she coaxes the snuff box out of her pocket and puts it on the table.

When she makes him do a half-turn and washes him under the arms, he sees the box lying there, he starts, and forgets to hold his underwear. Oh my God, his buttocks.

"Where'd you find it?" he asks in a tense whisper. The clock stops striking, she almost hears his heart beating under his ribs, she caresses him with the rag all the way down to his elbows.

"Behind the wash-stand," she says, standing still.

Then he gets so happy that he throws his arms around her, wet as they are; she returns him to the bed, pulls up his underwear, the shaft is now forgotten, but he's crying anyway.

"Who'd want a filthy old man?" he says.

"You're clean now, Pa," she answers. "And smell of Palmolive like a soap salesman."

She helps him into his black trousers, while promising: "I will shave you, Pa, without a single cut." She takes a little snuff out of the box and sniffs it in the way she knows he wants her to do. Suddenly he turns his mattress over, and keeps digging until, at last, he pulls out the dirtiest pillowcase she's ever seen. Probably worse even than Erika's.

"Untie it," he says.

She unties the black knot, and looks into the bag, it's full of money, bills, copper, silver, all mixed together. He laughs at the big eyes she makes, sticks his hand into the bag and searches through the treasure. What he is looking for he throws onto her lap.

"I don't want the butcher paying for the meat," he says. "The Snail isn't that poor. Oh, no! So now you're the one who'll take the bicycle to Simon and tell him that the Snail wants a fatted calf. Fed on cognac and white bread. Remember that."

Yes, she will remember, there's a lot she will remember, most of all this moment. May it last a long time, for what comes next? A clock strikes again, she puts her dry hot arms around the old man and cries, then it feels warm inside, a fire of dry wood and birch logs. The pillowcase with the money falls on the floor, he stuffs her apron pockets full of the soft currency of his love.

"Don't cry, my girl," he says quietly to console her, the sound of the striking clocks forms a safe cage around them, where it's warm and good.

"You mustn't cry," he adds. "It could have been worse. It really could. It could have turned out for you the way it did for Bjuhr's Anna. You could've ended up with somebody who brushes their teeth, girl."

Someday there will be a different star. It will be big and everyone will see it before they close the door in the evening. And everyone will talk about it before they fall asleep. It will be warm, not cold like all the others. It will shine most warmly on all those who love, it will be possible to take down and hang under your loved one's ceiling. It will not cause pain. It will have no name, it will shine whenever you want; you'll be able to touch it.

Siri is no longer crying. She has hung that star under her red shade, it shines gently in the room where she's been crying. It shines especially gently on her mother's picture, which she has just hung on the wall. She kneels below it; her knee hurts, but it doesn't matter. *Ave my Maria.* There is a star. And there is a song. There are tears that turn to song when you've been crying a long time. Sometimes she understands it all, then she becomes happy. Then she can believe that whatever happens, someday there will be a different star.

Then she thinks such fine thoughts, then she dreams such lovely dreams. Only the living are dead, she might think then. Only Mama is alive, the others are long since dead. And even when she's walking down the middle of the road to the Community Center, the boys crowding from right and left, she can feel that someday something different will happen. Someday someone will come who doesn't pinch and swear, but has different hands. Has a different language, and a beauty beyond all understanding. And then there will be other ways and other rooms where no one needs to sweat, where no one has pimples on their forehead, where it doesn't reek of liquor.

The Other bends down over the meadow, she is a meadow. She is a large sheath, she is a scabbard for a sabre. Someday the Shining One will come, he will walk lightly across the meadow, there'll be no rust on his blade. There will be nothing other than the star that shines and the Shining One that is coming, his shining sabre that comes to rest in her scabbard after the battle, red with blood, the scabbard filled to the brim, it doesn't hurt.

She starts getting undressed, sits on the floor under her mother's picture. The door is locked. Under the floor sit the dead, their hard dead voices pound against her floor, they sound like a farce in hell. Only the living shall forever be silent. There's a mirror attached to her wash stand, she turns it down toward her, leans forward into it and meets herself. Earlier, she'd feared it, then she'd fled from mirrors, hated her aching body, shyly hid in the corners of all rooms. *Noli me tangere* they've told her at school, she wasn't allowed to touch herself, she held her hands far from her body, that was before she knew that someday there would be a different star. That one autumn the gutters would be full of leaves from all the ugly trees.

Now she is pure and beautiful, only she knows it, it is her secret. She washes her whole body every day with hot water, she wants to be clean on the day when the Shining One arrives; he will enter a room where no one has ever been, only he has the key. She kneels in front of the mirror, kneels to herself, so far, she is the one who is coming, not the Other, the Shining One. *Ave Maria, my body.*

Her best outfit is laid out on the bed, a red blouse, a black skirt, she puts on the red blouse, she lets go of the mirror. The dead are choking with laughter in their hell, it doesn't concern her, she lies naked on the floor with the red blouse taut across her white breasts. Her mother takes her chair and moves close, moves all the way next to her, then everything else no longer matters. But someday there will be a different star, someday the Shining One will find the key to his only room, she closes her eyes and closes her mouth. A great beauty suddenly combined with an arc of pain. She cries for a while again.

Westlund laughs loudly. The shot just went down, number eight. He puts down the glass on the director's desk.

"Eight," he says, wiping his mouth.

But Simon has turned gloomy, and fiddles with the ring on his little finger. He lost the last round of five-card, they are playing for who will be executive, the standings are two-two.

"Seven," Simon says, knocking the ring on the table.

Westlund flares up, but soon he calms down. He stands up a while and takes a few steps. No staggering here. He turns the crank on the telephone and picks up the receiver.

"Six-three," he says.

Simon misunderstands, can't hold his liquor. According to Hagström.

"Two-two," he roars, "still undecided. Nothing is decided yet. And you've had seven shots. But stop if you can't take it!"

Westlund's call goes through to Bengtsson's café.

"Hello, Rullan," he shouts into the receiver, probably wanting to show off about his ladies for Simon, "it's Hilmer. How will you dress tonight? Put on the red jumper and that emerald necklace I bought for you last time we were in Gävle."

He casts a sly eye at Simon; oh yes, he's listening. But:

"Behave yourself before I send for the sheriff, you old goat," he gets in response through the receiver.

It must have been the old lady Bengtsson who picked up. He hangs up, not far from tears—that's how it goes when you're nice, you're just too nice, that's the whole thing. It's his turn to deal, so he deals. Simon wins, Simon becomes executive, he buttons his jacket and puts his hand over his eyes. Probably needs glasses now, gold-rimmed, managing director glasses. And sunglasses when he opens the safe.

"You mustn't think that I'm one to begrudge," Westlund says. "You're the executive. And that's that. But I've had eight, keep that in mind. Or should I get the adding machine."

He makes a gesture toward the chest-of-drawers in the corner, where he used to hide his liquor ration, at the time when he had to hide it. But Simon has already shut up, got something to think about. He doesn't have an adding machine, either.

Westlund goes on.

"But if I don't become vice-executive, then damn it. Then I'll take back my sawblade. Huh!"

"Seven," Simon says coldly and shuffles the cards, "we'll just have to play for that too."

But now Westlund becomes expansive, he downs the ninth shot, but the cards are just crap. Simon becomes vice executive too, nothing he can do. At one-thirty, Simon is managing director, vice managing director, office manager, senior slaughterhouse manager, senior cashier controller, senior sales director and senior butcher's trustee. Westlund is the personnel department second-in-command, so that's something, he can give Simon the boot whenever he wants. But it's not much, he becomes bitter, wants to vent his distress while there's still time.

"Simon," he says, "may I shake your hand?"

They shake, and shake again, the halos scatter like smoke, a great sorrow spreads through the room, Simon's truck stops outside the hedge. Westlund tries to keep from seeing it, but in the end he has to.

"A person should have somebody," he says with a sigh. "Don't get me wrong. I have my sawblade. I've got my thirty-five. And I've got a radio from Asea too. And I have ten or twelve books. And three liters of drink in my ration book. So can you tell me, why do people sneer?"

Now Simon, probably getting a little scared, lifts himself out of the chair, heavy from drink and from all the positions of trust. His butcher's assistant is cooling his heels out in the vestibule, he'll have to stand there awhile.

"Do I look too awful?" Westlund asks, concerned.

Now Westlund is standing too, they stand facing each other, Westlund mirroring himself in Simon. His sadness quickly passes, everything passes if you just wait.

"Take it easy, Westlund," Simon says, and opens the door for his assistant, "you look like a, well—"

"A Parisian," Simon adds.

And that does it. They toast for the Parisian but only in beer.

"The car is out front," Karlsson says.

Only the uniform is lacking, and Karlsson has two ears, Hagström is glimpsed behind him.

"Did you drive the car up to the entry?" Westlund asks him.

"Then you'll probably have to go and chop down a couple three apple trees first," Hagström pipes up. "Then I could drive all the way up into the hallway if Westlund so wishes."

Simon grins, Karlsson grins, they leave. The car is next to the slaughterhouse, Hagström scratches the top of his head, Westlund tests whether he is drunk, but no, he walks straight like on a tightrope down the steps. But Hagström has something to say, and stops under a tree.

"Well, is the idea that we should take the truck to the minister's?" he asks.

Simon's ears grow an inch, his assistant's as well, Westlund turns hot as an asphalt cooker.

"You damn well better believe it," he says to Hagström. "Shouldn't a thirty-five be good enough for a ride to the wedding! Who says otherwise? Huh!"

"No one," the assistant answers. "But I just heard from Lind that Hildur seems to have reserved his car for twenty past two. She was thinking that he has such soft seats in the back."

Now Westlund has to watch his step. He looks at the three men, they won't need to grin much longer. Before they have time to bat an eye he heads back up the steps, they follow.

"I'll give her soft seats, dammit," he shouts, boots on, boots into the office, the others at his heels.

"Lift," he hollers at the assistants, they lift.

So they lift the leather couch that had cost him three hundred eighty-five crowns, carry it out of the office, carry it down the steps, lift it up onto Westlund's '29. The couch sits there shining on the truck bed in the sun, looking like it costs at least six hundred. Rest your tired head it says on a big embroidered pillow. But no one is tired now, goddammit; Westlund climbs up and sits on the couch, but alone because Simon and Karlsson take off toward the Ford.

"Now we'll see who has the softest seats, Lind or Westlund," he shouts after them, puts a finger in his mouth and whistles for Siri. It's time.

And she comes just as Hagström turns, walks small and lonely down the steps, wearing a black skirt and a red blouse, looking into the distance, past all the dead here on earth. She appears to be going to a funeral, not to a wedding.

"Pull yourself together, girl," Westlund says, sinking deeper and deeper down into the couch of the upper personnel department.

He taps the window to the cab, Hagström puts it into first gear. The wedding journey begins. Simon honks behind the bayberry. Or is it Karlsson? So get to it! Honk and drive!

Now they've poked holes in the ground by the stoop, they've stuck the birch branches into the holes. And in the parlor, green garlands and red garlands and yellow and blue garlands are coiled like snakes in the Lord's jungle. Irma and her tramp brought the beer up from the cellar. It was pitch dark in the cellar, together they had lifted the crate up from the earth floor, together they put it down. "Gimme a kiss," Irma said. Water was dripping from the ceiling, suddenly she felt as heavy as the crate. But he had bitter lips, they tasted of blood.

Svea stands in her white coat in the kitchen, frying; Sören takes hold of her arm, not saying anything yet about the peddler's brooch transactions. He has tar on his fingers, she gets a smudge on her sleeve. "You made a stain," she hisses. "You've got a few already, haven't you?" He's hinting. She doesn't understand, she'll probably get it later.

Upstairs the old man has dressed for the wedding. He sits with his hands in his lap. Hildur has put on his wedding ring, it had all gone too easily. She'd cut him on the cheek, but there wasn't much blood. Sitting there alone, he starts reflecting. There is a staircase and he has legs, they smell like soap. But even so he can't go down, there are things getting in his way that no poor devil knows anything about, he is trapped like all of us. So he sits there, the clocks pick away at time like pigeon beaks. Once a fellow came along the road pushing a bicycle. *Why doesn't he ride,* someone said. It was hot, he had a hard time walking, that fellow. *Well,* he answered, *the fellow who owned it is dead, he drowned fifteen minutes ago, the bicycle was lying by the river. No one can ride a dead person's bike.* The old man sits there and remembers it all as if it were yesterday. Or was it yesterday?

The old tramp has written eight verses of the wedding poem, each with six lines each. Once there'd been another one who sat writing, in another arbor, while someone, a strong fellow, chopped wood nearby. The other one, he wrote verses too; the tramp sat a bit to the side, a bit above, and watched. He wrote about knives and night on earth, he had blood in his inkwell, the moon above casting its light on it. I'm not in my right mind, the tramp thought, no one is allowed to see such things, it's against all law. Then he forgot all about it, for some time at least. These days he just sweats; he sweats over the paper, he sweats out the words, he sweats out his whole life. At one o'clock while they are decorating with branches behind him, he thinks like so: Soon I will be The Other, the one who sits in another arbor and has an inkwell full of blood. Someone should write a poem about death before it's too late. Someone is chopping wood nearby even though it's hot, even though it's the month of August. Someone should write about death, not weddings. Like this: You little speck of humanity, you bride! Your bed is made for the final night, your wedding night. Your black bridegroom sets his clock, he moistens his lips in the only wine, and you know your lips shall dry them. Your only bridegroom is named Death, soon you will bear his name. Soon you will be loved by the only faithful lover; so get undressed now, his sheets are hot.

128

Soon the Singer, too, has dressed for the wedding, while his song lay in the forest under a bush, sleeping. It's midday, he has a hat on his head, the straw hat. He once had a straw hat in an opera, he should have eaten it so none of what followed would have happened. Instead, he wore it, and he had been drinking. He used to be beautiful at that time, and drank a lot. *I'm a danger to "public insecurity,"* he used to sing in his bathrooms. But this was another song, he took off his straw hat, a smile crept onto his lips, he drove it away, and sang. In the middle of the song the rigid faces in front of him billowed in over him like waves of the sea; he got as cold as if he'd fallen through the ice of a lake, getting stuck in the freezing water, he cries for help. He raises the straw hat like a shield, it breaks, the shape of his mouth disintegrates, the song falls to the stage floor, its throat cut, murdered by a violin. Good Lord, he thinks, confused; it's the wrong song, it doesn't belong here, it belongs in another opera, in another time, somewhere else. And after that, the dream lasts forever, the dream about the silence that always follows. Now, in his and Malm's room, he clips on the bowtie; the song isn't dead, it awakens under the bush, it yawns, it strides forth out of the forest, it lives at the poorhouse. Someday everyone will realize that they'd wrongly judged him, and then it will become completely quiet. Today he has written another letter and given it to the director for forwarding.

Gunnar has put the fish on the stoop, then he finds an arrow in Creek-Lasse's garden, he looks in the creek for lampreys, the only thing he finds is a leech on a stone, he sticks it onto a different one. The leech will hate that stone, it's a game too, moving all the small creatures to places they hate, it's his favorite game, the game that we like to play with our toys, that's the game others play with us.

Rudolf has taken the rake out of the shed; dressed for a holiday he walks around the farm and tries it out; it doesn't catch that much. But Rullan will get caught in it, he is going to rake her with it until the rake teeth break, in the meadow there's someone who's been raking for over fifty years. A fellow named Asp, Augustus; he wasn't all there, he raked and raked, the years passed, at last he died, even so he couldn't stop raking. In the mornings some ten years after he died there were broken off rake teeth in the grass, Ma still finds them, she's the only one, she's of the Asp family.

Hildur can't remain indoors, not since she got the letter. Gunnar came from the mailbox by the gate, mail in hand: the newspapers *Upsala Nya, Gefle Dagblad, Smålänningen*, a green envelope from the mortgage bank, a letter for the farmhand from home. "Hildur," Gunnar shouted, "you got a letter. There was no stamp on it, it was mean and thin." Alone in the parlor, she opened it. There weren't many lines, but the ones that were there were enough: *Who was knocking on the bride's window at four in the morning? Some people would like to know. But this is the way it is. You make do with what you have.*

She was dressed for the wedding, the letter went into her blouse pocket. "Come, Ma, let's step outside," she said. Hilma had just dressed too, Hildur had hooked all of her hooks, she had tied up the bun on her head, she had pulled on the black stockings, they went outside. They go to the tramp, who's in his arbor. "Not done yet but soon," he says, whistling. They walk farther, it's midday, the farmhand stands down by the lake, whistling too, washing himself, naked as far as they can see. Rudolf walks around with a rake, is probably crazy again now. Crazy for Rullan.

They walk even farther in the heat, she wants to have time to see all she will lose. She presses herself close to her mother as if she was a tree to hold onto, they walk under the lilac bushes, there was a swing there once, swaying in the wind. She was young, the world lay beneath her; I'm swinging on the highest branch like Zachárias Topelíus. There was someone who thought that was his name, he drowned later. They look into the shed, there is a sled up under the ceiling, one time she sat on it smaller than a calf under the pelts, the wind whining through the fences, she'd been woken up early. They took the winter roads, the stars burning high above the pelts, Pa held a kerosene lamp in his hand, Rudolf stood behind and howled with delight on the turns, the ice sparkled on the lake, the bells rung hard in the steeple. At church, they sat closest to the window; you can light the candles Victor, the parish clerk said. Pa stood up, he lit the branched candle in the window recess, he stood a long time so the whole church would see it. Never before had Hildur loved him so.

But you make do with what you have. She takes Hilma's hand, they walk toward the well and the manure pile, she takes everything in, she is a big suitcase, she packs it full, she locks it, she takes the key and tosses it onto the barn floor. Keys are always getting lost in barns. Or clocks. Or cigarettes. Or hair clips. Once she lost six during threshing.

A wagtail is hopping outside the arbor, it hops too late; they go in to the tramp, he hands over a folded paper, turning her back to the old people she unfolds it. She never gets past the first line. It is so dark, it looms so tall, it is a heavy gate. *Who can know my anguish?*

Leaving everything behind her, she rushes out of the arbor, scares up the wagtail, wants to be far away as if she could find him there, the one who knows. But she doesn't get far, doesn't get past the sawhorse. Because just then Lind drives in through the big gate; he has Swedish flags on the fenders.

Westlund rolls in, Simon rolls in after, they roll along the fence their gears in neutral, roll down toward the bride and retinue who are standing by the small gate, next to Lind's car. Lind himself stands with his foot on the running board, with a mocking look. So why not mock back? At first it looks like they're running him over, but no, they're just teasing; they block his Chevy in between their trucks, making sure he can't open a single door. Then there is life in Lind, and life in Rudolf and Sören too. Westlund is sitting firmly on the couch; Simon gets out.

"Are you planning to move in?" Rudolf shouts. "Because we have no rooms vacant here."

Westlund gets offended, he knocks ash off his cigar.

"What a brother-in-law," he complains from the depth of the couch, "who considers himself too good to go to the minister in his brother-in-law's car?"

"Get off the couch, you fool," Rudolf says, loosening the flap at the back of the truck. "Do you think we want to be the laughingstock of the whole village?!"

Simon intervenes.

"Is it prohibited to sit on couches nowadays?" the managing director says, standing on the ground, firmly holding onto the side of the couch. "For crying out loud, in Bomhus all we do is sit on couches."

"Knock it off!" Hildur shouts at them, "you're no better, none of you."

Too late. Lind, Rudolf and Sören are already up on the

truck bed. Westlund puts on a couple of kilos, they drag the couch backward, the butchers' assistants sit in the cabs and grin; they have the brakes on and the gears in second, so no one will be able to roll the trucks out of the way. None of this concerns Siri; she looks out the truck window, the dead can scream all they want; they get the couch to the edge, and Westlund tumbles down. They place it by the fence and brush off their hands, Westlund sits down on it, his cigar almost finished.

"How many shots did you have before you came here?" Irma asks him, shaking with anger, her nostrils quivering.

Simon is there at once to defend him.

"No more than eight," he says. "Not a drop more. Reymers and Bords. And then a couple of beers. But beer—"

"No, this person here is no worse than the folks in Skutskär," Westlund adds, and watches, with wrinkles on his sweaty forehead, as they push Lind's car free.

They push it right onto the intact mover shaft, it creaks, broken.

"Pa," Hildur screams and is gone, up the stairs in a dash. The door is locked, it's silent in there, it doesn't help a bit to complain. She comes down again.

Then a shrill signal overpowering everything cuts through the racket. Gunnar is in Simon's car, honking. Everyone falls silent, and it is strange: they don't have to be silent long to be full of laughter. They look at the couch where Westlund is resting, they look at the cigar, of which only the glowing ember is left, even the broken shaft looks funny.

"Get off the couch, Westlund!" Rudolf says, good-hearted now. "Get up and get married, you bastard!"

And Westlund gets up nicely, he goes to meet Hildur, takes her into his arms, someday he will write a whole book about all the people he's been nice to. They get into Lind's car. A hen has jumped up onto the couch, who cares as long as she doesn't soil it; they drive.

"Damned if they'll pass us," Westlund says to Lind, as the trucks rumble behind. "Faster, this ain't no funeral!"

But Hildur isn't laughing, the whole time they drive she is turned around; she sees the farm and she sees the window with the broken pane. But she sees no old man. In the last curve Karlsson passes them, honks and drives ahead. Hagström doesn't want to be left behind, in a flash, he's passed them, Westlund swells over the '29, and they arrive.

The parsonage has a hawthorn hedge, and an iron gate, Hildur slowly pushes it open, it whines, they are all silent. Hildur walks up the gravel walkway to the parsonage, a dog glares from the doghouse. She walks ahead as if she were alone; Westlund catches up with her. Gunnar picks up an apple from the grass, gets his hair pulled by Irma, whines like the gate just did. The parsonage has a short concrete staircase, six steps and an iron railing; it takes an eternity to get up. She takes one step at a time, *make do with what you have.* There is smoke from the pastor's washhouse, a mowing machine rattles from down on a lake meadow. The parsonage has a broad yellow door with a glass pane in it, it has a chain on the inside since the Tillberga murders, she takes hold of the handle, *make do with what you have.* She takes her handkerchief, a wet little ball—make do with the handkerchief you have—when she hears a strange sound from the other side of the hedge, and lets go of the door handle. Everyone hears it, a bicycle falling at the side of the road. The sound of steps approaching the gate. He hesitates a moment, then opens the gate and slowly walks toward his loved ones. He has dust on his trouser legs, a little grease from the bicycle chain; sweat runs down his collar.

"Pa," she whispers, as happily as if he were the groom.

But Westlund calls to Simon, his vest pocket is empty, Simon comes up the steps.

"The ring," Westlund pants.

They pull and tear on Simon's little finger, the ring just sits there, Rudolf comes over and pulls, they curse quietly so it won't be heard inside.

"It's swollen, that bastard," Westlund says. "We'll probably have to get the meat cleaver when we get home. Or the sawblade."

They tug a few more times, but the ring sits as if cast onto Simon's finger. Hilma pulls off hers, and sneaks it into Westlund's hand. The parsonage hall is dark, it has a large mirror and an oak stair. There's a white door to the left; they will go through it. The door has a cold brass handle. Hildur grasps it, *make do with what you have.*

Simon slinks in last through the front door, closes it hard, closes it irrevocably. Closes it with his left hand. His right hand he hides in his pants pocket.

Make Do with What You Have

But now it is evening and the moon is floating across the lake, the well cover is open, the well is filled with light, the liquid manure glistens like a pond at Löfsta Mill. Three vehicles are in the farmyard, the two butchers' trucks and one from town, a '32 Plymouth, its ship shines on the radiator. The hedgehog has been fed some wedding milk; now it's rolling through the moonlight, darned if a fox comes, it thinks, then it'll see a thing or two. The mowing machine has fallen asleep, its wings folded for the night, they've placed supports under the shafts, so the old man is satisfied. Because tonight everyone should be contented, even the ice is contented though the evening is warm, it's deep under the sawdust in the garden and not sweating any more. The horses have been fed bread and sugar, they're on their knees in their boxes, dreaming. One of them dreams about a forest: there the horses are brought to their knees tied to timber loads, they drag them through the juniper; there is no snow yet, they all have big bits in their small bloody mouths. The straw under the cows is warm and dry, the moonlight lies like shiny dust inside the small windowpanes, this is the hour when the horseflies have stopped stinging.

The apple trees stand in the garden with moonlit branches, the grass is slowly starting to tear, it will need many long trailing dresses to wipe it dry. The spiders spin their webs on the gates, the moss sways on the wooden fences—it doesn't care about anything, a sure way not to be fooled. The cats are on a moonlit hunt, they sneak in the jungles of the grass, they sneak into the virgin forest of the potato field. The evening is full of dangers. They sneak through sky-high rye down to the waterholes in the ditch to drink, the evening full of the trumpeting of the biggest elephants, the cats' world trembles.

The evening is full of shadows that lie resting sharp and still below the gates, and on the roof, the shadows of the chimneys don't move. But some shadows are in motion, some around the house, some around the barn and cowshed; quick and jerky, on constant flight from the light. One shadow steps out onto the stoop.

"Who's there?" the shadow calls, as it steps onto the fir branches spread out at the base of the stoop.

It gets no answer unless rapid steps are an answer, and tracks in the dew, dark tracks around the corner of the house. Another shadow emerges, staggers into the moonlight on the stoop, the gate over at the pasture creaks, the shadows who flee seem quite heavy.

"Stop and you'll get your ass full of rock salt."

It's the newly arrived shadow who calls, it falls off the stoop through the fresh-cut birch branches lining it, gets a laugh in answer, if a laugh is an answer. Then it becomes silent. The moonlight falls gently over the two shadows, it smells of wild herbs, the shadows smell of liquor.

"That's gotta change," one shadow says—a big one, it raises its hands over its head, "Calle Scheven's Waltz" drums against the windowpane inside.

The other shadow is not small either. It loosens its long tie, it sneaks toward the corner of the house, then, by the sunflower, its knees suddenly buckle. Unexpectedly, an explosion bursts out of the silence—there is a flash near the root cellar, and smoke rises in the moonlight, billowing toward the corner of the house. The house shakes its shoulders, the windowpanes quiver in their frames.

"That's gotta change," the biggest shadow shouts.

Then it becomes completely silent. Inside Gunnar has turned off the gramophone, another shadow staggers out on the stoop, bottle in its hand. All three shadows form a circle and drink, the moon puts on its new summer hat, darkness falls over the rye.

"Let's go in separate directions," one of the shadows whispers. "We'll meet down by the lake."

They sneak around the corners of the house, the gramophone starts playing again, two of the shadows stay together, soon the bottle is empty. But who is crouching by the cellar? They start walking on tiptoe, there's a smell of gunpowder, they cock their fists, about five meters to go.

"Hey," the two shadows shout, quickly they are on top of the third one.

They get their pockets full of sand, one gets a punch in the stomach, the other gets a kick to the knee, at last the third one is pinned down; he was strong. The moon takes off its hat, the light brightens, they raise up the one on the bottom and look at him. It's Westlund.

"It's just me," Westlund says. "I don't throw bombs."

Rudolf and Sören look at each other now, as brothers, brothers under the moon. Sören shatters the bottle against the cellar door. Smash.

"We were supposed to meet by the lake," Westlund complains, but he can't shake them off.

"Of course, but since for once you're on the bottom,

you'll get another punch," Rudolf says. "It would be a waste otherwise."

They take care of it. And order is restored.

"So how are things with Rullan nowadays?" Rudolf says amiably, sitting on Westlund's chest. Sören is sitting on his legs. "And how are things with Svea?"

Westlund grins, he's under them but otherwise he's on top, only dislikes the pebbles at his back.

"They're just fine," he answers generously. "Rullan's sitting on a chair in the arbor with one of the gentlemen from town. And—"

"There's only one chair," Rudolf snarls. He knows, he himself carried the others inside to the table.

"Exactly," the butcher says, "exactly." Now they let him off. "And Svea is probably in the kitchen making dessert. So there."

Then there is another explosion from behind the shed, quieter this time. The birches rustle, a bird screeches, that's all.

"Maybe we should go and look at the rake," Rudolf says.

He is almost crying. They rise, looking like road workers in their dirt-covered suits; suddenly they understand each other amazingly well, all three of them.

The rake is lying in the grass, it is long and beautiful, it is longing for hay, it seems. The fitting glistens, no one has ever seen such a beautiful rake, they stand in a circle around it, an odor of glue comes from the shed.

"Hell of a rake," says Westlund.

"You're right about that," says Sören.

Rudolf picks up the rake.

"Feel it," he says, barely able to utter a syllable, he's so moved.

The three of them touch it, caressing the shaft, it's soft as a girl's back. Westlund whistles.

"Feel the teeth," Rudolf whispers.

They feel the teeth.

"Not a splinter," Westlund says.

"You could comb yourself with it," Sören says.

"You should have something to comb," Rudolf says bitterly.

"You should have a little hay," Westlund says.

He guides the rake through the grass, creating a shiny path toward Rudolf's cut birches, Sören and Rudolf each fetch a handful of hay from the milk room. They spread it out under the moon, make a new meadow on the farmyard with it, Westlund walks backward and rakes, the fitting shines under the gray hay. Hildur comes outside and stands by the gate.

"Hilmer," she calls slowly. "Shouldn't we go home soon?"

One of the shadows in the yard answers.

"Go back inside! Can't you see he's busy raking?"

And tonight she is so afraid of the shadows, she just runs back in, crying probably.

Westlund rakes the hay into a long straight line.

"That's one hell of a rake," he says.

"Now it's my turn," the farmhand says.

Taking turns, they rake in the light of the moon, Rudolf makes a pile, he tops it off, there is a breast of hay.

"Guess you'll see me raking here from time to time," Westlund says; he is nice to the whole world now.

But just then the third explosion comes. It probably only shakes Rudolf, but it shakes him so hard he shatters. The third explosion is a laugh. Afterward it becomes completely silent, which is even worse.

"I'm done raking now," he says too quietly. "Pick up the hay! Come with me!"

He puts the rake on his shoulder like a rifle, the shaft is hot, the teeth are glowing. Sören and Westlund carry the hot hay, in a row the three avengers walk down toward the arbor. There is one white chair, two are sitting on it. Rullan's legs gleam between Wallinder's black trousers, he's the one with the Plymouth and a radio store; they are kissing.

"And I can get as much nylon as I want," Wallinder whispers romantically.

"And you can get even more of a beating," Westlund adds in a good-humored voice, in the style of his butcher's assistant.

Rullan jumps up, but Wallinder stays seated. He lifts his gaze toward the avengers and the moon, his mouth hangs open. He has a few fillings too, but small ones. Rudolf takes the rake off his shoulder, and supports himself on it; Westlund and Sören block the arbor entry with their hay; Rullan turns her back to all of them, she has a nice-looking back.

"I see, you're acquainted with Rullan," Rudolf says slowly. "I thought you only knew my cousin, Nisse Johansson, and his woman."

"Rullan—all of Gävle knows her from the time she worked at the hotel," Wallinder answers lightly; he looks at his car behind the three hicks. A car provides security.

But Rudolf feels the truth in that. He hugs the rake handle; damn, that hurts.

"Get up," he tells Wallinder.

Sören and Westlund have to help him, Wallinder doesn't seem able to on his own steam.

"Since I have the comb with me, how about we comb him?"

He looks uncombed; Rullan probably tousled his hair, she usually does.

"On what side do you want the part?" Rudolf asks.

Wallinder doesn't condescend to answer. They take him in a firmer hold.

"Let's try with a center part first then," Rudolf says, driving the rake into Wallinder's curls.

"We have better combs in town," Wallinder says. He's trying to keep a straight face even though Rullan isn't looking at him.

"Here in the village we have fittings on ours," Westlund talks back.

"In town they're made of plastic," Wallinder persists.

"But ours are longer," Sören says.

"A part on the left would probably look better," Rudolf says. One tooth of the rake catches Wallinder's ear.

"In town you comb yourself." Wallinder isn't done yet.

"But here in the village we have special comb bearers," Westlund says. "And they follow you wherever you go. If you want to be combed you just have to whistle."

"I didn't whistle," Wallinder replies.

Then Rullan laughs, Rudolf stops combing, Wallinder is released.

"Now you're going to rake," Rudolf says to Rullan, and roughly presses the handle of the rake into her tender hands. Westlund and Sören make a path of hay from the arbor up toward the small gate. Wallinder sits alone on the white chair, smoking.

"Now you're going to rake, Rullan," Rudolf says gently. "Because I made this rake for you. So now you should rake with it."

She sees no other way out. They each light a cigar, each of the three of them, while she rakes the path into a pile, she clenches her teeth, then drives the wooden teeth of the rake into the ground so hard it cuts into the hearts of the three master rakers.

"Are you done now?"

Yes, she's done, she throws the rake to Rudolf, he takes it in his right hand, and he takes her in his left.

"Bring the hay," he says to the others. "And follow us."

They walk toward the woodpile, Wallinder strolls a little behind, as curious as a magpie.

"Go get the chopping block," Rudolf says to the farmhand.

Sören rolls the block out of the woodshed, he has the ax in one hand, Westlund lets go of the hay; Rudolf lets go of Rullan, just then the moon puts on its winter cap; and all goes dark.

"Light the hay," Rudolf says.

Westlund sets a match to it, it burns slowly, it's a little damp from the dew. Now Rudolf lays the rake on the chopping block, and takes the ax from the farmhand. Rullan shrieks. First he chops it in two pieces, then he chops it into four. He chops in the middle of the fitting so the brass gets bent; the teeth fly in every direction.

"No one's going to be able to glue this together again," he says at last. He throws the ax firmly into the block, his eyes shiny from the dew of sorrow.

The hay stops burning; soon the moonlight will return. Separately, they go back to the party.

Wallinder tries to take Rullan by the arm.

"Let go," she hisses.

"I can get as much nylon as I want," he maintains.

"Shut up," Rullan answers.

Rudolf stops and waits for her. To his great surprise he suddenly feels her arm under his, to his even greater surprise he notes: that arm makes me happy.

"That was one hell of a rake," Sören says quietly, when they've reached the stoop.

"We should drink to that," Rudolf yells, mounting the steps between the birches with Rullan close beside him.

Wallinder stays behind at his car, smoking.

"You should have one too, Wallinder," he calls to him.

"Okay," Wallinder answers. "Wait. I have a flask made of plastic in the Plymouth."

"And here in the village," Westlund yells in response, "there's an old woman who has plastic buttocks. But she only uses them in church on Sundays."

So now they're nice and good again, all of them, the shadows have given way, the earthworms creep up toward the moon.

It's hot in the parlor, the garlands are withering in the heat, there's not much left of the candles. Drunken angels pass through the room. They take another plate of food; there are a couple liters of aquavit left and a couple of cans of herring and anchovies, they're all red and blue, only the bride is pale. The gentlemen from town debone the anchovies, Westlund eats his whole. The lady from town has been looking at Sören for the past three minutes, she wants to kiss him, her name is Mary, she's married to Nisse Johansson, the cousin. She walks around doling out kisses. Not her fault, she says, that she's passionate; she also has a powder box made out of plastic, it takes her fifteen minutes to eat a single lousy sardine. Svea wants to throw a meatball at her; she's sitting next to old man

Bjuhr, he pinches her on the back of her knee. Old lady Bjuhr sits there wondering how much the whole thing costs; she needs a pen and a piece of paper, or there's a risk she'll forget everything. But she won't need pen and paper to remember that the Singer and Hilma are sitting holding hands.

Simon is drinking the most, two shots per anchovy. That's how it's done in Bomhus, he says. Between shots he glares at Bjuhr, they aren't friends exactly; it's an old story. The first time Simon was in Bjuhr's stable: there was a horse on its knees in the box, it wasn't worth much, and Simon got angry. "This is the nag of a shady dealer," he yelled. Bjuhr got angry too, in his younger days, he was even more hot-tempered than he is now. "So you think I'm a swindler, do you," he said. "Exactly," Simon said, "a swindler." "If you'd said gypsy, I'd let it go but now I'll sue you at the Örbyhus courthouse." And Simon was sued, there were fines too. Never call an alternate on the Municipal Board of Road Maintenance a swindler! They haven't spoken to each other for eleven years and three months; not tonight either.

Hagström and Karlsson are sitting at the end of the table talking about cars, Westlund's is already a '38—so new that it might as well not even be made yet, as Karlsson says. But Simon's, you can get up to a hundred and seventy-five when you're drunk. It's probably best to put wings on it then, in Hagström's opinion, then you can fly to Furuvik and butcher the crocodiles, because you wouldn't get any other butchering here in the village.

Rullan and Rudolf are talking about rakes. Rudolf thinks that he can make another one like the last, with a name plate on it and everything; she'd only have to rake clover with it. She likes that.

But the later it gets, the paler Hildur gets. She feels as if she's falling, falling through the clinking of the glasses and all the candles and all the voices. Irma sits across from her, waiting; she keeps looking toward the windows. And sure enough, at ten o'clock there's a knock on the south window, Hilmer goes outside and Sören goes out and Rudolf too. They came back even more drunk, but without the knocker.

Siri is in the midst of them, feeling completely alone. She took food and drink to the tramps in the barn; they were sitting around a crate, a kerosene lamp on the floor. "There should be three of you," she said in surprise. "That's right," the young one said, "so you might as well stay." She fled but in the middle of the yard she stopped in the moonlight, feeling an overwhelming urge to go back. But she didn't go back; there were more stars in the sky, they were all wrong.

Gunnar is standing by the gramophone; he's the one who plays it, he's the one who winds it up; he is winding it up now, it's sitting on a wobbly chair. He puts on "See Grandpa Dance an Old-Time Waltz."

The Singer wants to sing, but he bides his time. I won't need persuading, he thinks. Well, resisting a little is just good tone, although not too long of course. Just so that they notice: it's not just anyone who's singing. But it's hard to be persuaded when no one asks you. And you can't say: So good folks, go ahead and ask, I want to give you a song from my heart. You can't very well ask someone to ask you to do something, that's just not done. But when the heart is overflowing, when your longing becomes too heavy for the heart's tender basket— what do you do then? You take what's there, you turn to the smallest of the small, seize the most rough-hewn of hands: So please, won't you at least ask me, when no one else does. And finally Hilma asks him:

"Now you should sing," she begs.

At once he stands in the middle of the parlor, he stands under the ceiling crown with the glass droplets, he stands under another light, he stands high above other faces. Suddenly Westlund is no longer there, the blinds quietly open; it smells differently, no longer of liquor and smoke and sweat; a new light falls, the light of darkness; and the bright faces disappear, only white shirt fronts shine like flowers in the deep meadow. In this darkness, he is an instrument he does not himself play, someone else plays; he fills the room, he explodes in song. But there is a cage for all our songs. In the midst of this exultation he begins to sweat, feels it running, he wants to touch his forehead but can't raise his hand; in both his hands, he holds a straw hat, it weighs more than anything else. An iron curtain slowly descends; it is sharp as a razor, it cuts him in two, it glides through his throat, it doesn't hurt.

Then he is wakened by another song, he is wakened by stomping. Horses? He raises his head, and looks over a table filled with cigars; he is lying on a couch with his shoes on.

"Lie still now," a voice says.

It is Hilma's, but he doesn't see her, he sees only a broad back moving up and down, he sees a large face, the mouth of the face giving off brilliant flashes. Slowly he returns to reality. Westlund has come to life again, Westlund dances an old-time waltz, he is red and sweaty, he is dancing alone. With a frightful disappointment, with a terrible anxiety the Singer takes everything in. He sees Hilma by the tile stove; she has never looked so ugly; he touches the door of the tile stove, it has never felt so cold; he is lying on Palm's couch, he is empty and dead.

"How did I sing?" he whispers.

"You sang so well," she whispers back; but she looks at Westlund, who has paused under the crown, his arms around his imagined bride, she is probably a full meter around the waist.

"Did you all see my moves?" he calls out when the record stops.

"Shouldn't we go home now, Hilmer?"

Hildur looks as white as a bridal sheet, Westlund falls into a creaky chair.

"Haven't you seen my moves?" he asks, offended.

Yes, she's seen it all. The Singer sinks into the couch pillows, he wants to leave, but he can't get up. Victor stands by the table.

"All of you shut up, because now I'm going to make a speech," he says. He has probably had a few too many; he picks up an anchovy from the can and holds it in front of him by the fin, as if that's who he's talking to.

"You have anchovies," he continues, and picks up a cheese. "You have cheese. You're not completely broke. You have sardines too. And Hildur, I just want to tell you that if the butcher ever runs out of ham, then come to me. Because here, so help me God, we have anchovies. And here we eat mayonnaise in the middle of the week! Don't forget that! And thanks for letting me have a word!"

He sits down, he is pale and drunk and now those who still can feel shame, feel ashamed. But Westlund is not ashamed, he's red-faced and angry, probably noticing how the butcher boys are grinning, how Bjuhr is sitting there thinking God knows what. So now it's his turn to say something. He takes his knife and taps it on a glass, it cracks; that was unnecessary, a shot of aquavit prematurely departed. Anyone who cares can lick it up, but Westlund is proud. He stands behind Hildur's chair, supporting himself on her narrow shoulders; for his heavy body, she is not much of a pillar.

"I'm no speaker," Westlund says. "But there are many who aren't but who talk anyway. So there."

"But no names," Bjuhr says, grinning. That old swindler, Westlund gets even redder.

"Please don't interrupt me," he shouts, "'cause then I'll get mad."

But it's Bjuhr's specialty to interrupt speakers. The first and the last time he was at Magistrate Jansson's he got thrown out. It didn't seem to do any good. It was on the magistrate's fiftieth birthday in '37. "Now as I stand here," the magistrate was saying, "now as I stand here on my fiftieth birthday, now as I stand here at my half-century, now as I stand here at my turning point and look around." "I think you're standing on the floor, magistrate," Bjuhr said. There had been eighty guests; three minutes later there were only seventy-nine.

"The last time I was in America," Westlund continues, now he's found the right thread, of cotton made in America. "The last time I was in America, it was jam-packed with speakers on the streets. Oh-estlund, they said to me. Oh-estlund, that is. Not Vestlund, like you say here in the village."

"Vest-land," old man Bjuhr says thoughtfully. "Vestland isn't too far from Tierp. I have a sister in Tierp."

Westlund raises his voice, soon Hildur can no longer bear him.

"Last time I was in America," he shouts for all he's worth.

"Last time I was in Gävle," Bjuhr says quietly, "there was a dog who went and drank beer by the harbor."

"Cheers," Westlund says defeated, taking Hildur's glass. The lady from town bursts out laughing, lying doubled over on the table like a used napkin, but that's all going to change.

Now Simon stands up, and his face is somber. He looks so

somber that gradually there is total silence in the parlor, even Hilma who had been sitting whispering with the Singer, falls silent. No light of mercy shines from Simon; and the shadows gather around Bjuhr; he has taken his hands off of Svea, he sits completely alone. One who is afraid is always alone. And all frightened hearts pound like drums, the frightened hands of those who know cling to the table, they know that in this village no injustice is ever forgotten, whether it's after eleven years and three months, or whether it's after thirty years and eleven months. Now Simon leans forward; his darkness descending heavily on Bjuhr, he holds his glass under Bjuhr's nose, not spilling a drop.

"Cheers," he whispers. "Cheers, you plastic fake!"

It takes a while before Bjuhr gets it. Then he stands up, glass in hand. It is dead silent in the parlor, a sigh would not go unnoticed.

"Say that one more time," Bjuhr says, not heatedly but cold.

"Cheers, you plastic fake."

"Cheers."

They drink, eyes locked, putting down their empty glasses at the same time. The blood rises like a fountain in old man Bjuhr's sunburnt face.

"What are you getting at?" he screams, almost breaking everyone's eardrums.

It is Nisse Johansson who replies, he will be the one who saves lives; he leaps to his feet, throws his jacket off.

"Look here," he calls out to Bjuhr.

Bjuhr looks; for that matter everyone looks; Nisse is standing there in his shirtsleeves, it's a blue shirt with red stripes, town fashion. Slowly he pulls off one sleeve garter, and holds it over the table in the light of a candle.

"This one here is made of plastic," he says slowly and with emphasis, he then takes the other one off and lets it be passed around the table.

But Bjuhr is no happier.

"I see," he says bitterly, "I'm the type who holds up your shirt. I'm a kind of sleeve garter. Am I perhaps another kind of garter too? Huh?"

Simon does not respond, he sits down, still in a dark mood. But Bjuhr feels an arm on his shoulder, the scent of powder in his left nostril.

"This is made of plastic too," the passionate Mary from town says, and shows him a cigarette holder, a black one and pretty.

"Well, I never," Bjuhr says, and gets a warmer sheen in his eyes. "That isn't bad. No. I'll be damned."

Now he looks really appreciatively at Simon, whose darkness lifts. Quickly Bjuhr takes a deck of cards out of his pocket, a new one, and Simon cuts. He has said what he wanted to say, so why decline?

"Last time I was in America," Westlund says with feeling, "we played poker for the dames. I won one whose name was Eunice. I couldn't pronounce it for the life of me. So I called her Oscaria."

Bjuhr shuffles; the Singer lies on the couch moaning; the old man is falling asleep. Westlund's car was made in '39. "1839," Karlsson adds. And Hagström keeps quiet.

"Last time I was in Gävle town," Bjuhr says, "I won a hundred and eight at whist."

"You ain't been in Gävle for four years," his old lady says; she shouldn't have.

And the lady from town shouldn't have gone outside, or if she did, Sören shouldn't have gone with. But she wiggles her plastic behind and he follows. As the door is about to close Svea fires off a meatball, but too late—it lands in the crack at the bottom of the door; as it falls she turns red from shame and anger. But Victor becomes sarcastic.

"Is it the custom nowadays that butcher-maids throw meatballs at doors?" he mutters to his son-in-law.

"Last time I was in America," Westlund answers apologetically, "they shot meatballs from cannons. So there."

Then Hildur turns the whitest of white. There's knocking at the window again, at the top of the south window, louder than the time before, louder than this morning. Anxiety shakes its dark crown inside her; she seeks her friend, but he isn't here. Then she remembers to make do with what she has, she makes do with the eyes that meet hers, makes do with Irma's spiteful ones and Svea's wicked ones. Suddenly she knows who wrote her the letter.

"Shouldn't we go home now, Hilmer?" she whispers to her husband. The eyes follow her all the way down to the place where everyone must be alone.

But Westlund has already stood up. He cuts the deck of cards.

"Just going to beat Bjuhr at poker first," he answers in a nice voice.

They all rise, only the Singer remains lying next to the cold tile stove, Gunnar puts on the "Good Night Waltz," it's cracked.

"How did I sing?" the Singer whispers.

This time he receives no answer.

The cats have fallen asleep on Westlund's couch, each in its own corner. They came prowling in the moonlight, their tails heavy with dew; the field mice danced in the rye. The cats sneaked across the clearings, threw themselves into the shadows to escape their pursuers; suddenly they stood still under the telephone wires, their hearts beating against the earth. But it was just the hedgehog, the one with spines instead of fur. *He's not in his right mind, let's take his milk,* they agreed, but the bowl was empty. That was when they saw it. They covered their eyes with their paws, they told each other that they must be dreaming. They leapt toward the couch, and it was really there; they felt it under their paws, they felt it with their whiskers, with their noses too. In cat-Paradise all couches are outdoors and all pastures full of soft inviting armchairs. *We mustn't sleep,* they said, *we must stay awake since we're in Paradise.*

But they fell asleep anyway, you always fall asleep right at the doorstep of Paradise, and when they awoke it was as if they were floating in a boat. They sailed forth in the couch across the grass, floating atop people in the moonlight. *Let's leave,* one cat said to the other, *we must be in Hell, there's people everywhere.*

The men put the couch down next to the well; they close the well cover, pour the green putrid water out of the barrels, then have a seat on the couch and barrels. The well pole stands like a broken gallows above their hot skulls; they pull down the well bucket and put it between them; it's full of moonlight, the moon fills the whole night, and it's very warm.

"Deal," Westlund says in a low voice.

So Bjuhr deals; there are five of them around the well, the cards are cool, their wallets glisten on their knees, this is a night for big wagers. Simon taps the cards on his knee.

"I pass," he growls.

"Tonight no one's going to pass," Bjuhr objects.

Then Simon opens with a two-crown coin, tosses it into the bottom of the wooden bucket. Bjuhr places his cap on the bottom, so the bills won't get wet. At the end of the game he puts the cap on, the bills tucked into its sweat band, the silver and copper jingling in his pants pocket.

"A person should've had a profit margin," Westlund says, business-like.

"Profit margin? It's better to take home the profit all at once." So Bjuhr takes it home, whistling. Off-key. A bicycle built for two. But you should be careful biking with him.

"If the post office was open," Westlund says, "a person could withdraw money from the bank. In America you've got your debentures of course."

"Exactly," Simon says. "I have mine with a cousin in Bomhus."

"But there are watches," Nisse Johansson says, his voice shaky.

He takes his off; it's a wristwatch with a plastic band. At last all their watches lie at the bottom with their faces showing; they lean down over the bucket and look, it is so indescribably beautiful.

"I remember one time in America," Westlund says. "I was in a watch store there."

"I was in a butcher shop in Gävle," Bjuhr says. "But I was none the wiser for that."

Dreamily Westlund takes off the ring, dreamily he lets the ring fall to the bottom of the bucket.

"Don't do that," Rudolf whispers, but as if in a dream he himself coaxes off his cufflinks.

"I raise," Westlund says, the ring glistening in the clear light of the moon.

Then another ring clinks as it lands in the bucket, Simon has finally gotten Hildur's off.

This is his first lady from town, it's not always easy. And she knows languages. As they're about to sit down on the grass under the maple tree, she says:

"Vot a night!"

She probably says it because it's wet in the grass.

"There must be some drier spots," he suggests.

He wonders if he should play all his cards right away, or if he should play piano-style. If he had a piano, he could play the "Good Night Waltz" and then say: let's go and get hitched.

"You really think so?" she says, smiling with white teeth. Colgate.

He hears someone in the lumber pile; a plank falls down followed by what sounds like a whimper. Then there is silence.

"How about we move," Sören says.

He gently touches her, he helps her up; lightly and carefully he leads her down toward the lake.

"Is it supposed to be drier in the lake?" she asks teasingly.

She might be around thirty-five, but if she asks you might say twenty-six, twenty-seven; he holds her tighter, she doesn't object. The lake shines yellow, reeds lean over the water, some people might ask themselves how the moon holds itself up the way it does.

"The moon is so lovely for us tonight," she says tenderly.

"Sure, you might ask yourself just how it can hold itself up the way it does," Sören says.

She doesn't say anything for a while, she's probably thinking about how the moon works; the cats sneak around the birches; that's the way to be, you can leave when you want, free as a cat.

"What's it like in town?" he asks.

Sometimes, when it's dark in the evening, they can see the

town's red glow in the sky to the north; some of them walk along the road, that red shining in their eyes the whole time. *I'll be damned how light it is in town*, someone might say. But Mary, or whatever her name is, stops.

"I think I have a hole in my stocking," she says.

And that's true, but it's so small that it's not worth stopping for.

"What's it like in town?" he asks again.

"Well, we have garbage chutes there," she answers; she lets out a sigh so hers is probably nothing special.

But there are others who like theirs, young guys who sometimes visit on Sundays. Who say, *we have garbage chutes, of stainless steel. You should probably get yourself to town so you can throw your garbage down a chute.* Here in the village you just toss it into a pile.

"A person should go to town," Sören says, as they stand in the moonlight in front of the washhouse.

At that moment the woman named Mary stops, puts her hands around his wrists like a pair of gentry handcuffs; he sees her in the light of the moon as if under a lamp, she's probably even older.

She's like a female embezzler on the front page of *The Workers' Daily*, her eyebrows like black arcs above her eyes, her upper lip an arc above her mouth. Where is the arrow for your bows, little sister?

"Come with me," she whispers and closes her eyes, only her eyebrows looking at him.

"How will we get there?"

"We should walk across the fields," she whispers, her eyes still closed, her lower lip swelling.

"But it's a good twenty kilometers to Gävle, and wet as hell in the grass."

She probably doesn't hear him, probably just hears herself, her mouth charging his red mouth like a mad bull.

"Though I have high boots inside," he whispers in confusion, as he opens the door to the washhouse with one hand, and with the other guides her in.

Just before he turns on the light, he remembers: he has to hide what's on the wall, he finds a few chairs in the darkness, stacks them and puts the radio on top. When he turns on the light, the lady from town elegantly sits on his bed; he is ashamed, ashamed of the room, ashamed of the wall, ashamed of himself.

"So, this is what a farmhand's room looks like," he says defiantly.

He doesn't know what to do with her, she seems much larger indoors, less manageable; to have something to do he turns on the radio. There are those who have nothing to do but be on the radio and talk all night, the world emptied of music, not a single note anywhere on this big earth. He pulls down the blinds, his boots are below the window facing the lake, he brings them to the bed. She is already barefoot. What he does he does slowly, he wants to take time, doesn't know what he should do next; it could all be plastic, he's not used to it. She has his boots on now, she closes her eyes again and stretches her legs out straight; he walked in dung yesterday, it shows. She lies stretched out, her arms under her head.

"I love things that are primitive," the lady from town whispers, hitting the floor with the boot heels. "I love what's original. Life itself."

Idiot, he suddenly thinks bitterly, you only love yourself and your garbage chute, you love garbage because you have a garbage chute, you love the dung on the boots because you don't know that dung is shit. You love farmhands because you don't have to be a maid. Furiously he gets up and moves the radio away from the carving on the wall. Her limp eyelids open wide.

"It's so ugly," she says, frowning and sighing.

But she stays lying there, and closes her eyes again.

"Remember that you're in a farmhand's room," he says furiously. "You can't expect to find angels on the walls."

Her lips separate, the little tongue peeps out, her bare arms extend toward him, like two cobras they attack, he doesn't have time to protect himself. He begins by trying to pull off her boots, she kicks herself free.

"I want to die with my boots on," she whispers ecstatically. "Nothing but the boots."

Just then there's a tap on the window; relieved he pulls up the blind, Svea is standing there under the moon, looking pale.

"Just come on in," he shouts.

He manages to put the radio back up before she gets inside. He takes her by the arm. The lady from town has sat up.

"This is my fiancée," Sören says defiantly, and doesn't let her go.

For the first time he realizes that they belong together, Svea is the one who fits here, she's the one made for his farmhand's room. She fits him, all the others are several sizes too big. She will have a child with another, all right, even that suits him. He strokes her across her ashen cheek.

"Please take your boots off me," the lady from town says, her eyes no longer closed.

Sören yanks the boots off her and throws them into the corner.

"You hurt me," she complains while she rubs her ankles.

Sören takes hold of Svea again, he sits her on a chair, he is so nice to her that he makes her cry.

"You shouldn't complain about that," he says to the lady from town, "since you love what's primitive. Primitive, that's what I am. That's what we are. We're in the middle of the shit. So love us, damn it!"

It turns out to be a whole speech he gives, Svea is sitting on her chair and she, too, notices what she never noticed before: we belong together, I'm the clay and you're the straw and the kid doesn't matter. A kid has to be someone's child. Whose then—it's all the same. And who is tapping on the window, that doesn't matter either. Mary takes out the plastic holder and slowly lights a French cigarette, her whole body is shaking, she is like a seismograph, with each tremble of happiness, she shakes. "It's not my fault that I'm torn up," she says. "Is it my fault that I'm not like other people? Why do I have such hunger?" She means for love. Only she's not really hungry, that's what's so terrible, she's only pretending; it's her hobby. She is sitting on Sören's bed, hating the two others for their little happiness, she hates those who are happy, like everyone does, it doesn't suit anyone's vanity for others to be happy. But she hates the true hunger too, because she can't experience it, and those who are truly torn apart, she'd like to tear apart even more. Only a little cracked teacup is to her taste.

Suddenly Mary from town starts; someone walked past the window. She has learned that movement carefully, startling at every little thing. Poor woman, everyone will think, poor little woman, all torn apart. There is a knock at the door, Hildur enters without having been invited. She must have run the whole way, can't get a word out at first, walks right up to Svea.

"Thanks for the letter," she says, loudly but not in any way accusingly.

"What letter?" Sören asks; Svea looks down.

"I didn't mean anything bad," she whispers, grabbing hold of Hildur's arm as if only Hildur could hold her up.

Hildur sits down beside her, Mary devours them with her eyes, the farmhand finally finds some music. There's always some station where there's music, after all; that's what's strange.

"But you said something true," Hildur says. "You make do with what you have. That's exactly what a person has to do. That's what everybody does."

"So what about it?" Sören says. "It's probably only embezzlers who take what they don't have. Isn't that so? Huh! But why did you come running here?"

"Pull down the blind," he gets in response.

Mary pulls it down, she is starting to look happy again, suspects that something is about to happen.

"There's someone in the lumber pile," Hildur whispers. "Someone who's screaming terribly. And Pa doesn't want to go outside. He's sitting with Wallinder at the table, drinking. Wallinder can't stand on his feet anymore. And the butcher boys are out on the road with the trucks, trying to get each other into the ditch. Pretty soon they'll wake up the sheriff. And the other men are sitting by the well playing poker, they don't see or hear anything. Siri says she thinks it's an animal, an animal in pain. Ma and Mrs. Bjuhr are sitting with the Singer on the couch, and say that it's probably Augustus, the ghost with the rake. You go outside and look, Irma says to me, maybe somebody's calling you."

"I think it's a cat," Sören says after a while. "A cat that's about to die."

And for a while, there is silence, even the singer on the radio got something to think about. Suddenly Hildur starts, turns even whiter.

"Do you hear?" she asks breathlessly.

Yes, they hear. Something comes rumbling down the steep hill, someone is coming toward them with very big strides, someone who is in a terrible hurry. The blind goes up again. A big fellow comes running in the moonlight, a big half-naked giant comes thundering down the washhouse path. It's Westlund, in a terrible hurry.

"Hildur," he bellows like a foghorn. "Hildur! Hildur! Hil-dur!"

Arrives, enters. Sinks down on the bed next to Mary. Sits there in trousers and undershirt, his head hanging between his shoulders like a bulging ear of corn. Hildur goes up to him.

"Hildur," he pants.

"Who was it?" she whispers, sitting down onto his lap, her body heavy.

"Can't you see it's me," he answers, still in distress.

"Where is your shirt and jacket, my dear?"

He takes her hand between his.

"I've been searching for you everywhere," he whispers. "In the attic and in the barns and on the road. You weren't anywhere."

"But here I am now," she says, she touches his undershirt; it is wet and he hasn't even changed undershirts for this his second wedding night.

But that doesn't matter, when all comes around nothing matters much, you make do with what you have and that's that. She makes do with his neck, the thick red one, and puts her arm around it. He makes do with her hands and presses them to his mouth's despair. Sören finds a different radio station. A waltz glides out of the box, the lady from town glides out on the floor, no one wants to dance with her, she dances alone. But she doesn't manage many turns, before they hear a piercing yell outside; it cuts through the surface of the lake and awakens the fish. They all stand and listen.

"Mary!" Someone yells at the top of his lungs.

The mountain on the other side of the lake throws the shout back, evidently not wanting it. Nisse Johansson rushes in, Mary puts her hands on her hips, Augustus Asp, the crazy ghost, stares at them through Nisse's black glasses.

"I see. This is where you are," he shouts. "You—"

But no words are strong enough, Nisse turns off the radio, but he can't turn Mary off so easily.

"Am I not a free person?" she screams. "And can I help that I'm not like other people? Can I help it that I'm more passionate than any of you? But in this damned country you'll have to be frozen solid to be okay. Copenhagen – that's another story."

"If you say one more word about that damned typewriter salesman I'll slap you," Nisse roars, losing his glasses.

Mary cries, she means what she says, she always does; it's just that she says so much.

"This is how high I tower above the whole lot of you," she shouts, getting on tiptoe, but she still isn't as tall as the rest.

But she notices that Nisse is shorter than usual, so she looks down.

"You're barefoot," she says with surprise. "And your feet are bleeding."

All of them look at Nisse's feet, there isn't all that much to see, free of corns for that matter, but he must have cut himself badly on Sören's bottle.

"Not because I want to be petty," Sören says, "but you could take a few of these magazines to stand on."

So he stands on some magazines and not only Mary notices that he becomes ridiculous; quickly she moves to crush him.

"So what have you been up to? You're bleeding like a . . ."

We all have names for what should not be named, his face turns white; it's still too early to go too far.

"You can at least say where you lost your shoes," she says instead, pretending she forgot the word she was going to use.

Nisse looks from his feet to Westlund, Westlund squirms a little, he's like a corkscrew, slowly turning toward the truth; his eyes wander, the corkscrew moves.

"Well, we were sitting and playing poker," Westlund begins vaguely.

"And then. . ."

"By the well."

"That has nothing to do with it," Mary interrupts him.

Blood is starting to soak through the magazines. And I haven't even read the comics yet, Sören thinks to himself.

"Of course it has something to do with it," Nisse says defensively.

"No, never sit and play poker by a well. That's what I've always said," Westlund says emphatically, you might think that he'd never said anything else his whole life.

"No, there's something treacherous about wells," Nisse says.

"Get to the point!"

Westlund twists and turns, Nisse browses through the magazines with his toes. And sure enough: soon he's standing atop the *Great Love of the Sheik*. But what else would you expect from someone from Gävle.

"Well," Westlund says cautiously, "we didn't win anything."

He squirms.

"And Bjuhr didn't exactly lose anything," Nisse adds.

"No, and then he took shoes and socks off you!"

"Oh no," Westlund says, to calm her. "From me he got my shirt and jacket and tie. Rudolf lost his cap. But you all should have seen Simon. I wouldn't want to be in his clothes."

"He isn't either," Nisse says.

"Do we have enough money so we can get home?"

"Depends on what you mean by money," Nisse says evasively.

"Money's not everything," Westlund declares.

"I probably need a thicker magazine," Nisse says.

He gets a couple issues of *Look*, Mary is standing with her shoes back on, filled with hate; Hildur rubs Westlund's cold right hand, his ring finger is empty, but it doesn't matter.

"Good thing you brought the bicycle," Mary snarls. "Because I won't ride in a car with someone like you."

"The bicycle, well. . ." Nisse says pitifully.

Westlund has to rescue him.

"Well, Bjuhr had to carry his winnings home on something. So it was just as well that he got the bike too."

"And the car," Nisse says. "We had to sell the front seat to Wallinder when I lost my driver's license. We got to keep the back seat."

"Tell me more!"

"Well, Bjuhr will come to Gävle sometime," Westlund adds. "And maybe he'll want to sit in the back seat and drive. Because the car, well, it's like it's his now."

Mary slaps Nisse before everyone's eyes, he doesn't budge, the pain enters him like a bullet into a moose. Sören can't bear to watch, he ransacks his drawers, takes out a shirt and tie and a vest for Westlund, a pair of socks and a pair of blue gym shoes for Nisse. Westlund can't bear it either. He stands up to his full height, stands in front of Hildur, so threateningly that she thinks he wants to hit her. But he himself wants to be hit; it looks the same, it's all the same.

"Hit me," he shouts. "Hit me too!"

He extends his hot face, she raises her hand, and caresses him.

"Hit me!" He shouts again.

Right then there is a tap at the door, weak and small.

"Come in," Sören calls.

The Singer comes in, or rather, he doesn't come in, he stands on the threshold; it looks like he's bringing a bit of the moon. Then, almost at once, they notice that they were wrong; it's not the moon he's brought, it's a bit of death. Already he's so much a citizen of that other world, one where a different moon shines, so much a foreigner, that they don't even dare ask him to enter, he'd never understand anyway. Without a visa, his gaze wanders from one to the other, no residence permit offered anywhere, nowhere a place where his soul can rest. What's wrong with me, he thinks, not yet having noticed his passport. At first, when he speaks they don't understand a word, but what they feel is very lovely. When a foreigner comes, you immediately feel: *I am not alone, I belong to a people, I am one among many who understand me.* They now all understand one another, that is why they love the foreigner on the threshold so much. When he finally speaks, they don't understand at first what he is saying, so he has to say it again.

"Well," he whispers, "I came to ask about something."

The question waits, hovering in the distance, he hardly dares come out with it.

"Well, how did I sing? You see, I never hear myself when I sing. That's why I have to ask people."

When Mary speaks she sounds as if she means what she

says; she can say anything at all, meaning every single word. She should have been a lawyer or a politician, some say.

"You sang marvelously," Mary whispers, enchanted; she dares to venture almost all the way to the border, all the way to the boundary of the land of the dead.

"Oh, how I love everything cultural," she continues ecstatically, rubbing her hands.

Westlund doesn't want to be outdone.

"Corusa couldn't have done it better."

"Not even Sven-Olof Sandberg," Nisse Johansson adds.

Finally, only Hildur hasn't said anything. No, I can't, she thinks. Is it worth lying to somebody who's as far gone as him? At first, it doesn't occur to her to think: What does truth matter for someone who soon won't need to distinguish one from the other? She feels his desperate look sliding off her face, off her steep mountain of truth; can she let him fall? Having made a decision, she looks up: his residence permit will be granted. For a few dizzying moments his life lives in hers, she feels his life inside her. Then, when he quietly fades, she understands: what does a residence permit matter for someone who seeks confirmation that he has lived? Filled by a wondrous joy she says, "No one has ever sung so beautifully for me."

Now he can leave. So he leaves. But those who remain now belong together in a new way, for a while even Mary and Nisse belong together.

"Now let's go down to the lake and wash my man's feet off," Mary says, together they walk down to the lake.

They stand there two and two by in the moonlight, Westlund puts on the farmhand's shirt, the vest is too tight, it splits.

"You've got yourself one big fellow," he says.

"You make do with what you have," Hildur says with

a smile, and looks out over the lake. There's no lake at Westlund's.

But it doesn't matter, you can't always have lakes. If there's a pond then you make do with the pond; if there's a puddle when it rains then you make do with the puddle.

"Tomorrow, let's bicycle to the air surveillance tower," Sören says to Svea. "From there you can see all the way to Eggegrund."

But then he sees the log floating beyond the reeds, and he imagines hearing the chopping of the axes echoing through the large hills and lake banks. And he remembers something that had been forgotten.

"Listen," he says to Svea. "Come with me for a minute."

They walk in under the birch trees, the birches are full of moon drops, he stands her against a birch, the brooch below her neck shimmering.

"Take off the brooch," he says. She unhooks it.

He takes the brooch in his hand, and raises his arm. Then he hears a familiar voice right behind him, and lowers his arm.

"You can take off your brooch too," Rudolf tells Rullan.

They emerge out of a glittering thicket, both wet all over, they must have been in the grass, swimming. Rudolf is as happy as a lark even though he'd lost his cap, watch and forty crowns.

"We've just been out looking for wood for a new rake handle," Rudolf says contentedly.

"You sure don't look like you stayed on task," Sören says. Side by side they walk toward the lake, break into a run, and lob the brooches into the water. Sören wins by a meter or two.

They walk over to the other couples. Mary is on her

nylon-clad knees cleaning Nisse's bleeding feet with grass; she pulls on his socks, she puts on his shoes, she ties the shoes. On her knees the whole time. On her knees atop hard stones. Oh my God, she thinks jubilantly, how wonderfully I suffer.

"You mustn't think I know nothing," Sören says to Svea, as he throws a flat stone; it skips eight times. "But let's forget about it all! None of us is better than anybody else. Let's do some dancing!"

"Hey, hey, hey!" Westlund hollers, and the vest splits all the way, "By golly, there's gonna be some dancing at my wedding!"

They make their way back to the house dancing a hambo, jumping and hooting, the cats trembling in their path. But as they reach the gate their hooting stops; they hear a howl that makes their hearts freeze, like the howl of a wolf. It's coming from the lumber pile behind the lilacs. The other women let go of their men, but Hildur whimpers, "Hold me, Hilmer. I'm so scared."

He holds her tight, they walk through the gate, Irma comes running toward them, white as the moon. Out of breath, she cries:

"You have to come inside. Everyone is so scared. Ma is scared because she thinks it's Augustus who's come to fore-shadow death. Old lady Bjuhr's teeth are all rattling in her mouth and she can't stop eating cake. Siri can't stop crying. And there isn't much left of the Singer, he's just lying on the couch rambling about an old straw hat. Bjuhr is at the table counting his money, over and over, he'll probably end up going crazy. Since Wallinder slipped out, Pa has been doing nothing. And Simon is standing on the road in his underwear, waiting for his butcher boy to come with the truck."

"Maybe it's Wallinder then."

Hildur's voice is full of hope.

"You'll just have to see."

Irma's voice is full of hate.

"Ladies, go inside!" Westlund says gamely, his teeth chattering like a chaff cutter. "Something's gotta change around here!"

The men remain outside. The north corner of the house shines church-white. They huddle down by the cellar, shifting from one foot to the other. Each of them hoping one of the others will step forward.

"Nisse, why don't you go first since your foot hurts," Rudolf says generously.

And you're from Gävle, the others silently add. Except for the night train rattling unseen through the forest on the other side of the lake, not the slightest sound is heard. Could the dying person already be dead? Nisse advances in his gym shoes, kicking up moonlit dust. At the corner of the house there's a water barrel, and there's a man. Wallinder.

"Is that you going around shrieking?" Westlund asks, and takes hold of him. There's not much to take hold of, the alcohol has dissolved him, he sways on plastic legs, clings to the water barrel with plastic fingers, all of him a mess.

"He's puking in our water barrel," Rudolf snarls, squeezing Wallinder's shoulder.

"That's probably how it's done in Gävle," Sören says. "That must be how they use water barrels in Gävle."

Nisse gets angry and goes inside to sulk. (*Keep in mind that we're the ones with the county governor,* he'd remarked.) Westlund grabs Wallinder hard by his plastic shoulders; the nerve, they're not even in Gävle County.

"Get away from the barrel! Or do you need some Marshall aid?" he roars.

No answer; Wallinder is as limp as a dead fish; he is heavier than he looks, they think as they lift him. Without as much as a sound, he glides down into the barrel; they feel his feet hit the bottom, and they let go. Right then, when their hands are again free, lifted out of the darkness of the barrel into the moonlight, the explosion comes, the fourth one, the mightiest. The buildings shake, the ground shakes, their ears are deafened by its rumble, flames shoot up behind the lilacs like an enormous sunflower; then wither. The cows wake and moo, the hens cluck, the neighing of horses bursts from the stable walls. Unbearably slowly the lumber pile begins to collapse.

They wait until it is quiet, then they run over, cold-sober, their hearts pounding wildly.

He is lying under the fifth plank, lying on his back, his legs together, he isn't dead. The moonlight falls slowly and softly into his wide-open eyes. They lift him up as if he were sick. But nothing ails him, except a terrible fright; he can stand on his own legs, his left hand bleeds a little; he puts it in his pants pocket.

"Let's all go inside for a drink," Westlund says.

They go together, feeling a little dazed, like when you arrive home in the evening after haymaking in the far meadow; he, who has been saved, carries his salvation across his shoulder like a newly whetted scythe with sharp edges on both sides.

In the parlor, the ceiling is low, the garlands under the beams quiver, no one has run outside. Nisse comes in, and hides his gym shoes under the table. No one says a word. Bjuhr jingles his coins. Hildur sits and helps him count them; she's pretending to count the two-crown pieces, but what she's really counting is the number of steps it takes to walk from the lumber pile to the doorway of the room. They are all counting those steps. Irma stands under the pendant lamp, her hand on her heart. Siri sits alone looking at the Singer; there is in those who are dying a purity that makes us cry, that makes her cry quietly, and unrestrained.

The small outside gate slams behind the ones who are coming from the stoop to the parlor. There are ten steps. Hildur drops a two-crown coin on the floor; she gets up, walks over to Irma; there's room for them both under the lamp. Under the lamp one is just as afraid as the other, under the lamp they become sisters, at last. The door opens, Hildur closes her eyes, Irma's eyes widen, their hot hands touch. The new guest is the first to cross the threshold. Westlund takes off his torn vest, and tosses it on the dresser.

"Look here, we're bringing you Ville," Rudolf says. "And he is perfectly okay."

And then they're all struck by the miracle of joy. He is there, alive and well, standing in the middle of the room with his hand in his pocket, the one they thought was dead, with only a little sawdust on his back. His horse face quivers a little, his eyes are clear as if they'd just been crying. With immeasurable tenderness, the sisters lead him to the table, to the place of honor.

"I'll get some new candles for the holders," Irma says.

He sits behind the tall candles, everyone looking at him, Westlund retrieves a fresh liter of liquor from the closet, they toast.

"That was one hell of a wedding salute," Westlund says.

It takes a while before Ville answers. They sit and watch him struggle to find the words; it's as if he's bringing them out of a deep well. And when he finally gets them to the surface, they are dark, dripping with strange water.

"It was no salute," Ville says.

"What was it?"

"I was trying to kill myself," Ville answers, filling his glass to the brim.

"Oh, my," says the lady from town. She feels a great desire to kiss him; as far as she knows, she's never kissed an almost-suicide before.

They all move closer, even the Singer gets up; they sit around the table, packed together as closely as possible forming a circle around a snake pit. A circle around death itself; they can see it crawling on its belly at the bottom of the pit.

"What made you think that way?" Hilma asks, pulling her sweater tighter around her.

So it was you, Hildur thinks. To her surprise she feels the initial relief giving way to disappointment. She feels terribly empty, like someone who can't remember a dream.

"Are you born a thief?" Ville asks, and leans heavily on the table, half-reclined below the candles. One by one, he looks them in the eyes.

"You're born, and that's that," Westlund answers. "I wasn't born a butcher. I just became one."

"So what were you born to be?" Ville asks. "A horse swindler?"

So he hasn't forgotten about the horse yet. Siri looks from her father to Ville, she would like to ask about so many things, but she doesn't dare. Bjuhr stuffs the two-crown pieces in his pocket.

"You're born to something great," he responds. "To something damned great. And then you become a piece of shit. Well, I've been an alternate on the Roads Maintenance Board so I'm not speaking for myself."

"And some who should've moved up quickly become snails," Victor says bitterly.

The lady from town says, "I would have become something great, something to do with culture. But then I married Nisse Johansson."

"You should be damned glad about that," Nisse replies. "Because you were born to walk the streets."

Ville looks down, he puts his bloodied hand on the tablecloth.

"I was born a thief," he says stubbornly. "And I've learned to be a thief. I stole nine sticks of dynamite from your shed and five meters of fuse. But then I thought I should take the life of a thief instead. So I went out into the woods."

"When was that?" Irma whispers breathlessly.

"At seven this morning," Ville answers. "Seven o'clock sharp if you wanna know."

Hearing this, the sisters look at each other and they are no longer sisters, just two rivals; they have never stood together under the same lamp.

"It was light in the woods, I lay down under a spruce, on Stora Kopparberg's land. You fucking thief, I thought, let this be the end of you."

"No one has ever said that you were a thief, my boy," Rudolf says.

"But if that applies to Creek-Lasse I'll leave unsaid," Victor says.

Ville sits with his hands over his face and sobs, even though he's not yet drunk.

"When I was six years old, I was taught how to empty other people's traps. First come, first served, Pa said. So when I was six I had to get up at four-thirty in the morning. When I was eight I got to go with him to the woods early one morning, it was in early September. After a while we went in the wrong direction. But this is Palm's forest, I say. So what, he answers."

"Did you get that?" Ville repeats defiantly, taking his hands from his eyes. "We were in your forest."

He looks into the eyes of the Palm family, his eyes have a wild sheen. See how wretched I am, his eyes scream desperately. So give me what I deserve!

"We came to a pile of spruce branches," he continues. "Underneath there was a butchered moose. Pa cuts loose a few pieces, and stuffs my backpack full. Go home, he said, I'll follow. But if you meet anybody, tell 'em you've got blueberries in your pack. It was a Sunday morning, I ran into three people, one of them was the parish clerk, the Sunday School teacher. My best lie was for him."

"Do you even know what it's like to lie?" he shouts suddenly, and his bloody hand hits the table so hard it sets off a moment of glass music, and candle wax drips down on his right coat sleeve.

They are upset by his sudden loudness. The snake is rising out of the pit, it reaches higher than they had expected.

"I guess we all know what it's like to lie," Sören says at last. "But you don't need to kill yourself because of it."

"Well, I've known some poachers in my day," Westlund says. "And some real thieves too. In America there was someone who went around stealing porches, dismantled them at night and drove off with them in trucks. But, hell, he didn't go and hang himself on account of that. He—"

But Westlund gets no further, Siri has placed her arm on his, placed her eyes in his: Be quiet, they say, be quiet because now someone who knows what he's talking about is speaking.

"When I was fourteen," Ville continues, calmer now, "I had learned to lie so well, I was really happy every time I could speak the truth. It was as if it was my only joy. But one day when I was sixteen, and was down on the field with the harrow, a car from Stockholm stopped on the road. How do you get to Karlholm? the Stockholmer asks. Now, we all know how you get to Karlholm from here."

"You ride a bike," Bjuhr says. He wants to lighten things up. You don't sit and win at poker all evening, and then have to sit at a wedding like guests at a funeral.

But no one laughs except Bjuhr.

"You turn left at the Co-op," Rudolf says.

"Turn to the right, I said to the Stockholmer. I knew I was lying. But I couldn't help it. The Stockholmer left, I struck the horse so hard that he bolted into the ditch with the harrow and all. Then I ran home and into the attic. What's going on? Pa screamed from the yard. I had thought of hanging myself, but instead I ran down and told him everything. I probably figured that maybe he'd understand. He was sharpening a knife. I'll teach you to lie when you don't need to, he screamed. Then he punched me."

"He was right to do that," Bjuhr offers, "because you shouldn't go and lie when it's not necessary."

"So is it better to lie when it's necessary than when it's not?" Ville asks bitterly. "Isn't lying always lying?"

This is a little puzzling to all of them, everyone has their reasons for lying, but it's not something to give a speech about. You might just as well drive into Gävle and show off your underwear.

"Stick to the subject," Nisse Johansson snarls. "You were going to kill yourself. That's what you were talking about."

"You had stopped under a spruce," Rudolf reminds him.

"Maybe you had even put a stick of dynamite in your mouth," Westlund suggests.

But now Ville is no longer under a spruce, he is far off in time, he is sitting and looking at death with absent eyes, he is sitting behind the candles looking at the dead past. The lady from town gets up and turns off the ceiling light. "I'm all about creating an artistic mood." She has slept with a couple of painters.

"You know where Kolbotten is," he says after a time. "On the other side of the clearing with wild strawberries, behind the commons. We went there one night, me, the old man, and the peddler. I was seventeen and it was the first time I had gone hunting. There was moonlight, it was in September. They posted me at Kolbotten, at three in the morning a moose came some fifty meters away from me. A cow. I let her go. Why didn't you shoot? they yelled. It's not moose season yet, I said. Then they hit me until I fell to the ground, I had to make my way home on my own the best I could. The next night, I took the rifle, and went out alone, I shot the moose on the road behind Luttman's pasture. I went home, harnessed the horse and left in the middle of the night with the wagon. When I came back, I smashed the bedroom window with the rifle butt. Come out and you'll see something, I yelled at the old man. He came out in the moonlight, I pulled off the tarps. Now you should have yourself a drink, the old man said. We sat and drank moonshine until dawn. And the whole time I was thinking: You're the next one I'll shoot."

"Why didn't you leave home if he was so difficult?" Sören asks. "You could've got a job at the sulfite factory like everyone else in the village."

But now Ville gets fired up, he's probably had too much to drink, Hilma signals to Westlund: don't pour him anymore!

"Doesn't anyone understand?" he almost shouts. "Doesn't anyone understand that he's the only one I have? Doesn't anyone understand that he only has me? Do thieves become better people if we desert them? Do liars lie less if no one likes them?

"If anyone says one more word about my old man, then I'll sock them," he shouts, getting up.

But just moments later, he seems to have forgotten his anger, the tears start running through his beard stubble, he sinks down onto his chair.

"Doesn't anyone believe you can love a bad person?" he whispers.

Then another low voice at the table says, "Yes, you have to."

It is Siri. It is so dark that no one sees how red she has turned.

"But this morning I hit him," Ville says bitterly. "He came home from the lake with bream. I like bream. Here's some fish for you, the old man said, I've just been out milking the traps."

Ville set his eyes on Victor Palm.

"They were your bream, Palm," he says.

"I don't like bream," Victor replies. "But if he takes pike, then you'd better watch out."

"Pa," Hildur says softly. "Let Ville tell his story."

"I don't know why I hit him," Ville continues. "I knew that he just wanted to be nice. But after I hit him, I couldn't stand to see him cry. Now I'm done for, I thought. Now you've hit the only one you have. I went out into the woods with the explosives, and lay down under a spruce."

"How did it feel?" the lady from town asks. She takes her plastic holder and offers Ville a cigarette.

"I felt damned happy. You bastard, I thought, soon this will all be over. But as I took out the matches, I started wondering what it would say in the newspaper. I lay there and went through all the regional newspapers from *Gefle Dagblad* to *Upsala Nya*. Maybe you'll even get in the Stockholm papers, I thought. It took me quite some time to go through the whole press. At last I decided that maybe it would even be mentioned on the radio. I closed my eyes. I imagined there was a loudspeaker high up in the tree, calling everything out just the way it is. Because when you're going to die, you go through in advance everything that will happen to you once you're dead. The obituary, the funeral, the reception and the whole nine yards. But finally, I had to admit to myself that the truth, kid, you'll never get at. Then I got mad. Now or never, I thought, and lit the match. I opened my eyes for the last time. But then I saw something remarkable and blew out the match."

"What did you see?" Siri asks softly, feeling that in some strange way this concerns her too.

"A spider," Ville replies.

"A spider," Nisse Johansson snorts, "What's remarkable about that?"

He probably means: Compared to Gävle, where we have the Pix candy factory, Hotel Baltic, Governor Sandler, and the rest.

"Poor boy," Mary whispers.

She warms to all that you can feel sorry for, she would like to bring them all close to her heart in her wide, soft bed. But Nisse is at home so much.

"It was only a spider," Ville continues defiantly. "But while my eyes had been closed, it had spun a thread between my spruce, or that of Stora Kopparberg rather, and another spruce. The thread sparkled in the sunshine; the spider kept on spinning. It spun thread upon thread, I'd never seen anything as beautiful as those threads."

"Then you should have seen *Gilda* with Rita Hayworth," Nisse adds. "Or the last issue of *Parisien*."

"What happened next?" Siri asks softly.

"'I'll lie here until he's finished, I thought. But the spider spun and spun, and never finished. That spider saved my life."

179

"It should get a Carnegie medal," Westlund says with feeling.

"But then I got angry," Ville says. "I didn't want to be rescued, I wanted to die. So I tore down the spider web and felt wretched. I understood what I'd gotten wrong: you aren't supposed to lie there and wait when you're going to kill yourself. Because then life shakes its head and says no. Let me run a while, I thought. I'll run to Kolbotten, and do it as soon as I get there. I ran as fast as I could, over logs and stones. As I ran across the clearing with the wild strawberries, I heard a strange sound and stopped. It was a child crying. The little French boy who stays at Luttman's was sitting on a stone sobbing, he was lost. 'I no find my way home to Luttman,' he said, and took my hand. I couldn't very well say that I was about to kill myself, so I walked with him through the woods, until we could see the farms in Fuxe. He was so happy that he took out a bookmark he had in his pocket, and gave it to me. But he was the one who should have been given something. He, too, saved my life."

"He should have a Carnegie medal as well," Westlund says firmly, striking his fist on the table.

"So I thought to myself, now I'll have to wait a while before I try again. I'll have to forget the boy and I'll have to forget the spider. Then I remembered a pond that I used to swim in as a kid. I so much wanted to swim there again; it'd be the last time you'll go swimming, I thought. It's the pond that's on the land of the Hunting Club not far from the cloudberry bog. I undressed and went in the water, I floated in the middle for a long time, I'd never before known how lovely it was to swim. I could have filled my pockets with stones and gone in with my clothes on, but no. I lay in the water, and saw the spruce trees, and understood that no one can take their life alone in

the forest. The forest is full of spiders and anthills and wild
strawberry patches and little French kids and they're all out to
save you. If you're going to die, I thought, it has to happen at
night and around people, grown-up people, because grown-
ups are the only ones who don't want to save you. I lay in the
forest until it became dark. Then I took my dynamite and my
fuse and came here to the wedding."

"Were you the one who tapped on the window?" Irma
asks, drawing Hildur's poor eyes toward her with the magnet
of her hatred.

"Why would I go around knocking on windows when
I have dynamite?" Ville says annoyed, sucking blood off his
torn hand. "I was setting off dynamite by the root cellar. I'll
stay here, I thought, and let them beat me. But when I heard
you all coming, I ran behind the shed. There I set off the
second dynamite stick, and didn't move. But no one bothered
to come. You can do whatever you please, lad, I told myself,
not a soul cares about you."

"What did you need us for?" Rudolf asks, "since you
wanted to kill yourself? You weren't hoping we'd light the
fuse for you, were you?"

"You can't die alone," Ville replies. "You have to have people around you to be able to die. But no one came. Finally,
I had to walk up to the window. I guess I'll have to knock,
since no one heard the dynamite. When they come out on
the stoop, then I'll do it. But I couldn't knock."

"Why not?"

Hildur asks, even though she already knows the answer.
Irma smiles.

"Someone was already standing there," Ville says. "So
I sneaked away, and made for the lumber pile, where I laid
down on my back. After a while I had an idea. I'll scream,

I thought. If I scream, then they'll have to come. So I screamed. But no one came."

"We thought it was a cat," Westlund says, lighting a big cigar.

But Ville gets back on his feet. Big and drunk and very mournful he stands at the end of the table with his head bowed; the candles flicker between his big hands.

"Did everyone think it was a cat?" he asks.

No one answers. He looks from one to the other.

"Did you all believe it was a cat?" he repeats, a good deal louder this time.

For a long time he looks at Hildur. At last Hildur looks away.

"Did you think it was a cat, Hildur?" he shouts.

"Yes," Hildur answers after a while, and looks steadily at Westlund.

"Okay then," Ville says tiredly.

And then, for the longest time of all, he looks at Siri.

"Did you think it was a cat, Siri?" he asks at last.

Siri looks him in the eye and answers, "I thought it was a person. Almost all of us thought it was a person. But no one dared to go look."

"Okay then," Ville whispers, and sits down.

After a while he continues.

"Then it must have been a cat that shrieked. Because no one came. A person should have somebody, the cat shrieked. But it had no one and never will have anyone. So suddenly the stick of dynamite was in the cat's mouth, it lit the match with its paws. But the stick fell out and the cat continued to live. It didn't shriek any longer, that damned cat. It was a good cat."

Now he's stretched out over the table, he must be tired, must be drunk. Rudolf touches his shoulder.

"Listen," he says slowly. "Your old man has been crying about you the whole day."

"You're lying, you bastard," Ville whispers from the depth of his sorrow.

"It's true," Sören says, "we were there."

Ville straightens up for a brief moment; he fills with a happiness so powerful that it hits him like a club. He collapses on the chair, and falls down to the floor. They pick him up and lay him on the couch, Mary turns on the light, Rudolf takes the six remaining dynamite sticks from his pocket. Standing under the light, they look at the sticks as if there was anything to see. They hear the butchers' assistants come back with the trucks, someone pulls up the curtain. Simon is standing in the moonlit yard in his shirt and underwear, waiting for them.

"They mustn't hit the mowing machine again," Victor whines.

He heads outside, Westlund goes with him, Mary falls on her knees beside Ville, Gunnar has fallen asleep under the couch with his hands over his ears.

"Shouldn't we go home now, Hilmer," Hildur calls anxiously after him.

"Just going to offer the chief executive officer a drink first," Westlund replies. "He'll probably catch cold otherwise, the poor thing."

"God knows I love drama," the lady from town whispers and kisses the defenseless sleeper for a long time.

And the moon, how does it still hold itself up this late? It hangs onto the air surveillance tower, spying for the sun's first airplanes. But night and peace still reign; although it is warm, autumn is in the summer air, it's there to increase our longing.

But Simon isn't cold, even though Bjuhr won his pants. And Hagström and Karlsson probably aren't cold either, they're standing in front of the trucks, arguing and talking big.

"Come here, Westlund," Simon shouts. He has buttoned his undershirt up to his neck so there won't be a draft, good thing he wore his winter undershirt; but his underpants, they're short.

Westlund comes and Victor comes too, this time nothing had happened to the mowing machine. Simon leans over, there's a scrape on the Ford's right fender, Hagström stands alongside scratching his head, steam rises from the '29's radiator.

"I beat 'im," Hagström whispers, nudging Westlund on the side. "I passed 'im right by Bengtsson's café. It got up to a hundred and five, that old goat. No one would've believed it."

But Simon remains gloomy, the scratch shines like a run in a lady's stocking. Westlund taps the chief executive officer on the shoulder, Victor takes a step back, probably scared that the '29 could explode.

"Don't be sad, Simon," Westlund consoles. "When my car was new, Luttman's bull ran into it and gored a hole as big as a mail slot in the middle of the passenger door."

"This was no bull," Simon snaps. "It was your assistant. And now he's going to get a thrashing."

"Did you hear that?" Westlund says sternly to Hagström, "you're going to get a thrashing."

"If he was also the one who ran over the shaft he'll get double!" Victor adds, getting into the fray.

But that was a mistake. Simon and Westlund send their butcher boys away behind the barn to fight it out the best they can, then they turn on the old man. They're not mean to him, of course, but there is always a rift between those who fatten livestock and those who butcher them, a rift that deepens when you're drunk. They take him lightly by the shoulder, one on either side. They only want to mess with him a little, and slowly move toward the barn. But the old man begins to notice what's going on.

"Where are we heading?" he asks worriedly.

He starts to feel as if he's in a jail with bars made of butcher arms, and wriggles to get free, which just makes it worse.

"Why don't we take a look at the livestock?" Westlund loudly whispers to Simon behind Victor's back, pretending that there are secrets afoot.

Victor becomes very afraid, good Lord, he's so unaccustomed to being outside, so that alone scares him: the moon hanging low in the sky, the sparkling wet grass, and the outbuildings where new rags to close up chinks in the logs hang like guts. Intimidation on the one hand, and a gloomy joy on the other: That's what I get for letting myself be fooled. Gradually he forgets completely why he is out here, and he forgets that it is his son-in-law who is walking to his left. Now they're here, he simply thinks, now they've finally come, the ones who are after the farm. He knows that there are many who are after the farm, that was why he added an extra floor and put a sturdy lock on the door; it's like a fortress up there. But now he's been lured down, betrayed, now he's on his way to defeat in the clear glow of the moon. He feels so terribly afraid.

"What kind of people are you?" he screams, bouncing between them like an old ball.

That makes the two others feel even closer, they nod and smile at each other behind the old man's back; the joke becomes eighty percent better when the third party seems to take it so dead seriously.

"This here is Simon, he's the senior butcher's trustee," Westlund says.

And there's some truth to that after their poker playing earlier that day, but the old man—what does he know? Doesn't even know what a senior butcher's trustee is.

"Don't you read newspapers?" Simon asks.

No, he has no interest in that, not since the war ended; then it was interesting, now there are only story serials. They wait before opening the door to the milk room; they hold him firmly in the moonlight and keep joking.

"Well, a senior butcher's trustee," Westlund lectures, "that's a fellow who goes around and counts animals."

"Then he should go and count Creek-Lasse's field mice," Victor snarls, "that'll keep him busy."

"No, he only counts the animals indoors, see," Simon explains. "That way it's easier for him. It's warmer inside. He doesn't catch cold."

But now the old man's knees are giving way, they barely can carry him out of the moonlight and into the milk room; there Westlund lights a kerosene lamp. Victor sits down on Hildur's milking stool, he made it for her once, it took him five days, it took two for the blue paint to dry. He put it next to the separator for her one evening, a Saturday. She looked at it and shrieked: *If you think you'll get me to the barn for this then you're a whole lot dumber than I thought.* She thought he'd bought the stool at the Co-op, that wasn't entirely her fault of course. No wonder things turned out the way they did, he thinks now. Everything has already happened. Here he is, sitting empty-handed on an old milking stool. Westlund, a butcher's trustee, lights up the void with his yellow lantern,

Simon-Superior lifts the latch on the barn door, and puts on Rudolf's cold wooden clogs.

"So what animals does the butcher's trustee count?" the old man asks, Westlund helps him inside.

In the barn the cows get up on their knees, their collars rattle, they probably think it's the sun itself stepping in through the door.

"Well, this is how it goes," Westlund explains. "Before the butcher's trustees go into a barn they decide that there should be so and so many cows and hogs inside. How many depends entirely on what color the barn is and how high the dung heap is. If the barn is blue and the dung heap is eight meters, for example, there should be eighteen cows and twenty-two hogs. And if that's not the case, you just have to pay the fines at the post office."

They step up into the first stall, May-Rose is there, chewing her cud, the old man weeps. In the dark, they don't notice at first.

"And the senior butcher's trustee," Westlund continues. "What does he do? Well, he's the one who counts the butcher's trustees. To be sure that more don't come out of the barn than went in."

"And vice versa," Simon adds. The old man is crying.

Now it's gone too far. The son-in-law becomes like a father to him, he wants to wipe the tears away.

"Father-in-law," he says when they stand in Yellow-Rose's stall, the fifth one. "We're just joking, you know. Don't cry, old man."

But they don't understand that it's too late, they don't understand that the old man has seen the sixth stall, the empty one. Suddenly he tears the lantern out of Westlund's hand, and shines it into the drain: Kulla's stall hasn't been cleaned out for a long time. He goes up to the feeding trough, feels inside it with his fingers; it has been cleaned out, there's no chaff on the bottom.

"Kulla," Victor whispers.

Whimpering, he falls to his knees beside the lantern; the empty collar is still there, he picks it up, caresses it. Westlund steps carefully into the stall, Simon stands by the pigpen and looks at the sow, weighs some seventy kilos, he guesses.

"Kulla," Victor howls, lying prone on the rotten wood floor of the stall.

"Father-in-law," Westlund whispers. "We had to take her. She went dry, you knew that."

But the old man doesn't want to hear, Westlund takes him by the shoulders to help him up, but his shoulders say no. The cows take it calmly, and lay themselves down. Then the milk room door opens.

"Get out, all of you," Hildur screams from the door, she is white with fury.

So the butcher's trustees slink out. There is a pair of overalls hanging on a nail in the milk room; Simon takes those with him. Westlund dries the old man's tears with a wad of straw.

"It's me," Hildur says, and leans down over Victor, he has the collar around his neck.

"I'm an old cow," he whispers. "And now I'll stay here until I'm ready for slaughter."

Hildur goes to get some hay in the feed alley, she blows out the lantern, moonlight fills the troughs and illuminates the webs of weavers under the beams. She helps him up on his knees.

"I'll put some litter out for you," she says, strewing the hay on the floor.

Then she sits beside him for a long time and waits out his bitterness. It's a thirsty little animal, that's all, it hasn't had tenderness to drink for many years. Thirsting, it creeps into its burrow, and listens with its thirst for someone to come and wait by the opening. God have mercy on those who have no one waiting with a ladle of water. After a long time, Hildur hears it come pattering down the dark passage, she brings it refreshing relief. She lies down in the stall, draping her body over her father's like a coat draped over a hanger.

"Pa," she whispers, removing the collar from his neck, "I was the one who did it. I put the collar on her, I led her out."

"Did she scream?"

"No, she was happy."

Finally he gets up onto his knees.

"Then she didn't know what she was going to," he says, still bitter. "Then you lied to her."

"I didn't lie," she answers firmly. "I told her what was happening. She went up the ramp herself. I saw that she was happy."

"As if you could be happy when you go to slaughter," he says bitterly.

"Pa," she says with the courage of despair, "This is how it is, I think. Make do with what you have. You have to make do with what there is, and be happy. If you don't have a life, then you have to make do with dying. And if a cow has no milk, then she has to make do with being slaughtered." And finally he seems to understand, his little animal has been drinking, again and again; now Victor is standing in the stall with the extinguished lantern and to him, it shines.

"You're going to the butcher. Are you happy?"

He meant to say: *You're going to slaughter*, but changes

his mind for his own sake. She answers, weeping: "Yes, Pa,
I'm happy."

She stands in the shadow, where no tears can be seen.
But he is standing in the bright light, and she notices with a
quiet melancholy how the moon sculpts death into his face.
For a long time she cannot tear her eyes from that sight. With
infinite patience, day by day, the greatest sculptor of all covers our faces with the small fine features of death. We are all
models for the sculptor of death. But one day, the sculptor
loses his patience, he lets the chisel work as if possessed; the
change is seen from one hour to the next. She doesn't get
scared, you get scared only when you are very young. When
you're young you watch those you love, see them come across
the yard with shiny milk pails swinging in the twilight; you
stand in the window and pray: Let it always be like this, you
who decide, don't let any of them die. But then comes the day
when you learn: Make do with what you have. And then there
is nothing to fear. She stands in the shadow and understands:
it has happened to him too. That now he makes do with what
he has. Doesn't build on anymore, doesn't build at all. He goes
down and stays downstairs with those he has. This is why he
is suddenly so full of death. Filled with gratitude, she thinks:
I'm the one who has been given the privilege of killing him.
I'm the one who gets to make his face so beautiful.

"Come, Pa, let's go," she whispers, and turns his lovely face
toward the shadow.

By now the Singer has posed his question to everyone, and
he wants to go home. The lady from town holds her right
hand up to the moon.

"Don't you think I have the fingers of a pianist?" she asks, standing by the car.

He is so tired, he has to hold onto the door handle.

"Yes," he answers, without knowing to what.

God, how she despises everyone standing there.

"There you have it," she screams. "I could have been a world-famous pianist if I hadn't been married to that one there."

Nisse tries to open the car door, but it's locked and stays locked. She had made him promise to drive the Singer home, saying: I really hope that you're not afraid, well, you yourself know of whom. But no names yet. Although he's drunk and his driver's license is suspended, he promised. It's the middle of the night, it's light outside, and the road is wide. But the car door is locked.

"Wallinder must have the key," he says.

Bjuhr is alongside the fence, loading the bicycle that used to belong to Nisse; he wears the rings he's won on his index finger, that's where they are most visible. I've never been as married as right now, he thinks. The losers are throwing stones against a target made from a piece of the rake handle. Bjuhr is thinking: Damn, if I don't have legal claim to both Hildur and her with these fingers. So he staggers over to Mary.

"We're as good as married, you know," he says, putting his hand onto something shiny that she's wearing.

"That's enough!" Mrs. Bjuhr throws in. "I'm going home, and tonight the key won't be under the spruce twigs. Just so you know! Old goat!"

And she takes off toward the gate, tramples on the rake target without noticing, her belly protruding as if she was balancing a banner on it in some demonstration. But Bjuhr has noticed nothing, he only notices Mary's breasts inside her blouse like two captive animals begging to be let out. He takes the big key out of his pocket. But Mary is now absorbed by her left hand, as that one isn't bad either.

"I could've played *quatre mains*," she calls out to anyone who wants to hear. "If I hadn't been married to that one there."

Old man Bjuhr puts the key into the lock.

"Cats or no cats," he says, "you would've been one heck of a player."

But she's not in the mood to be unlocked, now she's thinking about her future, and how Nisse Johansson has stolen it. She closes the lid of the piano, and cries over it for a while. But Nisse is caught in a fog of cheap cognac; he holds firmly onto the radiator ship of the Plymouth and searches, in his mind, for Wallinder. He can't find him.

"Where is Wallinder?" he cries out, suddenly afraid, he is hanging onto the ship trying to remember the last time he saw him. It was in Gävle outside his store.

Sören, whose turn it is to throw, stops dead with the stone in his hand; finally, it just falls to the ground.

"Let me see," Westlund says thoughtfully, winking at Rudolf, "didn't we last see him down by the lake? Come, lads, let's go look. No, Simon, you stay here."

They disappear behind the house, the others stay at the car and argue about Wallinder's fate. Bjuhr is in a great mood. "He's probably dead," he opines. "And he had the key and everything," Nisse says gloomily. Someone comes out of the barn; but it's not Wallinder, only Hildur and Victor.

They don't dare look in the barrel, they just stick their arms in and heave up. Wallinder is slack and heavy; water pours off him and runs into the moonlit grass; they don't dare look him in the eye.

192

"What if he's dead?" Sören says in a shy whisper.

"Let's turn him over and see," Rudolf suggests.

They turn him over, it's like opening a tap in a barrel.

"Maybe we should ask him something," Westlund says.

They turn him over again, he looks green.

"How are you doing?" Rudolf asks, softly so it won't be heard around the corner.

Their hearts beat like pistons at ninety kilometers per hour, their eyes are wide with panic, they stare at the green face. Wallinder's eyelids slowly glide up, revealing a pair of empty holes for eyes. His lips make a few swim strokes in the silence. Westlund places his ear close to his mouth. After a while he straightens up, relieved, and dries his hands on Sören's shirt.

"What does he say?"

"I think he's saying something about nylon," Westlund replies.

Before they even reach the others standing at the car, someone comes running. It's Irma; she wonders whom they are carrying. They hold his face toward the moon.

"It's your nylon man," Rudolf calls to Rullan at a distance.

Irma sighs. Relieved. As if she thought it was someone else.

"It's like we said," Sören says to the others as they carry him through the gate. "He was in the water."

"So now you'll probably get a Carnegie medal," Westlund says.

"No big deal," Rudolf says modestly.

"Water is water," Westlund says.

They carry him up the stairs, they lay him on the floor in Victor's room, they roll a rag-rug around him, a clock starts striking. The nylon man makes a few swim strokes on the floor.

"That should ring a bell for him," Sören says, Nisse gets the key to the Plymouth out of Wallinder's back pocket.

Outside Victor is lying in the grass by the stoop, stretched out on his back. They encircle the old man, standing so close that neither stars nor moon shine on him. He has fought with himself, his life has fought with his death, for the very last time life has won. He is lying pressed against the grass like a plant in an herbarium, he is lying in a well with the wedding guests as walls, their heads hanging like buckets. One slowly sinks down toward him. Hildur.

"Get up, Pa," she calmly coaxes him.

He doesn't move.

"Do you think I'd lie under the same roof as a nobody from Gävle?" he sneers from the depths of the grass. "No, I'm sleeping here."

But she sees in his face that he has but one wish, his whole being crying out to her: Lift me, carry me, tell me what I want to hear!

"The rest of you can go," she says to the others.

So some step inside and go on drinking, Nisse manages to open the car and shoves the Singer into the front seat, Mary squeezes in beside him, Bjuhr sprawls in the back, it's the first time he is the owner of a car back seat. They drive off in a cloud, ripping a piece of the gate as they go.

"That was the differential," Nisse explains, speeding up.

"I thought it was the lock of the gate," Bjuhr says.

Mary is telling the Singer about her lost future, the later it gets, the brighter her loss, it's always like that, Nisse knows that better than anybody.

"If you all knew," she says, believing it all so much that it brings tears to her eyes, "how that man there has ruined it for me. And you're not the only one who has said: Mrs. Johansson, you should have devoted your life to the arts. I knew this painter, for example. Your hands, Mrs. Johansson, he'd say, should have been holding a paint brush instead of, of—"

"A shot glass," Nisse suggests, getting control of the car. Bjuhr laughs out loud in the back.

They're all so unartistic that she cries for real. She can't come up with anything to say, but it doesn't matter. She thinks the Singer is listening to her and pities her; in truth, he hasn't heard a word. He is closed for the season. The only thing he may be hearing is the rustling of an envelope in his jacket pocket. It was Wallinder, before he collapsed, who had said: *Maybe you'd like it in writing.* True, he had addressed the Singer rudely, not using his proper name, but it was clear that he still understood a few things. It made the Singer believe that a written testimonial from a known, now living radio dealer, albeit from Gävle, who had heard most everything sung on the radio, would count for a good deal more than anything farmers would utter in their drunken fits. So Wallinder wrote on a piece of good Lessebo stationery with ink and big curves, then sealed an envelope with saliva and Bord's aquavit. *Read it when you get home,* he said. At home! *Such a great artist as you,* he went on, *must have the home of a singer with its own paid-for grand piano, and statues of both Beethoven and the Thore Ehrling Orchestra.*

The Plymouth zigzags its way alongside the hedge, drives its nose into it, but just a little and gently. Bjuhr is snoring, unartistically, in the back seat. But true enough: it's his seat now. The two others walk the Singer into the big dark building, snoring with all windows open, a light on in the director's office. He probably shouldn't have brought them in, not because he is ashamed because they're town people, but Göran was right in what he had said the last time they met.

Göran had invited him to Gävle, they met at a little dark café. *It's not necessary*, Göran said suddenly, *for you to advertise where you live. I've told Ellen and the kids that you're living at a boarding house, so that—well, you understand.* And he immediately understood: a stage comeback is a delicate matter and requires all sorts of precaution. In that state of mind, he says farewell on the front steps:

"Yes, so here's where I live. For the moment. Have a single room on the ground floor. In the corner. But only for the moment, that is."

Then it occurs to him that they are smiling. Scornfully. As if they knew better. As if they thought that fourteen years was one heck of a long moment. True, both men are drunk, but still. So he continues:

"By the way, I have a testimonial from an esteemed man in Gävle concerning my song."

He stands there with the envelope in hand, and politely asks them to open it, and read the testimonial out loud. The outside light is not turned on, only the moon shines, he himself sees too poorly. The lady slits open the envelope with the nail of her little finger, he looks at her hand, it is full of big rings. Suddenly he remembers her question, seems to recall that he hasn't answered it, and wants to compensate now. She unfolds the testimonial, holds it right under the moon's big reading lamp.

"One can't play piano very well with such fingers, such so to speak thick fingers," he says, expertly but amiably.

That decides the matter for her, that and Nisse's minute-long scornful laughter that follows. What had been a vile act, written on fancy stationery, against an old man who understands her, now becomes just one of Wallinder's good old jokes. So without a quiver in her voice she reads the testimonial from the esteemed man in Gävle.

"It is hereby attested by request," she reads out, loudly and triumphantly, "that the singer Johan Borg is one hell of a fellow to sing. It's just that not a single sound comes out when he sings. But maybe that's just as well. Respectfully, Fritz Wallinder."

Afterward, silence falls over the entire world. When she's in hell, she later thinks to herself, she'll stand on a stairway and read this scrap of paper for all eternity. They back down the steps, the envelope and paper lie on the second step where she has dropped them. He stands at the top, petrified, mute and black, as his own tombstone. What can they do other than flee? They briefly turn when they reach the hedge opening. He is still standing there. They wave in farewell, as if that could reconcile them. They get into the car as if into a prison, he turns it around with the engine roaring, then it cuts out.

"What have you done?" he screams as if it was also her fault the engine died. Bjuhr snores; she looks at her hands.

She tries to hide her hands, she knows they are nothing special and never have been, all they are good for is to press back tears in times of pain. Into them she anxiously asks: *Bin ich ein schlechter Mensch?* In German. Not: Am I a bad person? There's a story to that. Once she felt so terribly sorry for a young German refugee. One night she had woken up in his room with a dreadful sense that someone was looking sternly at her. A lonely light bulb shone in the ceiling, the boy was asleep, she discovered that he was very dirty. She pulled off the blanket, and saw that she was dirty too, it was as if they had wallowed in filth before they went to bed; they had been rather drunk. A mirror with a red frame was hanging on the wall, she looked into the mirror and encountered a different person than she had expected. She turned off the light and wakened the boy. How do you say in German "Am I a bad person?" He answered and fell back asleep.

Since then she always uses this. *Bin ich ein schlechter Mensch?* Saying it this way has its advantages. It sounds as if it concerns someone else, the foreign tongue serving as a buffer between the scream and silence. It turns the whole thing into a conundrum, and she often ends up thinking: Good Lord, I'm really an intellectual, you know. Fortunately she doesn't know enough German to ever be able to answer her own question.

She always exits their battles unscathed, the one who always loses is Nisse. It's more than enough to have to constantly live with a person to start hating him. So each time she has pressed her tears behind her eyelids, she lowers her hands and looks at Nisse, looks at him with ever-increasing hatred.

Even before he shifts to second gear, he knows that soon she'll say it. Beads of sweat appear on his forehead. Carefully, he lets the car roll slowly on the left edge of the road, down the long slope. It's the first time he has driven since it happened. The moon disappears, they roll in the blue-black darkness of the night. It was even darker back then when it happened. A road sign slowly appears in the night, then vanishes: Soft Shoulders. The white railing of a bridge shines in the beam of the headlights. It happened on a bridge. They slowly roll across the bridge as if there were fog. There had been no fog then either. She doesn't say anything, simply turns her hand slightly toward the railing. It happened by a railing. They roll past Bjuhr's green gate. After the accident he ran through a gate and disappeared, but they found him anyway. She makes a small gesture with her hand toward the gate, she'd followed him that far, then gone back and shown the others the way. The headlights catch a haystack, it takes a few steps back as if ashamed, and disappears. They found him behind a haystack. She still hasn't said anything, and before she can, he quickly steps on the gas, and the Plymouth jumps as if it wanted to catch up with its own light. Mary rolls down her window as far as she can.

"Bror Jansson," she screams out into the night. "Brorjansson! Brorjansson!"

He veers hard to the right to try and save him, the Plymouth spins, the road is rocky as a sea. He slams on the brakes, the car stands still but the wall of Palm's barn comes gliding toward them like a dark ship. Again, the left front wheel jolts upward and crushes a life. It's too late. The side of the car and the wall meet, and both scream, Bjuhr rolls down from his seat and falls back to sleep on the floor.

What happens next is not real but a dream, the dream that what has been done is being undone, the one we all have. He tumbles out through the left-side door, the only one that will open, and stands defenseless and blinded in the beam of the headlights. The one who was killed should be lying there on his stomach, his bloody head protruding from under the bumper. He himself should dive below the light beam, take Bror Jansson by the shoulders, and pull him out. He gets on his knees and throws his hands under the car; he only gets them full of grass. He lets the headlights shine on his hands; on them is not a drop of blood. He walks around the car, he calls out the dead man's name, but no one has been killed. No one has been killed anywhere; all that lies broken between the front and rear wheels is a rough gatepost. So: it wasn't Bror Jansson, it was a gate post. Relieved, he pulls out the post and drags it behind the barn. In the dream about what happened, he ran away through a gate. Now, he calmly climbs over. In the dream about what was undone, he slowly walks toward the haystack, wanting to feel what it is like to stand behind a haystack without having killed anyone. Mary follows, his shadow almost.

But behind the haystack, what has been done awaits him, as an amen at the end of a prayer. There lies Bror Jansson, on his back, his legs wide apart, his arms resting in the loose hay. Nisse falls on his knees beside the dead man and hates him because he will never allow what was done to be undone, he hates him because every time he chooses to die, never to live. The moonlight returns, and plays in his open, dead eyes. Mary glides out of the shadow of the haystack, soon they will hear the heavy steps of those who come to get him.

"Oh my god," she whispers, also falling to her knees, "it's Westlund's assistant."

No longer in any condition to distinguish between what was done and what was undone, Nisse pushes the tip of his index finger against a little ball on Hagström's bearded cheek. The ball disappears, what remains is a hole. No doubt: Westlund's assistant is reliably dead.

In their terror, man and wife both rise up at the same time; they run together through the long, cold shadow of the outbuildings. They leave him behind, lying there, legs apart, on his back beside the yellow-shimmering haystack.

It is when the car stops that he understands. He is still standing on the steps when it frees itself of the hedge, he hears it turn, gravel spraying, he hears it take off for a few meters. Then a dead stop and dead silence.

Good Lord, he thinks; suddenly he recognizes them, now

there's no time to waste! He understands at once whose faces those really are: they want him to believe that they've driven away. But in reality, at this very moment, they are returning on foot around the hedge, on their way toward the back of the building, on their way to the kitchen entrance which almost always is left open. He snatches the testimonial from the ground, and hurries inside; he turns the key, the light casts a weak, fire-red glow over the stairs that creak unexpectedly. Are they already inside? He walks on tiptoe toward the light, he crosses his arms; it is an invitation to their valor, if any were to exist. Gentlemen do not strike someone who approaches with their arms crossed.

Without having been seen, or in any case unharmed, he reaches the first step of the stairs. He understands that the most dangerous thing right now is to go to his room, as he so naïvely had revealed where he lives. Too late to take that back.

He finds the handrail, he feels his heart beating in his left hand. He ascends toward the moonlight, a white wall, a door behind which a light burns. On the landing he stops and listens; no, it doesn't seem they made it in yet. Or else they are already up here, and if they are already here, they are standing in the shadow to the left of the stairs. The director's door is to the right and directly in the moonlight. He understands that he must remain in the light, so he walks backward to the door, and carefully pulls it open without taking his eyes off the moon. He can't knock but his life is more important than knocking.

The director doesn't seem to think so.

"What's this all about?" he says, almost snapping.

Once inside the closed door, he can turn around, but holds hard onto the handle so that they won't be able to tear the door open. The director is sitting behind his green lamp, chewing, he is in the process of devouring a full plate of sausage sandwiches. It's a kind of German sausage that he buys in town, he has it with beer.

"Director," he whispers, "they're coming for me."

The director finishes a sandwich, stuffing sausage slices, one by one, into his chewing machine. The Singer feels sorry for the poor morsels.

"Again," the director says, smirking.

No need to smirk; to say "again". Admittedly, that's true. The gang that is after him is not lazy, it never goes on vacation; above all it has mastered the art of disguise. One day it's an old woman he doesn't recognize, who passes by on the road and throws sneaky glances at the home. The next day it's a girl on a bicycle who, as if by accident, rides into the yard and has herself a good look around. One time, one of them was on the radio, it's unfathomable how he'd managed to get there, maybe he had promised to read something entirely different. Instead the man had read a story aimed at him, from the very beginning to the very end; it was about an actor called Bergh. With an "h" and everything.

"Have a seat," the director says, picking up his letter opener.

Hesitantly, the Singer lets go of the door, walks over to the chair and sits on its edge, ready to leap up if anything were to happen. The director spears a slice of sausage on the letter opener. To get him to finally understand the gravity of the situation, the Singer starts to explain how it all fits together, how the gang has arrived from town by car to get him out of the way. He also talks about Göran's warnings not to reveal his place of residence to anyone, and many other related matters. The director spears sausage after sausage; when the sausages are gone, he spears the remaining bread slices; when they are all gone, he looks around for new prey and finds a cigar butt in the ashtray; methodically he murders it and inspects his victim for a long time under the lamp. He is still chewing, and continues to chew for a long time after the Singer has stopped his account of the gang's doings. He opens a book, which appears to be some kind of report, and carefully digests it.

"Perhaps they even arranged the wedding," he says at last, "to have a chance to get you, Borgh."

Now the Singer is not so stupid that he doesn't understand irony, malice or sheer ruthlessness. But sometimes it doesn't hurt him, on the contrary it can make him grow, he becomes stronger and even finds the strength to raise his shining shield. He has the power to think to himself: There was a time when I too could plunge young girls into happiness. Ready to saddle his tall horse, he smiles, almost with a sense of compassion, when something very strange happens. The director puts down the letter opener, he has probably speared enough for tonight. It shines sharply under the green lamp, but that isn't what is strange.

The strange thing is what lies below, it's a binder of Lessebo stationery. It's not that he now thinks that the director would be part of the gang, it's just that the forgotten peril again makes itself known. The horse falls to its knees and the shield rusts. His heart starts pounding. He gets such a desire to scream that when the scream comes at first he thinks it is his own. He thinks that it is because of him that the director stood up so abruptly, he doesn't understand why the director is hurrying toward the door. He wants to run after him, as if to press the scream into his hands. But the director stops and holds him back; he is done chewing, his jaws set around something that resembles a curse.

"Stay here," he says firmly, issuing an order. "I'll just have to go and calm down Klara."

Alone again, the Singer sinks down onto the chair, far from certain that it is all about Klara. True, Klara screams at night. She wakes up, God is standing outside the window, God wants to come in, the window is closed. Then she rushes up, tears open the window and screams so that God can find his way. But this sounded different. No one can fool me, he thinks like everyone else who gets fooled; he again becomes strong, remembers that the door isn't locked, gets up and turns the key.

It is the first time he has been all by himself in the director's office, and it feels strange. With no plan in mind, he walks toward the desk, and is on the verge of sitting down again when he remembers the binder with letters written on Lessebo paper. At first he just wants to move the letter opener a little so that he can see whether it really is Lessebo paper and not another brand. But not until the lock is broken does a thief become a thief. Trembling, he opens the binder; at first he wants to let it be, but his hands force him to pick up one of the many letters filling the binder. It is in an envelope with neither a stamp nor a postmark; he reads the address under the lamp.

His hands understand first because his hands drop the letter; then his knees understand, and he collapses onto the chair. When his brain finally understands, he stands up and without even a tremble puts the envelope back into its binder, then he takes the whole binder and walks up to the window. When he lifts the curtain he looks out onto the road, there is no car there. There's never been a car there. He lets the curtain fall. The binder is not large, yet it is heavier than anything he has ever carried, as heavy as a meaningless life. He doesn't have the strength to feel any bitterness toward the one who did this to him; it is the anguish of exhaustion that drives his steps toward the door.

I have never been heard, he thinks, unlocking the door. I have never been heard, he thinks, staggering out. In the light of the moon, he sees a mouth, this mouth is open and it sings. It sings but it is mute. I have always been mute, he thinks, and feels the stairs sink beneath his feet. The binder sweats in his left hand.

What is to come for the mute singers? What is to come for the guides who are blind? Only an even greater muteness, a deeper darkness. He drags his heavy burden down the steps, only in the forest, will he let it go. In the forest he will let go of everything; he will tear the muteness out of his chest. He hates himself without measure.

But before he has gone all the way down the stairs, he sees a face rise out of the moonlight by the door next to the entrance. The face rocks to and fro, as if floating on water, drowned. It blocks the way. The Singer stops.

"Any mail for me?" Mad-Anders whispers.

He must have seen the binder shining in the Singer's hand. He must have thought: *Finally a letter for me.* It is well-known that he gets up at night, and stands waiting, sometimes by the stairs, sometimes by the hedge. And if you ask him what he is waiting for, he answers: *For the mail, can't you see.*

Suddenly it becomes clear to the Singer: Why lug around these heavy letters, they aren't mine anyway? So it's for the sake of comfort that he gives them away, not for anything else.

"Yes," he answers, "there are many letters for you tonight."

Mad-Anders has his little room right by the stairs, there is a light coming from it. The Singer follows him, simply to give him the letters, not for anything else. But when he has given him the binder with the fifty white envelopes made out to the management of the Opera, the ones that were never sent, he can no longer leave as he had intended. Nailed in place, he stays and sees how Mad-Anders sits down on the floor and, quivering with eagerness, opens the binder, probably only expecting one letter or two at most. He must think he's dreaming, he has never received a letter before. Now he gets fifty-two, he can't count. He can't read either, he doesn't open them, he takes them one by one and sniffs them, holds them to his ear and shakes. Eventually, he puts them in a circle, and happily sits on the floor in the middle of a circle of envelopes, moving them now and then. Probably thinks that's how you read a letter.

The Singer stands outside the circle, for him it will never be broken. He is about to leave the room when behind him he hears a word so unexpected that it makes him turn around.

"Sing," Mad-Anders had whispered.

"I'm mute," he answers, wanting to leave.

"Sing," Mad-Anders whispers with happy eyes; he hasn't understood, his delight drools out of the corner of his mouth.

The Singer takes the towel from the hook and wipes his mouth tenderly. Closing his eyes, he takes a couple of steps back and begins to sing in a weak voice; he twists the towel around one wrist. Tighter and tighter. As his song grows, he twists the towel even harder, as if he wanted to sever a piece of his heart. I'm not heard, he thinks bitterly; he doesn't know what he is singing, just knows his voice is weak. No one hears you, he thinks, so you might as well open your eyes and look.

Still singing, he opens his eyes and looks at Mad-Anders. Immediately, with jubilation that knows no bounds, he clearly sees it: Mad-Anders hears him sing, Mad-Anders's eyes are firmly tethered, not to him, but to his song. The towel hangs loose in his hand like a banner, he closes his eyes and Mad-Anders's room bursts with his song, the banner flutters in the wind, stretched straight in the storm. Now, he is heard everywhere on the whole earth. The hedgehogs hear him and wake up, the algae sway to his song, his voice rises above the mountains, he is a hurricane that whips the desert bloody. He stands alone in the night with a straw hat pressed against his chest, it is the straw hat of the largest of giants, he will fill it with song. He puts it to his mouth and lets the song flow into it like a torrential rain, it will never be filled.

Some time after the Singer has collapsed on the floor, Mad-Anders rises up from his happiest night, he steps carefully out of the circle, he does not trample on a single letter, they should see that, the others. He leans down over the Singer and carefully pulls the towel out of his mouth. Entranced he unfolds the bloody banner in the light.

Never before has he seen anything so beautiful.

Everything on the Mustad crate has been eaten, and drunk too, all but a couple of beers. Filip is sitting on an upside-down bucket from the stable.

"I'm stuffed," he says, belching.

"The only thing missing were heated plates," Ivar says.

Ivar sits on the stool Rudolf uses when he shoes the horses, he pokes at his teeth with a fork, and looks at the third tramp. The third one doesn't say anything, he hasn't said a word all evening, he has barely eaten, barely had a drink even. There's something about him that they don't care for; sometimes he simply disappears, quiet as a lady disappearing out of your life. The barn door creaks, and he's gone. Then just like that he's back, sitting on the fire hose, staring down between his legs, there's only straw to see.

"You got to manage without heated plates when you're a tramp," Filip says.

STIG DAGERMAN

"There once was someone who made something of himself," Ivar answers. "How should you conduct yourself, he
went around asking, now that you amount to something?
Always ask for heated plates, said those who knew, then you'll
show them that you're special. So one day, they serve him
butter, cheese and herring, but the plate was cold. Bring me
a heated plate, he yelled. They serve him pancakes with jam,
the plate was cold. Bring me a heated plate, he shouted. At
last, they served him ice cream, the plate was cold. Bring me
a heated plate, he howled, and he got one."

"So what are you trying to say?" Filip asks, pulling off a
bottle cap. But the third one doesn't ask anything.

"I mean," Ivar answers, "that something is fishy here."

"And what is that?"

"We'll soon find out."

He takes the lantern, turns the flame up, and shines the
light straight into the third one's face, his eyes grow wide.

"You, for example, what are you looking for when you go
out?" he shouts.

The third one puts his hands in front of his eyes, his eye-
balls shrink, everything within him shrinks.

"There's moonlight outside," he answers at last.

Ivar gets up and opens the door, opens it wide and scoops
handfuls of moonlight into the barn. He takes a harness from
the hook and places it over his shoulders, it gleams. He raises
his hands up toward the doorframe, he is a horse rearing
toward the moon.

"Here's a silver horse, Filip," he says with a sneer, "since
you write poems. Just look at those silver hooves."

"Many things are beautiful," Filip answers quietly, and
knocks back some beer.

208

Moonlight drifts into the barn like smoke; it is burning on the moon.

"Please close the door," the third tramp whispers.

Ivar hangs up the harness and closes the door, then goes right at him.

"Finally, you've said something," he says triumphantly, again shining the light onto him. "You told me to close the door."

"Many things in this life are beautiful," Filip says. The bottle is empty.

Ivar lowers the lantern, the face of the third one is so white it almost is a light unto itself.

"You're afraid, you creep," Ivar says contemptuously. "You're so scared it's shameful. Is that beautiful to you?"

"I'm not afraid," the third one answers. "I think it's beautiful outside."

He is sitting down and brushing his pants; he's been doing that all evening, they will never get clean.

"I knew someone who had cleaning mania," Ivar continues, sinking down onto the stool. "If he stayed in a room overnight, it looked exactly the same in the morning as it did before he arrived. There was no trace of him in that room, it could just as well have been vacant. At first I thought that was a good thing. Then it occurred to me: if he is so careful to clean away every trace of himself, he must have something to hide. I was right. The cleaner had once killed a person."

"I haven't killed anyone," the third one says vehemently, no longer brushing off his pants.

"But I have," Ivar says, and raises himself up.

He stands upright, and lets the full weight of his shadow fall on Filip, the Mustad crate and the third tramp.

"Bah, all talk," Filip says, squirming.

Then Ivar puts his finger onto the third one's chest.

"Why did you become a tramp?" he asks sternly.

The third one does not answer but his head sinks even deeper toward the straw.

"I wanted to be free," Filip replies.

"Did you find yourself with a view of a brick wall from nine to five?"

"It was from seven to six back then," Filip answers.

Ivar hangs the lantern on the stable door bolt.

"Let's shed some light on the freedom of a tramp, shall we?" he says, and lies down in the straw, using the stool as a pillow. "What kind of freedom did you look for?"

"I wanted to be my own master. I didn't want to be owned by a fire insurance company."

"So the tramp is his own master? Maybe even the freest person on earth?"

"Yes," Filip answers proudly, grabbing another beer bottle.

"Yes," the third one echoes wearily.

Ivar becomes so angry that he throws the stool into the corner with the halters.

"Is it freedom to depend on the mercy of others?" he snaps. "You who are so free that you don't have any porridge. And sit and eat, without retching, the porridge of the unfree. You eat yourself full at the tables of those who are not free, and sleep until well-rested under the roofs of those who are not free. For what? To be able to despise the unfree? To be able to write your poems about how wonderful it is to be free?"

"Is it wrong to show how much beauty there is in our world?" the old man whispers; soon his eyes will fill with tears. "To speak of the flowers that grow along the road?"

"Listen, you have no world," Ivar continues mercilessly.

"You betrayed your world for freedom. And I'll tell you what freedom is. It's the hell of loneliness. And you can sing your heart out to loneliness, because that's all the unfree want to hear about. They want to hear about the free tramp who swings his gilded beggar's staff across the meadows. Otherwise, why would we tramps be so popular? Tell me!"

"Because we do what other people don't dare to," Filip answers. "We do what everyone longs to do but doesn't have the courage to."

"Exactly," the third one murmurs.

"Don't sit there talking bull," Ivar shouts. "Because everything you're saying is wrong. No one longs to be like us. There's no one who longs to be hungry, tired and dirty. There's no one who wants to wear the shackles of the freest person. There has to be a limit to the conceit of the freest man. I don't care about your Arcadia with its meadows and stars and stamens and pistils. You're no more remarkable than anyone else. And remember, every year there's the same number of suicides in London. A tramp isn't so free that he can't get caught in statistics too. Statistics exist but the Tramp's Arcadia doesn't. It's this goddamn world that exists, and that's what you should have furnished with all your marvelous possessions instead of running away."

"Don't all of us want it to be different?" Filip says defensively.

"Of course," the third one says, quietly as death itself.

"Different!" Ivar says scornfully, he gets up and walks over to the Mustad crate. "Different! The stones are always going to be hard. We're always going to get sweaty when we run. We're always going to get a stitch in our sides and sand in our shoes. We're always going to be jealous and envious. We're always going to try to run away. And we're always going to—"

Then Filip bangs his fist on the crate hard, so hard the bottles roll into the straw. The third tramp starts and almost falls off the hose.

"Then why are you on the road?" he screams, "A bastard of a grumbler like you!"

"Yes, why?" the third one echoes.

Ivar retrieves the stool, sits down by the lantern, and rolls himself a cigarette.

"Because I'm an asshole," he answers at last, licking his cigarette.

"How can you prove that?" Filip asks.

The third one comes to life.

"You said you'd killed a person," he says shyly.

"I was driving a trolley if you want to know," Ivar says. "There was nothing remarkable about that. Except that I perhaps wasn't your usual trolley driver. I had what you'd call a cultural bent, and was part of three study groups. A literature group, an art group, and a music group. In fact, I was on the verge of starting to write poems. In my mind's eye I could see a scrapbook filled with the finest reviews: No one could depict road salt in the trolley tracks at Hornsplan in such a vivid way as Ivar Lund. Or: no one within contemporary Swedish literature could surpass Ivar Lund in the art of portraying the cigarette butts in the gaps between floorboards of the smoker's compartment on Line Three. I was firmly convinced that I could make a contribution. But then Oskar Johansson went and got drunk."

"You would have been a much happier person if you'd kept writing," Filip says, drumming a funeral march on the bucket.

"Who's Oskar Johansson?" the third one asks.

"I'm glad that I never got started," Ivar says. "Oskar Johansson was an old guy who was sitting in a beer café at Storkyrkobrinken. By four o'clock he was drunk. At quarter past four he was down on Stora Nygatan. At twenty past four he fell from the sidewalk in front of the wheels of a trolley. It was my car. He died after ten minutes. At four-thirty, that is."

Filip reaches his hand across the Mustad crate, but gets no hand in response.

"It wasn't your fault," he says, moved.

"No it wasn't," the third one echoes.

But Ivar stands up again, casting his angry shadow over them like a sack.

"It was the trolley's fault, of course," he says mockingly.

"Exactly. Yes, exactly," the third one quickly responds.

"It didn't look that way to me," Ivar continues. "All I knew was that I had killed a person. It was the first time, so it felt a little unfamiliar. I felt I needed someone to talk to about it. So I went to the literature group and told them what had happened. *Don't take it so hard*, they said, *it was the old man's fault and the trolley's fault. Split about fifty-fifty. But tonight we'll be doing Kafka.* I want us to do Oskar Johansson, I said. *Oskar Johansson*, they asked, *has he written anything?* I understood that to them the only things that mattered were those that were written. Oskar Johansson was of no importance, he'd just been run over and probably all he had written was his signature in the liquor ration book. *Go read T.S. Eliot instead*, they suggested. *During this transition period, that is.* So I went straight to the art circle. *It was the trolley's fault*, they said, *and the old man's. But how do you like the Braque portfolio?* I don't give a damn about Braque right now, I said, I'm more interested in Oskar Johansson. One of the people there was your classic know-it-all. *Oh, Oskar Johansson*, he said, *he's no good, I can't stand his annoying moldy greens.* In their world only painters existed, and if you were lucky, what they painted. And there could be only one right opinion—if even that. *Take a look my boy, at Paul Klee, that's something other than that old Oskar Johansson of yours.* Right now, I don't give a damn about Klee, I said, and got kicked out of that group. But there was one left, the music group. I went there and presented my case. *Please be quiet,* they hushed. *Don't you hear we're listening to Shostakovich?* But what about Oskar Johansson, I said. *Shut up,* they shouted, *we're listening to Shostakovich's Concerto for Piano and Orchestra Opus 35.* And that settled it! I gave up on all of it. The trolley and the groups and the whole goddamn business."

"And what are you looking for now?" Filip asks. "Is there something here in the barn?"

"I'm looking for what's gone wrong," Ivar says, playing checkers with the bottles. "It must be somewhere, damn it."

Then, unexpectedly, the third one speaks up.

"It's the judges that make us into criminals. No one else! Don't forget that!"

"There's *one* thing you've got wrong," Ivar says. "When will you get into your big fat skull that you might just as well say that it's the criminals who make the judges into judges? I'm looking for something completely different."

"Like what?" the third one asks, showing his yellowed teeth, it's his turn to be scornful.

Ivar darts into the corner of the barn as if they'd thrown him there, his back right up against the wall, his face white now, too.

"Don't you get it, you bastards?" he screams. "Don't you understand that I'm going around begging the trolleys to run me over! I want to be done with Oskar Johansson. Is that so hard to understand? Heated plates—the biggest idiot gets that. And God have mercy on those who don't get Kafka or

Paul Klee. There's just one thing that no one understands anymore."

"And what's that?" the third one whispers, his back is stooped again.

Ivar takes down the lantern, puts it on the crate, and sits down.

"No one understands how to console murderers," he says. "But why are you a tramp?"

The third one shrugs his shoulders, as if he was trying to get rid of them. Trying to get rid of all of himself.

"Well, you know," he says at last, "somebody like me is just a nobody."

"Then you may as well take a halter and go and hang yourself right now," Ivar says, throwing him a halter. "Everyone is something in this world. You only have to look at the census to see that."

"There once was a guy who was in love," the third one continues after a while, the halter on his lap. "But the girl didn't want him, because he amounted to nothing. All he could do was the high jump. The girl's mother didn't think that amounted to much. *What does he do?* she kept asking. *Does he build?* No, the girl said truthfully, he jumps. *Jumps?* the old woman asked. Yes, the high jump, the girl replied. *Jumps upward, you mean?* Yes, said the girl. *So why doesn't he jump down?* the old woman asked. The girl didn't know either. So she picked somebody else."

"She was right to do that," Ivar says.

Straight across the crate, he looks into a pair of eyes that finally hate him.

"She was goddamn right to do that," Ivar says brutally. "There wasn't much to that guy."

"Can't even someone who is a nobody have feelings in

their body?" the third one asks, rising up over the Mustad crate.

"They probably can," Ivar answers, "but who said they'll be better for it?"

"You can die from those feelings," the third one says.

"No one gets any better from dying," Ivar says.

"No, but other people might," the third one says enigmatically.

At that moment, they hear a car driving wildly in the road. It careens toward them as if shot out of the silence, its brakes screeching with terror. At last it hits the barn wall so hard that the thresher shakes. The halter falls out of the third one's hand.

"That fucking Nisse," he says. "Now he's going to go to jail again."

But the moment he's said that, he seems to regret it; he picks up the halter; outside a car door bangs but no one screams. Filip slowly wraps the halter's lead rope around his wrist.

"You must be from here, kid," he says thoughtfully, and tries to catch the third one's eyes.

"Maybe your name isn't even Sixten," Ivar suggests.

The third one tears himself and the halter loose, leaps from the hose, and heads toward the door.

"Leaving?" Filip calls after him.

Yes, he's leaving, without a word. For a few moments you can see his thin high-jumper body outlined against the moonlight; then, quickly, he closes the door.

"He took the halter with him," Filip says after a while.

"So what," Ivar says. "Maybe he has a horse."

Ivar walks into the chicken coop, takes an egg from under a frightened hen, makes a hole in the shell with a horseshoe

216

nail, and sucks it. Then someone enters, not the third tramp but someone with a lighter step. It is Siri, moonlight bathes her body, a coffeepot glistens in her right hand.

"There should be three of you," she says surprised, like the last time.

Ivar drops the eggshell in the straw, she pours coffee into the glasses, the whole time he looks at her. It occurs to him that she has asked the same thing as before hoping to get the same answer. So he goes up to her and says, "When you're here then there are exactly three of us."

"That's not what I meant," she replies, but she lies.

He raises the glass, she stands still, her eyes fixed on the thresher.

"Are you thirsty?" he asks.

"Not for coffee. Maybe for water," she says hesitantly. The car's headlights seep in through the cracks.

"Then let's go to the well," he says, touching her for the first time.

She gently frees herself. Once at the well, she asks:

"May I pull up the pail?"

He opens the cover for her, she leans into the well pole with all her weight, she might have fallen into the well, he's the one there to rescue her. They each drink from their side of the well, the bucket full of stars. Across the water's surface, she dares to let her eyes seek his. There is an ocean between them but it is receding; she needs to know, before the bottom becomes visible, whether he is the one. He quickly raises his lips out of the water. Too soon. She lifts her gaze and, in confusion, looks into a pair of eyes that are all wrong. *No*, she wants to scream, *you're not the one*. But by then the ocean between them has receded, gone to the heavens; he makes the short step across the well cover, and takes her by the arm.

Desperate, she feels her will to resist wither; loud voices rise from over the stoop, it is too late.

"My dad is getting married," she whispers helplessly.

Ivar leads her out toward the road. Don't be an asshole, he thinks to himself, I'll kill myself if I do it. But killing himself, that's something he has always wanted to do. So he opens the gate, pushes her through, and follows.

"It's about time," he says, closing the gate.

The killer goes first, he tears out all the saltbush within reach and fashions it into a whipping wand. He talks fast and disconnectedly, like a dealer peddling junk; he probably wants to peddle his anxiety. But none of them wants to buy. A few meters separate him from the others, already he is being shunned, already a barrier exists between him and the innocent. He tries to advance more slowly, but the slower he walks the greater the gap. The others stand by the manure pile.

"You gotta understand," he says with a sob, "I didn't want to kill him. Didn't even want to fight him. But Simon kept insisting. You were right though, Simon, it was one hell of a scratch."

"You could have hit him in the chest, or in the stomach or wherever," Simon says, "just not in the head. You should have known that. But don't be sorry, I'll send as much beef as you can eat to the county jail."

Westlund is also tearing up.

"Hagström was a good butcher boy," he says, crying. "He would have gotten the Pro Patria medal if he'd lived and stayed healthy. Hagström was a—"

He probably plans to say more, but Karlsson calls out,

suddenly stops in the shadow of the stable, and points behind the barn door. There's no Hagström there.

"He's gone," he whispers, his eyes almost falling out of their sockets.

Nisse Johansson sticks his nose in.

"He's lying behind the haystack," he shouts.

"Was it Karlsson or you who killed him?" Simon asks angrily. "Karlsson knows what he's talking about and always has. If anyone deserves a medal, then it's him. Don't forget that. More than certain others."

They follow Nisse out into the moonlight, into the shadow of the haystack, they walk around it, straw crunching beneath their feet. Hagström isn't there either, but there is a hollow in the straw where he had been lying. Someone has stolen Hagström while they were gone. But while they stand there, indecisively, trying to solve the mystery, a sound comes from the other side of the barn, a whimper and a curse. They walk through the gate out onto the road.

Bjuhr has woken up, and stands behind the shipwrecked car, the back seat in his arms, Hagström is lying on his back with his head against the barn wall, his eyes glazed, his legs naturally parted.

"I got the seat out," Bjuhr says. "I won't be riding in that machine from hell any more, I thought, so I might just as well take the back seat and mount it on the bike rack. In any event, he was lying here, Hagström was. He's probably dead now."

Westlund falls to his knees.

"He was a good butcher boy, Hagström was," he says, touched. "I was about to give him a raise. And then this happens."

One of the women starts sobbing, Westlund unbuttons

Hagström's jacket, places his hand into the shirt, feels for Hagström's heart. It's beating like a hammer against an anvil.

"Not a beat," Westlund says softly, and looks accusingly at Karlsson. "Bjuhr, does your snuffbox have a mirror?"

He holds the mirror in front of Hagström's open mouth, wipes away the mist as he lifts it, shows the mirror in the moonlight. It is blank as water. Bjuhr takes a mournful pinch of snuff, and sighs. Westlund lowers his head, and places his big ear against Hagström's warm mouth.

"I'm just messing with them," the assistant whispers. "Let's say three hundred fifty."

"Not until hell freezes over," Westlund whispers back and gets up. "Now, let's carry Hagström in."

Karlsson gets to carry him by the head, Westlund says he doesn't want to deny him that, Simon takes the feet. Westlund walks ahead and opens the door of the '29; they put him on the front seat, Westlund dries his eyes.

"The thirty-five," he says, closing the door, "it was the apple of Hagström's eye. So it's only right that he gets to rest there. But let's drown our sorrows, let's go inside for a drink. The rest can wait until the sheriff wakes up in the morning."

They have just reached the small gate when Hagström rolls down the window and sticks his head out.

"What about the fireworks!" he hollers, and jumps out, a brown package in his hand.

There is a moment of confusion at the gate, before they understand what has happened. All they can do now is to accept it and give thanks, like Karlsson says. "But the next time," Simon says, "you'll give him a proper thrashing when you're ordered to." Russian firecrackers skip under the apple trees, a Bengal flare burns by the corner of the house. They save the best until last. Karlsson, Hagström and Simon get three rakes out of the shed, tie the casings firmly onto the ends of the shafts, and set them up three meters apart facing the rye field. Karlsson lights his first. A red burst shoots into the sky, somersaults under the clouds, turns yellow and green and blue, and finally comes floating down like broken northern lights over the water of Fuxe Lake. Hagström's thunders like the cannons of a firing range, they crouch to protect themselves from the burning flakes snowing down on their heads. Simon, wanting to be worst as always, is last. He holds the rake upright, his foot on its teeth, and lights his casing.

"Watch your foot," Westlund yells to him.

And then it's done, the rake turns over and the rocket goes off along the ground. Like a fire menagerie on the loose, it rushes off roaring in all directions. Howling with madness, the red tigers hurl themselves against the fence, and the greenest of snakes slither, hissing, between the legs of the shrieking guests, crowded at the front door. The rye is full of howling fire monkeys, the field mice watch as the world ends. A bloodied vulture falls burning into the lilacs, a small fire flares up inside the hedge. Hildur, who didn't have time to make it inside, runs over to put the fire out, a wet lilac branch whips across her forehead; she searches for more fire in the moonlight, but finds none.

"It's out," says a low voice behind her.

Martin rises from the ice stack; he comes toward her with the halter in his hand. She fumbles for support; there's no wall behind her back.

"Is that you?" she whispers.

He will not let her escape. He opens his arms wide, like large pliers they sink into her, and he pulls her toward him onto the ice stack.

"You shouldn't have come," she says, her hands now full of sawdust from the stack.

"Maybe I shouldn't have," he says with a sneer, swinging the halter. "But the thing is, you're mine."

She sees the halter.

"I'm not your horse," she says fiercely.

"Thought so," he answers, wrapping the lead rope around her sawdust-covered hands, pulling her closer.

He begins caressing her wildly; in an instant, he has her down on the ice in the shadow. She manages to free one hand, and hits him over the left eye. Quite lightly, but it surprises him, and he also sits up.

"You're mine," he says stubbornly, trying to get hold of her free hand; she locks it between her legs.

He gives up, and lets go of the halter.

"Don't you think I understand?" he says bitterly.

"Understand what?" she asks, burying the halter in the sawdust.

"It's no shame to be poor," he says vehemently. He stands up, grabs the lead rope, and starts pacing back and forth in the garden, the halter swinging around his legs.

She stays seated.

"It's no honor either, if that's what you mean," she replies calmly. "I guess it's like everything else. Of no importance."

He comes forward and inspects her. Righteousness stands by his side holding his hand.

He throws the halter in her lap.

"I guess it's better to be the butcher's cow than my horse," he says scornfully.

Strangely enough she doesn't get angry. You can't do anything to me anymore, she thinks, I've made do with what I have.

"I've made do with what I have," she says, and looks Righteousness in the eyes, Righteousness lets its gaze fall like an autumn leaf.

Then suddenly he becomes tame, and sinks down in a cramped spiral at her feet, it's the wettest hour for the grass.

"You have me," he whispers, arching his back, and falls over her, the halter scrapes against her hip.

He has never been particularly strong, she raises him in a bridge over her.

"Don't you understand that it's too late," she half-screams. "If you were going to come, you should have come before. I'm married now. My last name is Westlund."

Then for the first time, and by accident, she sees his eyes, until now he has been trying to keep them in the shadows, to hide them. As soon as she sees them she understands why.

"Why did you come?" she asks, eager for confirmation.

He lowers the bridge but not over her; he lies prostrate on the grass.

"I heard," he says sullenly, picking dew off the blades of grass.

"How?"

"An acquaintance wrote to me," he answers.

"Wouldn't you have come otherwise?" she whispers, trembling from tension and cold.

But instead of answering, he throws himself onto her, she has no time to even raise a hand in defense. He presses dew into her dry clothes, he brushes dew out of her eyelashes.

"Listen," he pants into her dry ear, "I've walked all the way from Västmanland. Only hitchhiked a few kilometers. I've been at it for a whole week. I've walked all day and night. I've slept in ditches."

"What do you want?" she screams without mercy, cold as the ice below the sawdust, cold as the rope on the halter.

With cold eyes, she sees his face melt with desire and drool over her in a sticky stream; his entire body melts and flows like a wave toward her mouth. At the moment just before drowning she hears him whisper, "Listen! I want you. I want you now. Now before he—"

She clutches the straw, she takes hold of the halter, she raises her face above the flood; the smell of sawdust and night grass again washes over her as a blessed swell. Long before he has had the time to recover, to again become solid, she is standing upright in the grass, the halter hot in her hand. Lying down, he turns onto his back, and deep below, she sees his burning eyes buried in a well of fear and hate. But only the halter can feel the pain when she understands that it was not for her sake that he'd come, but for the sake of a triumph, the triumph of celebrating a wedding night with Westlund's wife.

"If you only knew how I've suffered this week," he pleads as he slowly crawls toward her.

She throws the halter as hard as she can at his crawling face; he whimpers but keeps on crawling.

"Get out of here," she whispers. Her whisper is a scream. "Get out of here before I call for Hilmer."

With the halter over his shoulder, he steps onto the ice stack, stands on it as if it were a mountaintop, and leans over, threateningly. *I'll fall to my death at your feet!*

"You know what will happen if you call for him," he whispers, leaning even farther over the abyss.

She looks at him, already knowing what will happen. But that only fills her even more with hatred. She fills her lungs with the air of hate.

"Hilmer!" she screams for all she's worth. "Hilmer! Hilmer!"

He has been in the rye, stomping out a fire. She hears his heavy steps come thundering toward her, with an infinite sense of happiness, she sees, with lowered eyes, how the stack collapses but with the ice intact.

When she finally looks up, Martin is gone.

"It was burning so terribly," she calls to Hilmer when he arrives, and she leaps into his arms as if through a gate. "But it's out now."

"So let's go dancing," he says, twirling her in the moonlight. "Because now by jiminy everyone is rescued. And now no one will die. Hey, ho!"

Arm in arm, they run toward the house, out of the shadow of the lilacs. Suddenly she stops under the fading moon; frees herself, takes a few steps backward on tiptoe. She puts her hands on her head, holding them upright like a bridal crown, slowly she runs toward the gate.

"Dance the crown off me, Hilmer," she calls, letting herself be chased inside, to the parlor music, until the crown falls.

They walk on the road toward the forest, the rye stands white on both sides, the roadsides gleam deep green, the white potato plants blossom with their pale roses. Moonlight filters down over her shoulders, she walks in the right wheel track, bearing his arm slung onto her shoulders like a cross toward the moonlit Golgotha. She keeps on carrying her load, but he is not the right one. The right one will never come, she thinks, you have to make do with the one you pity the most. He looks across the fields toward the forest; a horse-drawn hay rake leans against an abandoned drying rack, the shafts reach toward the sky, two empty hands. He recognizes them, it's the trap.

Because for him, there is always a trap. A death trap. He is always going toward it, sometimes he can almost touch it. It gives him hope. Take solace, he whispers to his longing neck, soon the trap will close, soon the blade will fall. But soon is taking a long time; he gets impatient. He must do something again, something really vile. So he does, he takes his hatred of himself and throws it at someone else. He writhes like a worm during execution, but the trap comes closer, and that's the main thing.

It's not just a matter of throwing yourself in front of a trolley. You need a reason, a very weighty reason. There needs to have been an action that can only be excused by one thing: by the blade falling on your neck.

"What have you done?" he says to the girl, full of disgust, "You with such beautiful eyes?"

"What have I done?" Siri answers as the wheel track narrows. "I've been crying a lot."

"Why is that?"

"I don't know," she answers, stepping over a horseshoe.

"No, you probably cry first," Ivar says, looking at the hay rake that stands sharply black against the blue night. "Then you find the reasons."

"Maybe so," Siri says, his arm weighing on her.

They walk down a small hill leading toward the meadow with the hay rake, half way down there's an opening in the fence, wide enough for a cart. When they arrive at the gatepost, he suddenly throws her to the side, they fall down on their knees. Through the fence opening they see two animals that resemble a big mare and a little foal glide out of a ditch near the forest, and stand in the middle of the field of oats. He presses her close to him but she doesn't notice; all she sees are the moose. The cow raises her head and seems to look right at them, though they are well hidden, then chews at the oats. The calf stands still with lowered head, as if waiting for a reprimand. Suddenly, without them having understood how it happened, it's over, the mother has set off as if by magic. She sounds a warning, the calf runs across the ditch, and heads to the forest, she warns again, and disappears. A sound like the belch of a butcher, he's about to say, but remembers that her father is a butcher.

They walk close together down the hill; he notices how her resistance has relented; the moose have taken it with them into the forest. *Show a girl a critter and it's like you have her in a little box*, someone once told him in the dark of a hayloft. But that fellow got himself a punch to the face. I can't stand you saying that, Ivar had screamed. He can't stand it now either, so that's why he does what he does. He leads her toward the hay rake, lowers the shafts, places himself between them, stands in his death trap, and plays his role.

"Let's rake," he calls, Siri stands at his back with her hand on the release lever.

He pulls the rake over the embankment, bringing Siri with him toward the stone bridge at the oat field; on the bridge, he sets the shafts down.

"We don't dare go into the oats," she whispers, withdrawing a little.

"What the moose dare, we dare," he says, taking the first step; he hears her follow.

They climb toward where the moose had been, the oats are wet, cooling their legs, but soon they no longer feel it. They have taken slightly separate paths; in the middle of the field he goes over to her, and turns her around.

"Look," he whispers, pointing at their two trails in the oats. "Someone drove here with a cart."

"No," she says, "those are our tracks."

"We're two wheels on the same cart then," he says, and feels ashamed.

Deep in thought, she continues toward the forest, he follows her tracks.

"This was where the cow stood," he is behind her and he lies, he steps out of the track, lets her see it.

Like a coward, he lets her say it, as if she herself had thought of it.

"Now we're just one wheel," she whispers.

A moment later her arms are around his neck, the wheel starts turning. It rolls over the oat field, it rolls into the forest, it rolls through many warm lakes. In the end, it rolls against a rock and is crushed into small, small pieces.

She stays lying while the earth absorbs her blood, and sees him looming through the oats, standing with his back to her, moonlit, searching in his pockets until he finds what he is looking for. While she lies still resting on the earth, he stands turned away from her and smokes. She follows the smoke and finds a star. Perhaps stars feel pain too, she thinks, that's a small consolation. Perhaps everyone feels pain. She is lonelier than she has ever been; the oats stand like a wall between her and the Shining One. But the Shining One does not exist, has never existed, and will never again spring to life. Her heart beats hard and anxiously; she doesn't have the energy to get up.

"Listen," she whispers, barely audibly, but he hears and turns around, his smoke like fog over the oats. "Listen, there was something—"

Then she changes her mind and falls silent; he pulls her up.

"Speak up," he says and starts to walk back.

She tries to keep up with him.

"Yes, I was thinking," she says, "but it was a silly thought. I was thinking that you can never really rest your heart against the heart of someone else."

He answers over his shoulder.

"Some have their hearts on the right side. So you'll just have to advertise."

After this, they walk in total silence back through the oats and the dew, through the grass and the dew, in the wheel tracks and the dew, retreat squelching around their legs. Oh God, what a bastard I am, he thinks, his hope ignited but the moon is losing its light. White as a corpse, it hangs a thumb's breadth above the forest; dawn interfering. The headlights on Wallinder's car are on, staring across the road like sickly eyes, he can't bear to see them suffer, so he goes to turn them off. Nisse Johansson is lying on his back on the couch by the well, snoring. Then the wheels, their hubs cold, come loose from the broken cart and slowly roll, in opposite directions, through the gray grass.

At three-thirty there is a soft knock on the parlor door, so soft the first time that no one hears. "The Key to Your Little Heart" is playing on the gramophone.

"Water is water," Westlund cries. "When Wallinder has dried out, he'll have to write a testimonial to Carnegie himself."

"Let's see who gets the last laugh!" he roars at Simon.

"Now we're going to open a little heart," Mary whispers.

Siri stands under the pendant lamp and unbuttons her blouse, Mary takes a little key out of her handbag, and inserts it into the lock.

"Not that one," Siri whispers, "it hurts so much."

"It should hurt," Irma says. "Isn't that right, Ma?"

"Stand still now," Mary says to soothe her. "We're just going to open your little heart."

Hilma brings her wicker chair closer.

"Yes," she answers, "of course it should hurt."

Mary turns the key and the hinge groans.

"I think this little heart is sore," she says, kissing it. "How did that happen?"

"We can find out later," Irma says. "First we need to take a look at the little heart."

So Mary unhooks it from the hinge. Blood falls in heavy drops from the pendant lamp onto Siri's neck.

"You're hurting me," she says, panting, and looks at her heart in Mary's hand; it is breathing like a newly caught fish.

"Of course it hurts to open small hearts," Mary consoles her. "But I think we should bring it closer to the light."

"Maybe it hurts less out in the oats," Irma says sharply.

Hilma takes Irma by the arm to calm her.

"Let me have a look," she says, reaching up curiously. "One of you, go find a candle."

"Don't get a candle," Siri calls desperately, "I don't want you to shine a light on it."

"He, of course, didn't get to shine on it," Irma says with a sneer.

"No," she answers truthfully, "he didn't even ask about it."

"What do you need the candle for?" Hildur asks when Irma comes and gets it from the table.

Mary places the heart in Hilma's outstretched hand.

"Such a little one," Hilma says, weighing it in her hand. "It can't weigh much."

Siri stands and looks at the hole left by her heart, it's not bleeding, only the pendant lamp bleeds. Irma holds the candle over the little heart.

"You need something to turn it over with," she says. "So you don't get your hands dirty. Isn't there a cake server around here?"

"It's in the drawer," the old woman answers.

"Water is water," Westlund repeats, pouring whatever is left over. "Soda water or well-water or water for shaving— it's all the same. But if you pull a fellow out of the drink you should have the Carnegie. Enough said!"

"And if the water is heavy, you should get two," Simon adds and empties his glass.

"You can't talk. You weren't even there," Rudolf protests, making his point with a big bang to the table.

Because now everything is coming to an end, it is that time of day both inside and outside; a gray dawn mingles with the smoke and light, surrounding faces shiny with sweat. The Singer is still trying to open his gramophone heart; he will no doubt, like Ville, eventually resort to dynamite. Ville is lying on his stomach on the couch, his palms pressed against the seat cushion as if against the shoulders of death. He is drunk but he's alive; for now, the dynamite sticks lie on a beam, tucked in between beams and ceiling.

Bjuhr has already left, he stood outside by his bicycle holding onto the fence, he kept on counting, and puking, without it ever adding up. Either a pair of pants was missing or else there was one tie too many. There was still some light from the moon, and he held his right hand in his pocket so they wouldn't take the rings off him. He wasn't really feeling well, he had managed to put the cushion from the car backseat onto the bike's carrier rack.

231

"You'll never make it home with all that junk," Rudolf had told him. Bjuhr cursed and felt sick.

"Since you've been an alternate on the Road Maintenance Board," Rudolf said, "you ought to have the sense to puke on the road and not in our yard."

"Help me up, and I'll go," Bjuhr shouted angrily, he'd had enough of counting. They lifted him up onto the bicycle. "Give me a push so I'll get some speed," he shouted, "push me so I'll get home with my loot." They all ran, Rudolf, Sören and Westlund, to get the bike going. Bjuhr got the pedals moving, then rode right into the couch, Nisse fell off.

"I thought the gate was open," he said. They got him started again. "Turn," they screamed as he passed through the gate. He turned toward Uppsala instead of toward Gävle. "Now you'll have to ride all the way around the globe to get home," they shouted after him. "I'll be home in five minutes," he shouted back, he didn't understand what he'd done, he had only followed the road. *Lordy, how it has gotten hilly*, he thought as he passed by the parsonage. *But just go along, if I get off I'll never get back up again*. So he rides on under the moon, rides straight into dawn with the rings, the seat cushion and the suit, the two-crown pieces jingling on the hills.

No one hears the knocking the second time either.

"What are the ladies up to?" Westlund asks, because suddenly seven sweaty men, all danced out, sit alone at the table. Well, Victor has not danced, he is just sweaty. The Singer fiddles with the lock.

"We should take up a collection to put a dead bolt on it," Hagström says guilefully.

Westlund gets up to have a look, and suddenly shouts:

"What have you done to the girl?"

Irma stands with Siri's heart on the cake server, its blade glistening in the light. Hildur tries to stop him from seeing it.

"If any of you is more pure than she is, prove it!" Hildur's bitterness encompasses them all.

But Westlund doesn't like seeing Siri's heart cut out like a piece of cake.

"What have you done to the girl?" he shouts again, and now they all come and crowd together under the pendant lamp.

"We've just opened her little heart," Mary explains,

"There's nothing more wonderful than opening small, small hearts."

"When did you get this?" Irma asks in a scathing voice, and she points to a deep wound with festering edges.

"As long as I can remember," Siri whispers, "I've always had it."

Standing under the pendant lamp is like a dream; it is a nightmare to see a cake server carrying your heart going from hand to hand, defenseless, under the scrutiny of sharp eyes. This is something that only happens to me, she thinks, the back of her neck wet. No one unlocks other people's hearts.

"Well, what do you all say?" Irma asks when everyone has had a look.

Some say nothing, they probably think it is none of their business and that the whole idea is dumb.

"It was an ugly wound," Westlund says assessing it, "but—"

"It's an old one," Siri says stubbornly. "I've had it as long as I can remember."

"You didn't by any chance get it tonight, did you? In the oat field?" Irma puts the cake server aside.

Siri only shakes her head no.

"Put her heart back in place, right now," demands Westlund. "But what oats are you talking about?"

"Our oats," Irma answers, and Victor pricks up his ears.

"If you go and trample down my oats, you'd better start behaving," he threatens.

"Don't say!" Hildur cries, "it's nobody's business. Which of us hasn't been out in the oats?"

"Not me," Irma answers.

"No, not tonight," Hildur says, "but there've been other nights."

Through the wall to the bedroom, they hear Gunnar crying in his sleep, soon he'll wake up and find himself all alone. Then he'll cry while awake. Westlund buttons up Siri's red blouse.

"Have you been out in the oats tonight, Siri?" he asks quietly.

But the other men have heard and only now does the whole thing make sense. They look at her with X-ray eyes, to see if she's wet from the oats; one gets wet from oats at night.

"Yes," Siri answers without hesitation, without shame.

Simon stands there thinking about a girl in Bomhus who wasn't particularly attractive; she went to buy herself some lipstick in Gävle, her first. *Good for kissing*, the clerk had said. *It cost me five crowns*, the girl said, *but nobody would kiss me anyway.*

"There's nothing like oats," Mary says with a sigh.

"Did a lot of the oats get trampled down?" Victor is worried.

"I'll pay whatever the cost," Westlund says magnanimously and digs for his wallet, but he remembers it's in Bjuhr's pocket and Bjuhr is now somewhere along the Uppsala-Gävle road.

"I only saw at a distance," Irma replies, "but from what I could see, most of it was trampled."

"No one wants to know what you've seen," Hildur shouts.

But everyone wants to know. Westlund places his heavy hand on Siri's shoulder.

"Were you alone in the oats?" He asks quietly, but everyone hears anyway.

"No," she answers without batting an eye, "Ivar was there with me."

"The young tramp," Irma adds quickly.

Everyone has heard, Westlund turns deep red. He takes the heart from the cake server.

"Say it's a lie," he cries, "say that it wasn't a tramp. Otherwise I won't give this back to you."

"I felt sorry for him," the girl answers.

"You don't go into the oat field with someone because you feel sorry for them," Westlund says. He doesn't understand.

"Why else would you do it?" his daughter asks.

"I'll throw your heart out the window," Westlund screams, "you'll never get it back."

"Next time," Svea snorts, "it will probably be with a Negro." She does not hide her disdain.

"Oh, there are no saints among any one of us," Rullan says, wanting to hold Westlund back. "And he is good-looking, that tramp."

"Then say that it was because he was good-looking," Westlund shouts.

Tensely, they wait and look at her; it becomes completely quiet; Gunnar cries, now he is awake.

"No," she says and sees her heart withering in her father's hand, "I felt sorry for him."

Then, they finally hear someone knocking at the door, it's the third time and it is strong.

"Come in," Rudolf calls.

Filip stands on the threshold, holding his beard. He bows and taps on an invisible glass as if to give a speech. But Rudolf jumps in before Filip can open his mouth.

"We don't want any more tramps here," he screams, "not in the oats, or anywhere else."

"But," the old tramp whispers, completely shaken, more shaken than he already was.

"No buts but out!" Rudolf roars, grabbing the old man by the scruff of his neck—he gets that a lot – to throw him out.

But now Hildur, too, is standing under the pendant lamp, in front of Siri, shielding her so Siri is barely visible.

"Taking pity on somebody," says Hildur on the verge of tears, "that's the only thing you can do."

Dawn is pouring through every crack, and suddenly Westlund doesn't know what he should do with Siri's heart. Mary takes it.

"Song is the key to the heart," she chirps, and before anyone can bat an eye, she has put the little heart back in place; she's good at that. The record has ended, next comes a waltz and almost everyone begins to waltz, the garlands bobbing in time.

Siri takes a chair and climbs up, she looks down into the pendant lamp, there's a heart lying there, bleeding. She feels a soft hand on her hip.

"It's mine," Hildur murmurs, "I don't want it. I have no place for it."

"I know a place," Siri says eagerly, "in my room. I have my big chest there, it's on the balcony above the porch, no one can get there."

They stand together under the pendant lamp, two sisters with one heart, while the shiny faces of the dancers sway like dim lanterns in a storm. At that moment, someone comes running outside and the parlor door is suddenly thrown open, as if by a gust of wind. Siri turns pale. Ivar walks through the door, the waltzers begin their final turn, the lanterns flare up. But he doesn't have time to wait. He strikes his fist like a sledge hammer on the dresser, the glass shakes in the mirror frame, the hairpins fly, the pictures tumble down. There is dead silence, like after a nearby clap of thunder; everyone stops, as if they suddenly had been frozen into a photograph. This time no one has the time to silence the tramp, he straightens up and screams:

"Who is hanging dead in the barn?"

The photograph in the room remains frozen.

"Who is hanging dead in the barn?" he whispers, looking around for an answer.

Hildur answers with a lonely scream.

They leave the women waiting on the grass outside the closed barn door, then lock it shut from the inside. The women stand waiting in the early morning light, grieving; they don't expect a resurrection, the harsh daylight washes their faces clean of every impure hope. Only those who grieve have clean faces. Over the forest to the east, the sun launches a few emergency flares. Bjuhr's rooster crows five times, then falls silent. A loon calls out from the lake, as if it knew all about life. The wind rustles the poor tired leaves of the lilacs; Nisse Johansson snores softly on the sofa next to the well. The women stand waiting, the way women have always waited for death to open the gates for a dead man.

Inside the barn, it is no less quiet; they stand unmoving in the straw, seeing the blacksmith's knife glisten as Rudolf gets on top of the thresher. They see him crawl forward like an assassin on the roof of the thresher, making his way toward the still shadow. They hear when he cuts, his breathing growing very loud, the shadow seems to lengthen. Next, they hear the body's muted fall onto the floor between the thresher and the barn wall. The severed halter falls with a whistling sound into the straw, like a bird on the hunt.

This may be the time to say a few words. Filip gets up on the hose.

"I was in the stable," he begins. "I'd gone there to piss. I thought I heard someone coming. Running. Then it gets quiet. Except that I think I hear something fall from the thresher. I stayed in the stable for a while because I like horses. When I come out again, somebody had dimmed the lantern. I can hardly see a thing. I'll sit a while longer, I thought, because I'm not tired. But the stool is gone. That's strange, I say to myself, it was here just now. So I take the lantern and go looking for it. I come behind the threshing machine, and there it is on the floor. And he, well—he was ill I suppose, it all seemed so strange."

By the time the women are let in, the men have placed him on his back in clean straw in front of the fire hose; they have spread an empty flour sack over his head and neck. Everyone leaves except Hildur and Irma. Irma removes the sack; she puts it on the hose. Holding each other, Hildur and Irma fall on their knees beside Martin, but they've known it could happen for so long that now, when it has finally happened, they can't even cry. They can't even whisper: Poor you. The defunct halter lies next to him. Hildur can't bear to look at it, she gets up and hangs it as far in as possible behind the live halters. Irma does not move.

"Go now," she whispers to Hildur, and Hildur leaves.

She finds the letter in his left inside pocket; she quickly folds it up, and puts it in her blouse pocket like a little handkerchief.

When Irma steps outside, the morning has arrived. The lake is full of small sparkles, the ailing moon has sunk into the dark forest. Irma sees that they have all been waiting for her. Mary stands with her face toward the sun, crying, her hands by her side; she feels every tear, it is a moment she will never forget. Victor slowly walks away from the group and toward the barn; everyone is quiet as he locks the door on the dead man. He walks over to Rudolf and hands him the key; it is more than Rudolf can bear. He stands and looks at the key until he can no longer see it for his tears.

They stand there staring at the locked door; standing and staring somehow makes what has happened seem comprehensible. Even Simon sheds a tear; and Hagström gets moist behind his ear, touching it now and then with his hand to dry. But Ivar cannot cry, what he feels is liberation; the death trap has never been so close to snapping. It pushes its cold walls against him, it tightens its rope around his neck, he can barely make the sounds that he still must give voice to. Almost suffocated by the trap, he stands across from them all and screams as best he can:

"I was the one who gave him the halter. It's all my fault!"

He beats his chest, he waits for them to throw themselves onto him, but no one even makes a move. Desperately, he steers toward his only hope. Suddenly, he is in front of Siri and forces it out:

"And I've slept with you. It was nothing special. But don't go around bragging about your innocence anymore!"

But the slap he expects doesn't come, she doesn't crawl before his whip. Standing upright, she looks him in the eyes and whispers with infinite compassion.

"Poor, poor you."

Then, finally, he cries, and lets his eyes pour out their despair. He turns his back on all of them, takes hold of Filip's arm and pulls him out toward the road; the old man can barely keep up. They walk toward Gävle, the dew clings to their frayed pant legs, the old man is half-running.

"Do you have a pencil?" Filip pants, but there is no answer.

"I thought of a poem, you see," he continues, he already has a stitch in his side, "if you don't have a pencil you can at least help me remember it."

Ivar walks in the middle of the road, but no trolleys ever pass along this road. He had taken out life insurance right before it happened *for when Mr. Lund dies*, the agent had said, it sounded so simple.

"It goes like this," Filip says, out of breath. "'When morning on every leaf comes down / the dove will cry in farm and town.' Do you hear me?"

"Do you hear me?" he wails. Finally, he understands that never again is Ivar going to hear as he once heard. The sun is behind them and bathes their backs, in the sky, the telephone wires start to sing.

"When daylight comes to farm and town," Ivar declaims until he is laughing so hard that he doubles over, and the more it hurts the more he laughs. The more his laughter hurts Filip, the more he laughs.

The steel sole no longer shines on Ivar's shoe, the key weighs heavy in Rudolf's pocket. Only Westlund is crying.

"Don't cry, Hilmer," Hildur whispers, drying his tears as they fall.

But they are endless; his grief knows no bounds. I could have saved him, he thinks. He should have been on my list. And if only there'd been no dog! Now it's too late, now the door has been locked, and he, Westlund, is the most wretched person who has ever raised an ax. But before it all comes to an end, Hildur feels a sister's arm around her, Siri. She looks from the one Westlund face to the other, from the damp to the dry. I am a Westlund, it suddenly occurs to her, I belong with them. Feeling strong, Hildur Westlund leads her family to their truck.

The sun has risen over the wedding night; soon it will dry every tear. It will dry Simon's single tear and those of Hagström behind his ear; it will dry the grass and all the wet roofs, wept on by the night. It will dry the water hole in the cat's ditch, and it will dry the wet wings of the clouds. It will pass its towel over the moist rocks of the lake. If you just wait long enough, it will dry everything, it will dry the Plymouth and all wet halters, it will dry the oats where no one is walking, it will dry the leaves grazed by the moose. It will dry all the weeping of the world.

And, finally, it will dry Westlund's tears.

Where Is The Friend I Seek?

At the end, everyone falls asleep—all except one. Everyone always falls asleep at the end—all except the blessed. But before everyone falls asleep, a chase has taken place. Where to find the friend I seek? Each of them, before they fell asleep, had been searching. In the mornings, we find them sleeping everywhere, many in the strangest positions. In the mornings, the seekers are sleeping. Some sleep in the forest on black stones, stretched out across the stones, their nails torn. Some come floating along the current, their hair flowing in the opposite direction. Many are lying in meadows; in the mornings some meadows look like battlefields, but battlefields without blood. Some lie in hollows. This small, black hollow—could it be my home? But no one asks, all the seekers fall asleep wherever they have found something; and if they haven't found anything, they fall asleep where they are. In the morning, we find many on glaciers, their arms melting, and some are hanging in the trees, vertically as if they were standing on air.

Yes, in the mornings we find them in all places, those who have been searching for their friend.

But where has the old man gone? At first, they didn't know. Those who didn't belong on the farm had left, they had lifted the couch up onto the truck bed, Nisse went along. The trucks drove off in the sun. "The girls are sitting on the couch in the back, crying together," Hagström told Westlund. "They're sitting!" said Westlund, "in America you *stood* and cried, on Wall Street. Like this," he said, and bumped his head on the roof of the car. Annoyed, he told Hagström to go faster; "Take the lake road so we get there before Simon." They were soon up to a hundred, it became hard to hang on to the couch.

But no one knew where the old man was. They wondered if he might have done something foolish. They didn't understand that he had simply gone on a quest to seek what everyone was seeking: A Friend. They, too, went out looking; it was sunny but the ground was not yet dry. *Pa*, they called, they went down into a long ditch its bottom covered by clay; there they saw his tracks. Quietly they crept up on him, he was standing in the rye, almost buried in rye. They could see how he stood there, feeling the rye swelling around his body, swimming in rye. When he came out onto the roadside he was carrying an ear of rye in his hand, they saw that he had nipped off a grain and bit into it; he didn't see them, he only had eyes for the rye.

"Pa," Rudolf called, going ahead of the others. Victor was not surprised to see him, he stepped down into the ditch. They could all see that he had found something he'd been missing for a long time. He was happy and even-keeled; it must be the rye, they thought. It must be death, he thought to himself. You go downstairs to the others to die, but wherever you go, you carry death with you. That's why you're so afraid of yourself. In the end, it's the others who will carry you out, and you only have to say thanks and accept it.

He said, "Tomorrow you should cut, Rudolf."

Rudolf said, "You've come down now, Pa."

He answered, "That may be. But tomorrow you go ahead and cut."

He walked in front along the ditch, the others followed in a compact group. It was as if they were protesters, down in the ditch, carrying banners of rye. The rye was not the friend they were seeking, that is why they were protesting; they hated their banners. When he stepped up onto the roadside he asked Rudolf for the key.

They did not cover his naked, lovely face. They carried his body across the yard as it was, raised toward the sun. Victor took his feet, he was not heavy, his arms swung calmly in the calm rhythm of the bearers. They did not close his eyes, they wanted the last thing he saw to be what they saw—a lovely Sunday morning. They opened both gates, even though one would have been enough, they opened both front doors too, that was more necessary.

Irma had prepared the parlor for the visit. When they came in the table was bare, the parlor aired out, the curtains drawn. The garlands were still hanging but they weren't in the way. At one end of the table was a candleholder with three burning candles; there they placed his head. Rullan and Svea had been outside cutting dahlias; they placed them by his feet. Mary made sure that everything went into the right place. Hilma searched in the sideboard, and at last she found the small box she'd been looking for. In the box were two coins from the reign of Charles XII. They were small and cold, they had been placed on Augustus Asp's eyes, the night he died. Irma said, "I'll do it, Ma." He lay outstretched, looking up toward the beam with Ville's explosives, she closed his eyelids as gently as she could. The coins lay on his eyes like two seals. She said: "You can go. I'll watch over him." They answered, it's at night that you keep watch. But she wanted to watch over him anyway, she needed to, she thought there was something she could come by before it was too late.

After Rudolf and Sören had carried out the sleeping Ville and the others had left, she was there alone. She took a chair and sat down beside him. She remembered his hands. She crossed his arms over his chest and placed his hands on top of each other. In a few hours it would be too late. He was hers, it was so strange, he no longer had anybody, he only had her. Until this moment, she had never had anyone; when milking time came, she was asleep on her chair.

Ville was heavy. They tried to get him to stand, but it didn't work. Sometimes they had to put him down, they sat beside him in the grass and smoked. Toward the end, they carried him only a short stretch at a time; but even so, it felt good to carry him. They sat quietly and wondered what Creek-Lasse would say. He'll come out with the gun, they agreed. They smoked and looked out over the lake; the birch had floated almost all the way across; a whole lifetime had passed since they had swum and blown up the fish. It was almost as if they could poke each other and say: Do you remember that time? It was quiet in the village and in the surrounding forest. Sometimes Ville sighed and writhed in the grass. They got across the creek without getting wet. It was harder to get him up the bank; they tugged and pulled, their sweat pouring; finally, they rolled him up like a rolling pin—that worked. They laid him down on the porch, very quietly. Rudolf pounded on the door with his fist. After a while, they heard steps, and the sound of dragging suspenders, like rat tails. They hid behind the corner of the house. The rifle barrel poked out, and they pulled their heads back. They heard the gun fall, and looked around the corner. Creek-Lasse was on his knees beside his son. "What have they done to you, those bastards," he wailed, "if I get hold of them I'll shoot them to pieces."

Then Erika came outside. "He's probably drunk," she said, she was wearing the dirtiest nightshirt they'd ever seen. "He's home," Creek-Lasse said, "tomorrow he'll get as much bream as he wants."

"He's drunk as a skunk," Erika said, picking up the rifle.

"My boy," they heard Creek-Lasse say. He was sitting on the floor of the porch, and raised Ville's head up on his lap, "I'll shoot you a moose, the biggest one we can find."

"Should he just lie here?" Erika asked. The two of them tried to carry Ville in, but got nowhere. "Get some blankets, woman," Creek-Lasse shouted, "and some pillows." They saw Creek-Lasse stretch out on the floor beside his son; Erika came with pillows and blankets, she covered them. When she had gone, and it had become quiet inside the house, they heard Creek-Lasse crying; they stole forward toward the porch, and watched. They saw him lying there, struggling to get Ville into his arms, to hold him close. He tried to turn him over but Ville just lay there like a rock, no matter how hard the old man struggled.

Victor lay down in Hildur's bed; he had the ear of rye with him, he had placed it on the covers. After a while, Hilma heard him get up. She didn't dare ask him why, she just opened one eye and realized; a moment ago the clocks had struck over Wallinder on the floor upstairs. She heard Victor walk up to his room, the stairs creaked, his floorboards squeaked, very soon he was back downstairs again. She could hear that he was walking slowly as if he was carrying something. He didn't return to her bedroom, he went outside. She lay there wondering, but soon she got her answer. Someone was walking past the bedroom window. She pulled back the blind to see. It was him and he was pushing a bicycle. On the carrier was his best clock, still ticking, the pendulum shining in the sun. She knew where he was going. Dear God, let him get there, she prayed. She got up, took the ear of rye and placed it between her breasts.

But it was far. I must go through with it, he thought, or else it would bring eternal shame. He did not look up, just kept walking the best he could. He passed by the parsonage, he passed by the sheriff's, past the smith, and from time to time the clock struck. He never counted the strokes, and he never met anyone; this is the last time you'll be in the village, he thought. He must hurry now before the clock would stop. Beyond the church, the road was newly graveled; as he walked looking at the ground he saw a track, it went right across the road and off to the side. There was a bicycle in the ditch. He took the clock down, and laid his bicycle next to the other one. He crossed the ditch and into Luttman's pasture; there Bjuhr lay on his back in the grass. He had his head on the seat cushion, his winnings were scattered around the juniper bushes, the two-crown pieces sparkled, the rings glistened on his index finger. Victor put the clock down, he lifted the hand with the two rings and pulled them off. Then he stood for a long time filled with regret. As the clock ticked, his thoughts went back and forth. I'll rest a while, he thought, stuffing the rings in his vest pocket, then I'll decide. He had never stolen anything before, and couldn't decide whether what he'd done was wrong. He fell asleep in the grass just as the clock struck six.

Some time earlier, Westlund was sitting in his kitchen together with Simon. Time passed. "Shouldn't you go in to the bride?" Simon asked. The trucks were parked outside the window. No one had won, their fenders had collided where the lake road turned into the main road.

There was something Westlund wanted to know. *You go ahead*, he'd said to Hildur, *I have something I want to talk to Simon about.* The butcher boys went to Hagström's to continue their drinking.

"Simon," Westlund said, "I could've done something."

"About what?" Simon asked.

"About the boy," Westlund replied, "about the one who died. It's like it's all my fault."

"If you had hidden all the halters, he would've gotten hold of a drying line, the barn was full of them," Simon said.

Is that a consolation?

"Simon," Westlund whimpered, taking his hand, "I was mean to that boy once. He was here begging, wanted me to give him some scraps; his mother was sick, he said; this was long ago. And what did I do, bastard that I am? I had just bought a dog, and I didn't know what the dog would do. Get out of here, I shouted, before I let my dog on you. He didn't have time to get away, and his pants leg got torn apart."

Simon replied: "He didn't hang himself 'cause of that."

"How can I know?" Westlund went up to the window and opened it. "I'll never know," he shouted. He had turned his back on Simon, and stood there talking to himself or no one, shouting things like "I'll shoot the goddamn dog," or "tomorrow I'll get rid of it." He gulped mouthfuls of his drink, it was strong and he was weak. "And I'm supposed to go into her bedroom," he cried, "I'm not worthy even of being her dish-rag!" He stood in front of the window, and with each gulp, his sense of worth diminished until, at last, only rags remained. "In America," he said, "they got rid of people like me in big machines and what came out they used as road filling."

"But Simon," he murmurs with his glass empty, his face blank and wobbly knees, "even if you make do with what you have, why would anyone make do with a bastard like me?"

He turns around to encounter a friend, but he only encounters a void. Simon has been gone for some time. He had left without making a sound.

"A person should have somebody," he weeps, sliding to the floor.

Don't look at him, she thinks; she wasn't crying. He can have all he desires, I just won't look at him. She didn't know yet how close she was to losing her wisdom: to make do with what you have. Not until he opened the door did she feel how far gone she was. She not only closed her eyes, she turned her back. She heard him undress by the side of the bed, she curled her body into a tight knot. But one thing got in the way of her resistance: she could not help hearing how his clothes fell. When she knew that he was naked she uncurled herself; he raised the covers. I won't look at him, she thought as she turned toward him. She saw anyway.

She saw, but she did not strike Simon in the face; she caressed it. She raised herself toward him; she hated it, she did it anyway. She did it with a kind of joy.

Something makes us choose the greater degradation

before the lesser. But what is that something, she would later ask herself. Once someone had written a letter on the subject to the editor of a newspaper; it wasn't printed. "Why do we love sinking?" was its title. The letter read:

I wonder if anyone in your readership could help me answer the above question or at least tell me whether the answer I've arrived at is completely in error. In our present-day society there is an unfortunate tendency among people, often emphasized by the press and other media, to seek out defeat. From my own line of work, I know many such cases of self-mutilation, where valuable individuals reduce their possibilities for development by their own free will. A whole category of people spend their entire lives passing themselves off as being sick, with such persistence, that in the end it becomes impossible to distinguish between sickness and health. The purpose of that form of self-imposed disability is relatively easy to see. The idea, no doubt correct, that our modern society demands one hundred percent effectiveness from its citizens, has understandably evoked a fear of failure in many members of society. By passing themselves off as being defective, to this percent or that, they obtain a kind of insurance against failure. This, for more people than we think, is the only thing that makes life bearable.

But this sinking is only one stage, one station on the way. The more noteworthy phenomenon is the growing desire to seek out total defeat, complete disability, the deepest degradation. After musing on this puzzle from multiple directions, I have come to the following conclusion, framed as questions: Have we perhaps experienced the misery of victory, success and glory too often to still be able to believe that this is how we can achieve salvation? What then is salvation? I think that salvation is the process by which we are suddenly able to bear the fact that this life is without meaning; empty, cold and indifferent, in itself nothingness. If we assume, which one should, that the capacity to bear this is the most valuable kind of knowledge there is, then an unavoidable question arises: In what situation are we most receptive to salvation? Do we dare answer: Victory offers no support, and glory is a desert in which our soul languishes? All of us wonder: What do other people think of when they are alone? If they think like we do, why don't we ever find that out? And do all of us perhaps know the same thing without daring to reveal it to each other? Perhaps we all ask ourselves: Where is the friend I seek everywhere? Do we perhaps find him only once we ourselves are lying bloody and beaten at the bottom of the abyss into which our despair has made us fall? Fall deeper, ever deeper, our longing calls, so we do not stop the fall. We do not fall because we love to fall, we do not crawl toward darkness because we love to, it is not because we love death that we seek it, for we know that death is only a punishment for having lived. But perhaps we believe that in the darkness we might find a light that light itself denies us, perhaps we believe that in loneliness we can find a friend that community denies us.

Is this what happens? I do not know, for if something truly is worth knowing there are only guesses to be had. But if any of your readers has an opinion on this problem, the undersigned would be grateful for an answer.

Long-term newsstand buyer

When she found what she was looking for, she was completely alone. Simon had staggered off satiated; the light brightened outside. She was on her knees by the bedside, its wooden edge pushed against her forehead, the floor was cold, as it should be. It was dark at the bottom of the abyss, she crawled around, naked, searching for something. There were only stones and between the stones, dirt; she arrived at what she felt was a body of water; she was lying on a dark rock, and beneath her was the water. Something grabbed hold of her to throw her in, she screamed desperately, but no one heard. She fell and sank; it was not ordinary water, it was acid. Piece by piece she dissolved, her arms last of all; finally, she was reduced to nothing. She was water in the water; someone had lit a fire, she was fire in the fire. She owned the fire, as a flame owns fire, she owned nothing. I am nothing, she dreamed, as she dissolved into a new life; whatever happens to me is of infinite indifference. But I must exist. Because there is a house.

There is a house, it stands on free ground. In that house I am the window and you are the door; in that house, all of us are something. Therefore the house needs us all, it needs even a dirty stone under the foot scraper. It needs the threshold that sighs for freedom, as if there was any freedom to be found outside the house. Outside the house there is nothing, but inside the house there is purpose.

Is there anything else in that house? Is it an uninhabited house for us to shape, or does someone live there inside us? We have to find someone to open us, the doors sigh. We have to find someone to step on us, the floors complain.

My friend, she thought, we must wait. The house cannot seek the one who is homeless, the homeless one must seek the house. The house can only wait. I know now what that wait is called. It's called peace.

So when the one who let loose his dogs asks her: "Can a criminal know peace?" she answers, with jubilation: "Yes, lord, only he."

In the mornings we find them sleeping, on their sides, on their backs or even hanging; they have such dear faces. They meant no harm. They are asleep all over the earth and no one has the heart to wake them. They are sleeping so deeply; it turned out the way it did, but they meant no harm.

Bjuhr is sleeping on his back in Luttman's pasture, the rings again on his index finger. Victor is sleeping in Luttman's ditch, his head next to the clock. Svea is sleeping with Sören and Sören with Svea. Rullan is sleeping on Rudolf's couch and Rudolf is sleeping there too. The tramps are sleeping on either side of a hay-drying rack. Now we'll go our separate ways, Ivar had snarled, Filip merely lay down on the other side of the rack, in case Ivar were to change his mind. Gunnar is sleeping in the kitchen, he doesn't know he is alone, one day he will find out. Martin is sleeping on the table with dahlias at his feet, Irma is sleeping on the chair and dreams that Martin is alive. On Creek-Lasse's porch, Ville is sleeping with his head in Creek-Lasse's arms, and Creek-Lasse's arms are asleep. The Singer is sleeping on Mad-Anders's floor and Mad-Anders is sleeping on letters. Wallinder is sleeping on the Snail's floor and a snail is sleeping in his house. Mary is sleeping in the Plymouth, and Nisse is sleeping on the couch on the bed of the '35. The director is sleeping with sandwiches next to his bed and Klara is sleeping in the same room as God. Hilma is sleeping in Hildur's bed, and Westlund is sleeping on Westlund's floor. In the barn the cows are sleeping; the moose sleep under the aspen. Simon is sleeping outside Siri's door, and Siri is sleeping on the balcony, where she has Hildur's heart safely locked up, the key under her pillow. Old lady Bjuhr is sleeping in the bedroom, and Karlsson is sleeping at Hagström's table, and Hagström at his own. In the reeds, the pike are sleeping, and in the lilac bushes the hedgehog. In the well, the frog is sleeping, and in the clouds the rain. In life, death is sleeping and in death, life. On the rock, Lorelei is sleeping, her long hair gray.

But the bride lies awake.

And the wedding night passes.

Acknowledgments

The helpful responses of Bengt Söderhäll and Kristina Söderhäll from the Stig Dagerman Society to queries about terminology, especially vernacular expressions from the rural setting of the novel, have been greatly appreciated.

Thanks to Brian Levy for his feedback on early drafts, and to Max Levy (Stig Dagerman's grandson) for his clever suggestions for the translation of the folk ballad on page 120.

Many thanks to Maivor Hallén and Bengt Söderhäll of the Dagerman Seminar at Gävle University for sponsoring this translation.

Finally, this translation would not have been possible without the initiative, enthusiasm and persistence of Lo Dagerman.